ONE TRACK MIND

Bethany Campbell

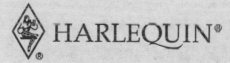

D0100859

HARLEQUIN®

TORONTO • NEW YORK • LONDON
AMSTERDAM • PARIS • SYDNEY • HAMBURG
STOCKHOLM • ATHENS • TOKYO • MILAN • MADRID
PRAGUE • WARSAW • BUDAPEST • AUCKLAND

Recycling programs
for this product may
not exist in your area.

ISBN-13: 978-0-373-18525-2

ONE TRACK MIND

Copyright © 2009 by Harlequin Books S.A.

Bethany Campbell is acknowledged as the author of this work.

NASCAR® and the NASCAR Library Collection® are registered
trademarks of the National Association for Stock Car Auto Racing, Inc.

www.eHarlequin.com

Printed in U.S.A.

To Majicka—
...the difference is to me

NASCAR HIDDEN LEGACIES

The Grossos

Dean Grosso
m.
Patsy Clark Grosso

Patsy's brother ········

Kent Grosso
(fiancée Tanya Wells)

Gina Grosso
(deceased)

Sophia Grosso
(fiancé Justin Murphy)

Dean's best friend

Patsy's cousin

Kent's agent

The Clarks

Andrew Clark
(divorced)

Garrett Clark ⑯
(Andrew's stepson)

Jake McMasters ⑧

Kane Ledger ⑦

The Cargills

Alan Cargill (widower)

Nathan Cargill ⑤

The Claytons

Steve Clayton ⑩

Mattie Clayton ⑭

Damon Tieri ⑪

Business partner

The Branches

Maeve Branch
(div. Hilton Branch) m.
Chuck Lawrence

Will Branch ②

Bart Branch

Penny Branch m.
Craig Lockhart

Sawyer Branch
(fiancée
Lucy Gunter)

① *Scandals and Secrets*
② *Black Flag, White Lies*
③ *Checkered Past*
④ *From the Outside*
⑤ *Over the Wall*
⑥ *No Holds Barred*
⑦ *One Track Mind*
⑧ *Within Striking Distance*
⑨ *Running Wide Open*
⑩ *A Taste for Speed*
⑪ *Force of Nature*
⑫ *Banking on Hope*
⑬ *The Comeback*
⑭ *Into the Corner*
⑮ *Raising the Stakes*
⑯ *Crossing the Line*

THE FAMILIES AND THE CONNECTIONS

The Sanfords

Bobby Sanford
(deceased)
m.
Kath Sanford

— Adam Sanford ①

— Brent Sanford ⑫

— Trey Sanford ⑨

The Hunts

Dan Hunt
m.
Linda (Willard) Hunt
(deceased)

— Ethan Hunt ⑥

— Jared Hunt ⑮

— Hope Hunt ⑫

— Grace Hunt Winters ⑯
(widow of Todd Winters)

The Mathesons

Brady Matheson
(widower)
(fiancée Julie-Anne Blake)

— Chad Matheson ③

— Zack Matheson ⑬

— Trent Matheson
(fiancée Kelly Greenwood)

The Daltons

Buddy Dalton
m.
Shirley Dalton

— Mallory Dalton ④

— Tara Dalton ①

— Emma-Lee Dalton

CHAPTER ONE

SHE'D HAD no choice.

Lori Garland had put the Halesboro Speedway on the market eight months ago. And when the For Sale signs went up, she felt as if someone had cut out her heart.

Before her father died, he'd begged her to keep the speedway alive —it had been his greatest dream and his proudest accomplishment. She'd pledged all her energy to granting his wish. He wanted it to be his legacy, a monument to his place in North Carolina racing.

She'd quit her job at the high school to devote herself to that legacy. But all Lori's energy, all her determination and dedication weren't enough. The speedway needed money.

The track had once stood out, a state-of-the-art facility, scrupulously well-kept. But when Lori's father was dying, it had sunk into decline. Had he understood how far? Did he really comprehend? By the time of his death, it was dilapidated, unprofitable and mortgaged to the max.

And her father, full of unwarranted resentment, had given up his single NASCAR race, believing it came too early in the year. He demanded the date be changed *or else*. It was *or else* that came to pass. Halesboro gave up the right to host the race and took a terrible blow to its importance in the sport— and to its finances.

When her father passed on, she sold her parents' house, she sold her own, but there still wasn't enough cash. Now if she didn't catch up with the speedway's mortgage payments by the end of June, the bank would foreclose.

For seven long months, nobody'd showed a jot of interest in buying the speedway. Then, in the middle of May, a real estate outfit in Miami, the Devlin Development Corporation, contacted her.

Lori knew she had to sell, but she'd vowed to do it with one nonnegotiable condition: the speedway must remain a speedway. Those were her terms; she wouldn't change them, and she told Devlin so.

Devlin's reply was that it wanted only the land. It intended to raze the speedway and build condos and time-shares. Their representative rejected her condition, then stated the company's offer. It was insultingly low.

She took the offer to her friend Liz, a Realtor. Liz urged her to accept it, but Lori held out. There was haggling and dickering from Devlin, which finally issued an ultimatum: Lori would sign the contract as it was by the sixth of June, or Devlin would withdraw its offer.

"I won't do it," Lori told Liz. "I can't."

"Lori, take the money. It's all you can do. The bank's going to foreclose. Devlin will turn around and buy it from *them*. You'll still be in debt and for what? A speedway that's a lost cause."

"I have to think it over," Lori said, squaring her jaw. She had only three days left to accept Devlin's bid. She knew her situation was desperate and she was about to lose everything, including her honor—for she'd given her word to her father, and she couldn't keep it.

But she wouldn't quit without one more try. Quitting wasn't in her nature. She'd go to her banker, old Martin Grott, and give his arm another twist, the kind she was famous for.

The Carolina morning seemed promising, balmy with a tender blue sky, a kindly sun and vireos warbling in the maples that lined the sidewalks. As Lori approached the bank she kept her back straight, her stride sure and her chin up. *Never let them know you're scared,* her Uncle June used to tell her. *You know who wins? Folks who believe they can win, that's who.*

She was a small, shapely woman, a former teacher who looked young for her thirty-seven years. She had an unlined face, wide green eyes and an upturned nose. Today she'd covered her freckles with makeup and pulled her long red hair back into a sleek, no-nonsense chignon. She wore a slightly out-of-fashion summer suit of lavender, hoping it made her look like a woman intent on business.

She moved with such energy and easy confidence that a stranger would think she hadn't a care in the world. She tried to act as fearless as her father and his closest friend, Junior McCorkle—the man her family always called Uncle June—would want her to act.

It was a quiet day in Halesboro, unnervingly quiet, and that was part of the problem, not only Lori's, but the whole town's. She saw no other pedestrians, only two elderly men sitting on a bench outside the boarded-up hardware store. A dog lay by their feet, idly scratching fleas.

Occasionally a car sighed over the asphalt of Main Street, on its way to somewhere more interesting or important. The highway was only a quarter mile away, and she heard the cars and trucks traveling past Halesboro toward destinations that bustled instead of drowsed.

Well, Halesboro had bustled once—more than any other town around. And it could bustle again; she knew it in her mind and she knew it in her heart. But she had to convince other minds and hearts.

She slowed her gait as she neared her destination. The Halesboro People's Bank building was the oldest bank in town. It was also the last bank open in town. It had stood on the corner of Main and Park for more than a hundred and forty years.

The building had once been a small showpiece of Victorian architecture, two stories tall, made of blocks of pink Carolina granite, a roof of pinkish red tiles and a cupola topped by the finest brass weathervane in three counties.

The bank still occupied the first floor. But the second story, which had once housed the offices of a dentist, a doctor and a law firm, was now vacant, its windows dark and empty.

The bank building, like Halesboro, had known better days. In her heart of hearts, Lori feared her trip there was probably hopeless. But one more try—just one more—couldn't hurt. Could it?

She remembered her father's favorite saying: "No guts, no glory." She opened the door with its tarnished brass trim, took a deep breath and marched inside.

MARTIN GROTT, the bank president, was eighty-one years old and claimed he did not intend to retire until he was one hundred. He sat behind a desk so massive that it dwarfed his wizened body. The fluorescent lights glowed down on his pink scalp and his few unruly white hairs. He looked at her with something akin to distaste and demanded, "You? Again?"

"Me. Again," said Lori. She was not by nature a demure woman, but she sat demurely as possible, because Martin expected ladies to be ladylike. She gave him her most innocent Southern belle smile.

He leaned toward her and lower to his desk, peering at her like an elderly lizard assuming a predatory crouch. "Didn't I just see you yesterday at the Chamber of Commerce luncheon?"

"Yes, sir. I was there." She smoothed her skirt and kept her ankles daintily crossed.

Grott pointed a crooked finger at her. "And at the Chamber, you gave your spiel about saving the speedway and revitalizing the town and our heritage, blah-blah-blah?"

"I mentioned the Renewing Halesboro project, yes," Lori said.

"Hmmph. I thought so. And weren't you at the city council meeting night before last?"

"I'm *on* the city council," she reminded him. "I'm supposed to be there."

"And weren't you saying the same damned thing?" he

asked. "Renovate the speedway? Pump new economic blood into the town?"

"Sir, since the speedway's been in decline," Lori said, "the whole community's felt the effect. Pump fresh life into it, and it'll pump fresh life into Halesboro."

Grott narrowed his eyes. "Don't beat around the bush. When you say 'fresh life,' you mean 'fresh money.' And you want to shake it out of me. The answer is *no*."

Lori sat straighter and lifted her chin. "What's good for the speedway is good for the town *and* this bank. All I need is a second mortgage and—"

Grott crouched lower, as if deciding how hard to pounce. "No. Forget it. For your own good. Be off. Be gone. Goodbye."

She didn't budge, only clenched the worn wooden arms of the chair in determination that she feared was futile. She called up all the passion she could muster, and the amount surprised her.

She cocked her head and said, "The Halesboro Speedway is part of North Carolina's heritage. Motor racing's heritage. It's a legend—"

"It *was* a legend," Grott hissed. "It isn't anymore. It's *insolvent*. It's unsustainable. It's past saving."

Her green eyes sparked as stubbornly as his cold blue ones glared. "Halesboro Speedway is a historical legacy that—"

"You're mistaken," he informed her. "It's not historical. It's history, period. Dying, done for, over, kaput."

"But—"

"You're mortgaged to the hilt. Your credit's run dry. You've got no collateral left. Nobody with the sense of a gnat would loan you a dime. And you ought to know better than to try to go even deeper in debt."

Her face paled with resentment.

He sat back in his chair and shook his head. He gave her a look that was almost sympathetic. "I know that you promised your daddy you'd do your best to revive it. You've done your best. It's unrevivable. I know about the Devlin offer. Everybody does. Your father would want you to take it. And get on with your life."

Lori wanted to protest that the speedway could have another golden era with enough hard work, enough faith, but most of all, enough backing.

But before she could speak, he said, "I've already given you a loan modification. A second mortgage? Impossible. Take Devlin's money. It's the only sensible action. Do you know how close to bankruptcy you are?"

And then she couldn't speak, because she knew. She'd given every ounce of her strength, every last resource to save the track. And she was going to fail. The knowledge made her feel ill.

"Stop fighting the inevitable," Grott said. "I know what Devlin's offered. It's not much, but it's the best you'll do. I mean that."

Lori's jaw clenched in rebellion. Tears stung her eyes, but she fought them down. She realized that Grott, in his crotchety way, was trying to give her good advice. If she took the Devlin money, she would be able to pay off her debts—just barely.

She swallowed hard. "I want to follow my father's wishes, that's all."

"You can't afford to be sentimental," Grott said with an air of finality. "Devlin's offer is your only lifeline. I knew your father well, and he wouldn't wish you to compromise your economic future. And I won't help you do it. I won't do it for your sake. And I won't do it for his. You know he wasn't himself in his last years. The man he was at his best would never have asked this of you. Do what the best in him would have wanted."

He looked her up and down. Then, he picked up a document, adjusted his glasses and began to read it. He had said what she always avoided admitting.

In her father's last years, he slowly lost his hold on reality. That was why the speedway declined. The truth pained her, and she could tell it bothered Grott, as well. He was not a man who liked speaking of such things. The conversation was over; she'd been dismissed.

She realized that the old man was actually trying to be kind to her. "Thanks for your time," she said softly.

"Goodbye" was all he said. He didn't look up.

She rose, squared her shoulders and left.

LORI FELT mercifully numb as she walked back to her car. She unlocked her ten-year-old blue Mustang and got in. Like a robot, she turned the ignition key and put the car into gear.

As if to spite her, the Mustang began performing its new trick, a dramatic act. It became deeply recalcitrant before consenting to go into reverse.

Clunk. Sputter-sputter, it proclaimed as she finally backed out of her parking space. *Wheeze. Hockety hockety-thud...*

"Please don't let that be a death rattle," Lori begged the car. "Please just have the hiccoughs. Give me a break."

The Mustang quieted itself to a low groan and behaved until she reached the highway. Then she pressed the accelerator. Nothing accelerated.

Clunkety, thunkety, the car said. But then it sped up. "Don't do this to me," she told it. "Learn another way to express yourself. I can't afford to repair you."

But then she thought she'd have the money because she was going to sell the speedway to Devlin. She'd played her last card and it had been a joker with an unsympathetic grin. Her fate was sealed, and so was the speedway's.

"Never feel sorry for yourself," Uncle June always used to say. "Worst waste of sympathy in the world."

She smiled in spite of herself, thinking of him, her family's friend and her godfather. She supposed all of her talk of renewing the speedway and Halesboro was a delusion of grandeur—as if *she* could somehow both save the track and revive the town.

Once thousands of fans and tourists had poured in during the racing season. Restaurants flourished, the town hotel prospered, motel units popped up like orderly, geometric mushrooms. Her father opened a campground and RV park. Shops and stores did a brisk business, and so did nightspots. She smiled nostalgically. Think of it—Halesboro used to have nightspots! Now it had only two small, rather sad bars left.

Her smile faded. So much was changed, so much was gone. Halesboro, the only place she'd ever known as home, seemed to be fading away. Someday it might live only in memories, and then the memories, too, would die. The thought sickened her.

For years, Halesboro's textile mills, owned by Uncle June, and the speedway had made the place secure, even prosperous. But the mills had shut down ten years ago, the speedway hung by a fraying thread, and Halesboro was becoming one more little rural town on its way to oblivion—or radical change. For who knew what the Devlin Corporation might do to it?

She'd always loved Halesboro. Her family roots here went back for generations. Yes, she'd been some sort of megalomaniac to think if she'd save the speedway she could help revive the town.

Well, she couldn't do anything of the kind. She wasn't a heroine, only an ordinary woman, and not a very successful one at that. Her father had left her a failing business, and she couldn't stop its failure. She'd been married at twenty-two to the athlete who'd been the homecoming king in high school his senior year.

Her husband came to realize that he'd peaked in high school. He worked for his father's insurance company, but he made only middling money, and he felt as if all his promise had somehow deserted him. He began to drink and mourn his lost youth.

When he reached thirty, he tried to cheer himself up with younger women, a long, embarrassing series of them. Lori divorced him when she was thirty-three. They'd had no children, and she realized that was probably a good thing.

She had no family left except her aging Aunt Aileen, her father's sister. Martin Grott was right; dammit, it was time to get on with her own life. Maybe she'd go back to teaching high school again. The thought cheered her.

The Mustang rounded a curve, and Lori saw a full vista of the foothills of the Blue Ridge Mountains. That was one thing the Halesboro region had a wealth of—natural beauty. And high up on the highest peak, was one unnatural beauty, McCorkle Castle.

Over the years, North Carolina's scenery had attracted millionaires, even billionaires, who'd built opulent and historic homes, including the world-famous Biltmore House at nearby Asheville.

McCorkle Castle was far more modest, but it was still a castle, a thirty-five room residence built in the Scottish revival style. It had a breathtaking view of the surrounding mountains, and its grounds included hundreds of acres of forest, a lake, brooks, gardens, stables, and a carriage house.

The property was formerly the estate of Junior McCorkle himself. Uncle June had inherited it from his father, a mogul in the textile business. Lori once knew the castle well, for her father and McCorkle had been close friends from boyhood. Now both men were dead, and Halesboro seemed diminished by their loss.

The castle, like the speedway, had fallen into neglect. It stood uninhabited, but wonder of wonders, it had recently been purchased by a mysterious buyer who planned to restore the buildings and grounds. Did he mean to make himself a truly lordly retreat? Or did he have grander plans—ones that might help the whole community?

And who was this person? Among guesses were a politician, a famous entertainer, a reclusive millionaire, an Arab potentate, an award-winning film director—gossip abounded, as always in a small town.

In the meantime, the buyer's people—architects, decorators, landscapers and so forth—were busy, but the buyer, it was said, wouldn't appear until renovations were complete.

Well, Lori reasoned, if McCorkle Castle came back to its full glory, maybe that would help at least the city of Halesboro. Uncle June used to give special tours of the gardens and part of the castle itself on special weekends. Lori had loved going to the castle, where Uncle June always teased her by calling her princess.

Well, she was far from a princess now. Her whole life had changed. On a plateau below Bin Birnum, the mountain dominated by the castle, was Halesboro Speedway. She looked at it from the distance, not believing that the Devlin Corporation would wipe away every sign of its existence.

Well, whatever happened, she'd pick herself up and go on. Somehow. But the taste of failure was like bitter ashes. She headed for the road to the speedway, and the Mustang tried to distract her from her larger troubles by sounding as if it were gargling bottle caps.

She finally reached the parking lot. She tried not to notice how badly the building needed paint, the fence needed repair, and that ragged verges of grass, untended, were balding in spots. The lot should be repaved. And inside? Inside, she knew that things were worse.

She pulled into her parking place. Other vehicles were in the lot because she had to rent the track out for summer sessions of driving school, and she heard the sound of motors that roared and buzzed like giant wasps.

The battered Ford truck belonged to Morrie, the caretaker, and the perfectly restored '57 pickup was Clyde's. Clyde was the aging maintenance supervisor, who'd somehow kept the place patched up enough to handle the little business it had. The rusting foreign compact belonged to Jimmy Pilgram, a young high school dropout and Morrie's part-time assistant.

When she put the Mustang into Park, it tried to keep moving. She stopped it, at last, and swore under her breath, for she had to admit it, the car was giving off signals of transmission trouble. And what would *that* cost?

She got out, slammed the door and went to find Clyde. Well, the Devlin money would pay for the transmission, she supposed, trying to find the silver lining in the cloud. She met Clyde, his Halesboro cap pulled down to cover most of his gray hair. His basset-hound expression told her there was more bad news.

"Clyde?" she said apprehensively.

His seamed face twisted in disgust. "Last night, some kids or somebody shot out two sets of the night lights. I don't know what gets into kids these days. And there's graffiti on the outside of the east fence. I got paint to cover it, but those lights are expensive, and this is the fourth time this year somebody's done it. Damn delinquents..."

Lori patted him on the back, thanked him for keeping her informed and asked if he had time to glance at her transmission. He said yes and he'd ask the driving school's chief mechanic to look, too. He shambled off, looking depressed. He, too, knew the track's end was near.

She went inside to her father's old office, which also needed painting, and sat at the antique desk that had belonged to her grandfather, Judge Simmons.

She'd been outlining the next year's events calendar. She'd hoped to line up seven more driving school sessions, a 500-mile race, and a car show—pretty much the same as this year's schedule.

But now there wouldn't be a next year's schedule. She stared, half-sad, half-philosophical, at the tentative list. She picked it up, folded it neatly in half and dropped it into her dented waste can.

She looked at the room's dull green concrete walls lined with photos from better times. In a folder on the left hand side of her desk was the contract from Devlin. She supposed she should phone their representative and say she was going to accept it so they'd start the final procedures.

But then she pushed the folder farther away, setting her mouth at a rebellious angle. She'd tell them later. At the last possible minute. She'd take them down to the last lap before giving them the satisfaction of letting them know they'd won.

What she needed to do was start drafting letters that Halesboro Speedway was shutting down. The employees should know first. She was down to a skeleton staff, but at least with Devlin's money she could give them two weeks' severance pay.

But it was going to be hard, and it would hurt. Some of these people had been with the speedway for more than twenty years. Clyde had been there thirty-one. She'd hoped to give him a retirement party in four years; it wasn't going to happen.

That almost made her teary, but she brushed angrily at her eyes and started making a list about closing down. The driving school would have to find a new home, so would the Super Stang Fest in August…

Would there be contractual troubles? Lawsuits? She prayed not, thinking again of Martin Grott's question: did she know how close she was to bankruptcy?

Until her father's decline, she'd never had to worry about money. She'd never had to *understand* money, and she and Scott were at least comfortable on two salaries. When she could no longer bear her husband's coldness, lies and affairs, she'd been too proud to ask for alimony or any more than her fair share of what they owned.

She kept the house and the furniture she'd inherited from her grandmother. She was naive, for she'd never wanted for anything in her life.

Like Uncle June used to tease, she'd been a princess. Well, she was a princess no longer. That wasn't as painful as failing to save the Halesboro Speedway, even though she knew now she'd been playing Don Quixote, tilting at windmills, believing she could triumph over giants.

Yes, pride *did* go before fall, didn't it?

Well, suck it up and get to work. She gritted her teeth, picked up her pen and on a legal pad began to draft the hardest letter she'd ever written in her life.

"Dear staff and friends,

"I deeply regret to inform you…"

She'd written and scratched out and rewritten, and re-scratched her way through a paragraph when the phone rang. Startled, Lori almost jumped, for few people called her these days.

Who needs money from me now? she wondered, but she thought she knew. Clyde was calling her to tell her the transmission was fading fast and had to be replaced. She picked up the receiver with foreboding. *Not the transmission,* she thought. *Please.* She'd have to buy a whole kit. How many hundreds would that cost?

"Hello?" she said, trying to disguise the quaver in her voice. "Lori Garland here."

But it wasn't Clyde; the voice belonged to a stranger. "Miss Garland, this is Judith Stribley of Jennings, Jennings and Jennings Law Firm "

"Yes?" Dark thoughts danced through Lori's mind. This must be another agent of Devlin. They were out of patience and withdrawing their offer. The bank would foreclose. She *would* file for bankruptcy.

"Ms. Garland," said the Stribley woman, "You have a property, a speedway for sale about two hours from Charlotte. I've asked about for information on the property and the terms. My client would like to offer you a contract to buy. He's willing to pay the full asking price, and the speedway, as per your wishes, stays a speedway."

"Good grief," Lori said, light-headed with disbelief. Was she dreaming? "Who? Who's offering to buy?"

"I'm not at liberty to say at this point," Ms. Stribley stated firmly. "But I assure you it's a legitimate deal. The buyer prefers to stay anonymous for now to avoid publicity. He's a very private man and a long-respected client of our firm. He'll personally introduce himself to you and offer you the contract."

Lori, too astounded to be businesslike, said, "I don't know whether to laugh or cry." Her hands shook so hard that she had to grip the phone more tightly.

"Well, I hope there's no need to cry," said Ms. Stribley kindly. "Our client does have one condition of his own. He knows the speedway's been a family business for years, and that you, as acting president, know it better than anybody. He wants you to stay on for one year, with pay, to help him make the transition to get the facility fully functioning again."

"He'll *pay* me to stay on?" Lori asked in amazement.

"Yes. Three and a half thousand a month."

Good grief—that's a lot more than I'm clearing now, Lori marveled. It seemed like a fortune. The speedway, to her sorrow, had become a bottomless money pit.

"Our client is an efficient and decisive man. He wants to meet you and have you give him a tour of the place. *Tomorrow.* At 10 a.m. sharp. Are you amenable to that?"

"Oh, yes," Lori answered, fighting to keep from stammering. "I'm amenable. I'm completely amenable. I couldn't be more amenable."

I'd meet him at 3 a.m. I think I love him.

"Very good," said the woman. "I hope that this works out well for both of you. You'll see him at the facility tomorrow at the designated time. I'll give you our number in case you need to get in touch with us later…"

When Lori set down the phone, she was ready to fall to her knees in thanks. She was saved. She put her face in her hands and indulged herself in a few tears of gratitude.

Who was her rescuer, her knight on a white horse? A wrinkled old millionaire who remembered Halesboro Speedway in its heyday and didn't want its rich history lost? Or some eccentric who wanted to keep a once-great track open and functioning?

Whoever he was, she blessed him. She hadn't failed her father after all.

Again she thanked this unknown champion. Even if he were as odd and ugly as a troll, she wanted to hug him and give him the longest and most heartfelt of kisses.

CHAPTER TWO

THE NEXT MORNING, AT fifty-nine minutes to ten, Lori sat tensely in her father's office.

In summer, she usually came to work in shorts and a T-shirt, but she hoped she looked like a semiyoung professional who had neither overdressed nor underdressed. Feminine, but not too feminine, sensible, tidy, and orderly—that's how she hoped to appear.

She wanted to impress the man who'd be the new owner, so she'd rooted through the pathetic contents of her closet until she'd found a modest white linen sundress with cap sleeves and only a barely visible stain at the hem. It had been a long time since she'd had money to spare. A very long time.

Her old white sandals were polished to a snowy sheen. She wore her hair pulled back and pinned decorously into place with a white barrette. And once again she'd covered her freckles.

She'd given the staff orders that she didn't want to be interrupted for any reason that morning, although she'd told nobody of her mysterious visitor. For the last thirteen minutes, she'd been doing deep-breathing exercises to calm herself.

She didn't want to show her anxiety or to burst into tears of relief—or, as she was still tempted to do, fall on her rescuer's neck and embrace him as if he were a hero delivering her from barbarian captors.

So she sat very straight in her chair, her hands on her knees, her eyes closed. *Breathe in to the count of fourteen seconds. Hold breath seven seconds. Exhale smoothly for eight. Breathe in to the count of fourteen seconds—*

A knock shook the door so hard that it rattled on its elderly hinges. Lori's eyes snapped open. The clock on her desk told her that it was exactly ten.

"Come in, please," she said, forgetting to exhale. It made her voice come out too high, almost squeaky.

She leaped to her feet, moved quickly to the door, and swung it open to meet her guest. She looked straight at a male chest clad in a slate-gray silk shirt. She raised her eyes to meet those of the visitor. Their eyes locked, hers green, his dark brown.

"Ms. Garland," he said. "I came to make you an offer on your speedway." His face was lazily expressionless, except for a hint of a sardonic quirk at the edge of his mouth. There was a slight scar next to that quirk.

She blinked in disbelief. She now found herself wanting to weep with rage rather than relief.

She no longer felt impelled to kiss him, but wanted to turn him around forcibly and kick him in the seat of his obviously expensive pants.

He cocked a dark eyebrow. She could tell he enjoyed her dismay, even savored it. "We used to know each other," he almost purred in the low voice she remembered all too well. "You were Lori Simmons then. We were in high school together. I'm—"

"Kane Ledger," she supplied. She wished she could pry up a few tiles from the office floor and burrow down into the earth, deep out of sight.

He was the boyfriend from her past that she most regretted and most wanted to forget.

"May I come in?" he asked in a tone that was half-silky, half-sarcastic.

"Please do," she replied with her finest imitation of calm. She waved him inside, and suddenly the little office looked twice as shabby as before. She gestured for him to sit in the extra chair. It was upholstered in ancient imitation leather, and its seat was patched with an uneven X made of duct tape.

Kane nodded and stepped into the room, laying a black leather folder on the edge of her desk. He still had the long, lean body he'd had as a teenager and that air of being at once both casual and dangerous.

And, to her discomfort, she saw that he still had that same sell-me-your-soul grin. It made her pulses quicken and her nerve ends tingle. His presence galvanized the little room like a gathering lightning charge.

She sat and gestured for him to do likewise. *Get control of yourself,* she scolded. *What happened was half a lifetime ago. We're adults now. We were hardly more than children then.*

But there was no longer any vestige of boyishness in him. His shoulders had broadened, and his face no longer bore the haunted, too-thin look of someone who knew what it was like to go hungry. He'd finally grown into those beautifully carved cheekbones, and they no longer cast hollow shadows on his face.

As a teenager, he'd already had frown lines etched between his brows. But as poor and underprivileged as he'd been, he'd been handsome. Oh, how handsome. And he was more so now.

He looked tan and fit, and the frown lines were balanced by the laugh lines at the outer edges of his eyes. His hair was no longer ill-cut and tousled. He still wore it a bit long, but it was expertly barbered and still as dark as night, no hint of early graying.

Long ago, there'd often been something troubled in his expression, an almost constant wariness. That air was gone now; he seemed confident. Perhaps too confident and too hard-edged.

He crossed his leg over his knee and studied her. "You haven't changed."

Liar, she thought, with a twinge of deep sadness. She was twenty one years older; her marriage had failed; she was no longer the town's princess; and although she hated to admit it, he frightened her more than a little.

All those years ago, she'd encouraged him to want her. She'd loved him, but in the end she'd treated him abominably.

He'd quit high school and disappeared from town, and for more than a decade she'd worried that she'd ruined his life.

Then word had come that, in spite of the odds, he'd made a success of himself. He'd become a lawyer, then a sports agent, a powerful one. She'd been sincerely glad for him, but to tell the truth, she'd felt more glad for herself—she wouldn't have to carry so much shame over what she'd done. But she still felt guilty and knew she should.

Something in his face told her that he knew it, too. She'd made him suffer. Was that why he was here? Had he heard about her distress and decided that it was payback time? She didn't like the cold gleam in his eye or the self-satisfied twist of his mouth.

"I've changed, all right," she said. His sudden reemergence had shaken her, but she held his stare with one as steady as his own. "So have you. You've obviously done quite well for yourself," she said.

He gave a small, noncommittal nod. "Well enough."

"I'm happy for you."

"Thank you," he said. "But you deserve much of the credit."

He said this so coolly, with such studied poise, that she felt a palpable sense of menace.

But Lori refused to play the ingénue. She didn't widen her eyes or act innocent or ask him what he meant. She simply studied that impossibly handsome, unreadable face and waited. Let him explain himself.

He stretched the silence out for half a minute and then smiled, almost to himself. But he kept watching her.

"You did me a big favor once," he said. "You threw me over."

Oh, good grief, she thought. *He doesn't want the speedway. He came here to get even somehow, to play some twisted game.* But he'd always known where her thoughts were heading. "I'm not trying to play some sick joke here," he said quietly. "You found somebody else. And it was the best thing that ever happened to me."

She lifted her chin. "Am I supposed to be flattered by that? I'm not."

He gave a low chuckle. "But I mean it. Back then, I actually wanted to get you pregnant so you'd have to marry me. Then where would I have been? A teenage father with no prospects."

He shrugged. "Your dad might have put me on the payroll here—for your sake. And I would've ended up spending my whole life in this lousy town. I'd have watched your father run this place into the ground and be right where you are now. And you're in a pretty helpless situation, princess."

Lori's ire rose dangerously. "Kane, don't pull your punches. Just rub my nose in it really hard, why don't you?"

He grinned, showing those dimples that could seem so cheerily sinister. "You're something," he said approvingly. "They could tie you to a stake to burn you alive, and you'd be trying to spit in the eye of the guy lighting the match."

"It'd be smarter to spit on the match, wouldn't it?" she retorted.

The dimples deepened. "No. Because you'd be tied up, and there are too many matches in the world. Like I said, Lori, you're trapped."

"I'm glad you're not gloating over it," she said acidly.

He laughed again, which infuriated her. She wished she had a brick to throw at him.

But he said, "I didn't come to gloat, babe. I came to help. I have the offer in that folder." He nodded at the black leather folder on her desk. "I came to buy this place. At your asking price. And to keep it a speedway. To restore it."

He was being deliberately cruel. Tears smarted in her eyes, but, furious, she blinked them back. "Why?" she demanded. "Why would you want to do such a thing? A minute ago, you called this a lousy town. You said…you actually *said* my father ran this place into the ground."

She put one fist on her hip. "And that *my* situation, which means being in charge of this speedway, is like being condemned to burn at the stake. You want to take my place at the bonfire? *You* want to go up in flames? Why?"

He narrowed his dark, dark eyes. "I don't think I'll go up

in flames. Bring this place back to what it was? You can't do it. But I can."

"You *think* you can," she shot back.

"I *know* I can."

"But," she said, more frustrated than before, "why would you *want* to?"

Any trace of a smile he'd had faded. "I told you. I owe you. And frankly, I don't like owing you. Let's call it paying off a debt."

She squeezed her eyes tightly shut. "Again, this is not flattering, Kane. Nor funny."

"I'm not trying to be funny," he said. "I've got no reason to flatter you. But I do have reason to do you a favor."

She opened one eye and studied him suspiciously.

"I know exactly what you're facing," he said. His half-smile flirted near his scarred cheek. "I know how much Devlin offered you. I know when their deadline is."

She opened both eyes, now more distrustful than before.

He raised a speculative brow and looked her up and down. "I know you have to take Devlin's offer—unless you get a better one. Otherwise, at the end of June, the bank owns this speedway."

"You've been spying on me," she accused, her voice flat, yet accusing.

"My business is in sports. That includes motor racing. I know what goes on in the racing world, Lori. I know what happens. And who it happens to. And why."

She shook her head dubiously. "And you think *you* can transform Halesboro?"

"It can be turned around with enough sweat, money—and connections. I'm an agent. It's a good life. I enjoy it. But my accountant says it's time I diversify. Invest. I'm making some extremely safe investments. And I'm also making this one. Because I also enjoy a challenge. And Halesboro Speedway is a big one."

Lori frowned. Had his wealth made him insufferably

smug? Was he working out some crazy adolescent issues about growing up poor in Halesboro? And some even more crazy fantasy about evening the score for how she'd treated him so long ago?

A small, icy, pragmatic voice inside her head whispered, *To hell with his motives. Make him prove he means it.*

"I want to look over the contract," she said.

"Fine," he said. "Look it over. Take your time. Take all day. I'm staying over. Meet me tonight for a business supper. We'll talk about it."

"A business supper?" she echoed.

There was no so-called fine dining left in Halesboro; all such restaurants had closed. And she didn't intend to go out of town with him. He unsettled her too much. She wanted to be on her own turf.

Again, he seemed to know her thoughts. "I saw that The Groove Café's still open. Does Otis still run it?"

"Otis died ten years ago. His son runs it."

"Do they still make that hamburger steak with fried onions and hash browns?"

"Yes," she said. The menu hadn't changed in almost thirty years. Nor had the décor. It was the Eatery That Time Forgot.

"Then let's eat there. It'll almost be like old times."

She couldn't help flinching. She and her friends used to buy cheeseburgers and malts there on their nights out. They'd linger and giggle and use half a bottle of ketchup on their French fries. The most popular boys would seek them out and linger with them.

Kane had been in the kitchen, washing ketchup off the plates and the lipstick prints off the glasses. But he gave her that mysterious half smile of amusement.

"Should I pick you up? What time?" he asked.

"I'll meet you there," she said crisply. "How about five o'clock?"

Five o'clock was too early for most diners. She wasn't looking forward to having people stare at them. And stare they would, even if nobody recognized Kane at first. And when they did recognize him, they'd stare like the very devil. All of them.

SHE OFFERED to show him around the speedway, but he asked if Clyde was still there. He remembered Clyde, had worked with him and would like to see him again; where could he find the older man? She called Clyde, her throat tight, and told him Kane Ledger was here and wanted to be shown around. "Yes," she said uncomfortably. "*That* Kane Ledger. I'll send him to you."

She closed her phone. "He's out by the scoreboard," she told Kane.

"Fine. You want me to keep quiet about the offer?" Kane asked, standing by the door.

"Please. He'll know soon enough," she said and sighed. If the offer was for the asking price, she'd have no choice but to take it. Then the bank would know, the title company would know, her whole staff would know and the news would be all over town in minutes.

When Kane left the office, she made herself look carefully at the contract, which seemed to contain the best of all possible offers. But her temples pounded, and her lungs burned as if she'd run a long and grueling way.

When Kane had first appeared, it was as if he'd forced most of the oxygen out of the room and now it came seeping back. Slowly her breathing became almost normal again.

But she still didn't feel normal. Her heart beat too hard, her stomach fluttered in a way she'd forgotten it could flutter. She felt as if she'd opened more than a physical door when she'd answered Kane's knock.

She'd opened a door that seemed almost supernatural in its power. There, beyond it, was a lost world, the past, as clear and vibrant and vital as if it were happening for the first time.

SHE REMEMBERED that first time, that summer day when she'd been sixteen… She and her parents and older brother lived in the big, beautiful house on McCorkle Avenue. Her father, Andrew Jackson Simmons, was one of the most influential men in town, his speedway one of the most prosperous businesses.

The Victorian house in Queen Anne style had an elaborate porch and small second-story balcony with a delicate spindle-work frieze extending round it. There was a similar balcony in the back, between Lori's bedroom and that of her brother, A.J.

The lawn was slightly more than two acres and meticulously landscaped, with Lori's mother's prize rose garden near the patio, and beyond the roses, flowering shrubs and an octagonal swimming pool.

It was summer vacation, a warm but mildly breezy Saturday, and the rest of Lori's family had gone to the speedway to watch a qualifying race. Lori had opted to stay home and read by the pool.

She loved being outdoors, but with her red hair, she never tanned, only burned or added to her freckles, so she sat in a lounge chair under a big green-and-white striped umbrella. She wore a modest two-piece green bathing suit that she hated, but it was the closest that her mother was going to let her get to a bikini.

She had a gauzy white cover-up she wore unbuttoned and white flip-flops for padding to the pool for her very short dips to cool off. Her hair was heaped atop her head to keep it from getting wet, but the breeze had loosened long tendrils that danced on her cheeks and the nape of her neck and played games with her oversized sunglasses.

But Lori sat, happy to be alone at home as only a sixteen-year-old could be, and feeling *quite* grown-up. And she was reading a quite grown-up book, one her parents probably wouldn't want her to read. She'd secretly borrowed it from her Aunt Aileen's private library. If Aileen noticed frequently that books would disappear then reappear from her shelves, she never mentioned it.

Lori was paging solemnly through the book, when the

back gate opened. She barely looked up. Her mother had told her that old Mr. Merkle, the man who owned the lawn service, would be over to tend the rose garden sometime this afternoon. So Lori paid him no attention, for Mr. Merkle liked plants better than people and never talked if he could help it.

Except, from the corner of her eye, she noticed the figure heading toward the garden shed moved too fast to be Mr. Merkle. She stole a furtive look over the top of her sunglasses and was unpleasantly surprised to see *that* boy.

She knew little about him except that he went to her high school and he didn't fit in. He was one year ahead of her and had seemed to appear out of nowhere at the beginning of the spring semester.

Her friend Shana said he was poor white trash, that he came from a broken home and his mother was a barmaid, and "was no better than she ought to be," whatever that meant. Worse, his father was in prison for fraud. The boy's name was Kane Ledger.

Lori had secretly thought he was very handsome, and she suspected she wasn't the only girl who did. But he had none of the things that most people in school had—no nice clothes, no stylish haircut, no car, no decent house or respectable family and apparently not even lunch money.

He could've eaten the government-assisted free lunch with the other poor kids, but he didn't. He sat alone in the lunch room, his nose in a library book. He looked like a hoodlum, and he never smiled or acted friendly. When he walked through the halls, he radiated a fierce solitude. It was as if he were the only real person in a teeming hoard of ghosts.

Lori thought he was strange and probably no good. As her mother would say, he wasn't one of "their kind." That meant many things, including that he'd be lazy, slipshod and undependable.

But he went straight to work, got the wheelbarrow and pruning shears and lopping shears out of the garden shed, leaned the leaf rake next to its door and then set out to work with an energy it was hard to ignore.

He certainly didn't move like Mr. Merkle, who plodded through the plants like an elderly tortoise, slowly going snip, snip, snip. No, Kane Ledger moved with speed and strength, so much that Lori suspected he didn't really know what he was doing.

She decided she should watch him carefully, because if he ruined her mother's roses, there'd be hell to pay. Lori knew something about pruning because people couldn't live in the same house with Kitty Simmons and not know more about roses than they ever wanted to.

She narrowed her eyes to focus on him harder. She was almost disappointed that he *did* seem to know what he was doing. Was he Mr. Merkle's apprentice or trainee or something?

Well, it was good he was learning a trade. Shana had said she'd seen him digging ditches with some workmen along the highway during spring vacation. If he applied himself, he could be a gardener instead of a common laborer.

The sun beat down harder. His dark hair was long and hung nearly to his shoulders. He took off his garden gloves, reached up and tied his hair back neatly with one of its own strands. It was a strange, efficient movement, and made him look rather like a young Native American brave.

She was growing hot and wanted to go into the pool, but she wasn't sure she should take off her cover-up. Her mother had let her have the two-piece bathing suit on the promise she wore it only at the family pool and that she didn't "parade around" in front of members of the male sex.

This particular male, however, hadn't so much as glanced in her direction. It was as if she were so unremarkable that he didn't realize she was there. But as the sun blazed down more hotly, he stopped, stripped off his damp white T-shirt, and she certainly became more aware of *him*.

He was almost too lean, but his shoulders were surprisingly wide. He was totally snake-hipped, and his bare torso was all muscle, no fat. He was tanned, so tanned that she felt disgustingly pale.

But she noted all this almost subconsciously because what struck her most about his bare skin was that he had *tattoos*. They covered his upper arms, his shoulder blades, and when he turned in her direction, she saw he had some kind of small tattoo above each of his nipples.

She ducked her head, embarrassed, but fascinated, too. No respectable boy at Halesboro High had tattoos, but he had half a dozen or more. What kind of person was he?

Not a person she should give a second thought, she decided, especially since he gave none to her. She stood up, put on her flip-flops, laid down her book and sunglasses, and slipped off her cover-up. She flip-flopped to the pool with as much dignity as possible, kicked off her footwear, and climbed down the ladder into the water.

She secretly watched to see if he saw her, but he wasn't looking at anything but roses, roses and more roses. She swam for about five minutes, until she could feel the burn of the sun on her tender skin, then climbed out again, dripping. She went back to the lounge, and for all he noticed, she might as well be invisible.

She patted herself as dry as possible, taking her time. She put her gauze shirt back on, but didn't button it. She tried to smooth her hair a bit.

He threw a batch of canes and twigs into the wheelbarrow. She jammed on her sunglasses and sat on the lounger again, determined not to look at him, either.

But she did. He had an uncanny smoothness in his movements, and he radiated a quiet intensity. He was a man in his own world. So she tried to be in *her* own world and concentrate on her book. She almost succeeded.

The shadows lengthened, although dusk was still far off. Kane Ledger did so much work in so much less time than Mr. Merkle that she almost wanted him to slow down. After all, he was probably being paid by the hour and needed the money. It must be awful to be poor. His jeans were faded and raggy, but not at all in a fashionable way.

He saved the hardest chore for last, tending the big wooden trellis loaded with the Don Juan roses. A windstorm last week had made the trellis tilt unpleasantly to the left, and the climbing vines covered it so thickly they were pulling it over further.

Really, she thought rather disapprovingly, this didn't seem like a job for just one man, even one as agile as Kane Ledger. But his tan, his long, tied-back hair and tattoos gave him a look of primitive strength, so she trusted that he could probably handle a couple of overgrown rose plants.

He trimmed the red roses so the mulch around him was littered with green leaves and withering petals. But just as he was straining to heave the trellis upright again, something in it snapped loudly. He tried to wrestle it back into place, but she could see it was useless, it was bearing down on him, and he couldn't stop it.

It fell halfway over, and he went down to his knees, still fighting to hold it in place. But it had fallen as far as it could, with only the vines themselves managing to hold it up. Kneeling, he tested it, made sure it would fall no further, then stood up and began to limp toward the shed. He held one hand against his ribs, and blood oozed between his gloved fingers.

Lori, snatching off her sunglasses, sat straight up, horrified. Red scratches, red as the roses themselves, lacerated his arms and torso. Blood ran down the side of his jaw.

She leaped to her feet and dashed toward him. She reached him just as he was opening the shed door.

"What are you doing?" she demanded, trying to keep the door shut. "You're hurt. Sit down."

She wasn't strong enough to stop him. He yanked the door open. "I need stakes and twine to prop up that trellis till it can be fixed," he said from between his teeth. "Lemme alone. Go 'way. I'll take care of this."

She tugged at his arm and felt the slick of his blood beneath her fingers. "You need to take care of *you*," she insisted furiously. "Stand still. Let me see your side. You're bleeding like a stuck pig."

"The stuck pig is busy," he said, trying to shake her off. "Let go. You're going to get your shirt dirty."

She looked down. Scarlet already flecked her cover-up, but she refused to be shaken off.

She hung on tighter. "Come over to the hose, wash those cuts," she ordered.

He looked down at her. His dark hair had come loose, his face shone with perspiration, and a deep scratch ran along the edge of his mouth, seeping red drops that mixed with the sweat. His eyes were so dark they seemed black, and they flashed in anger. "Let go of me, you little pip-squeak."

Pip-squeak? Nobody talked to her like that. Nobody. She yanked at him harder, trying to drag him back from the door.

"Ouch!" he said involuntarily. "That hurts, dammit. You're pushing a thorn right *into* me."

She lessened her pressure. "Then stop fighting. Look. The stupid trellis isn't moving. It's not going to fall any farther. So get over to the hose and wash off."

His mouth took on a warning twist, and he brought his face closer to hers. "Just who do you think you are, short stuff?"

She squared her chin. "You work for my father, and you're bleeding all over his lawn," she shot back. "And you've got blood on his shed door, and if you don't do what I say, you'll get more blood on me, and you'll never work in any yard in this town again."

"Oh," he said with an indignant toss of his head, "the princess of the manor has spoken. All right, all right. I'll wash off. Now leave me alone. And let go."

Again he tried to jerk away, and again she held fast. His arm was warm to her touch and knotty with muscle.

"Ouch!" he cried again. "You're pressing on that thorn, for God's sake. What do you *want?*"

"I want to see you do this right," she said stubbornly. "Stop being so macho."

"Stop being so bossy," he countered, but he allowed her to lead him to the hose coiled up on its holder beside the faucet.

She let go of him and unscrewed the nozzle, then turned on the water. "Come here," she ordered.

"I can do it myself," he said contemptuously. "Who are you? Florence Nightingale? Give me that."

He snatched the hose from her and began to let the water run over his chest. He kept his left hand pressed to his side, and the blood still dripped from under his fingers.

"I've studied first aid," she said. "I've got a certificate." Actually, this was a white lie, because she only had a Girl Scout badge in first aid, but she knew telling him that would only make him sneer. She could already see that he was a master of the sneer.

"Whoopty do," he muttered, letting the water run down his arm.

"Let me see your side," she commanded, trying to pry his hand loose.

"Quit!" He smacked at her fingers, but lightly, as if shooing a butterfly.

She glared up at him as imperiously as she could. "You did this to yourself on my father's property," she said. "What if you've got internal injuries? A...a severed artery? Or get blood poisoning? Or gangrene? Then he'd be liable, and I won't stand for that. I will not. I demand you show me that cut."

He rolled his dark eyes in disgust. "Yes, my lady." He drew away his hand and held it, bloody in the air. "Look. Does it make you happy?"

Actually, it was a wide, nasty cut, and it made her rather sick. She was glad she was pale by nature, because she could feel her own blood draining from her face. But she kept a stoic expression.

"How'd you manage to do that?" she asked.

"The trellis broke," he said slowly, as if explaining it to a child. "The slats cracked, and one shot into my side. I think it bounced off a rib. It's not as bad as it looks. It's not deep. It'll heal."

"You've got a splinter in it," she said, staring at his naked side. "More than one. Let me get the tweezers. I'll pull them out and patch you up. But then you should go get a tetanus shot."

"You don't get tetanus from wood," he informed her. Then he faced away from her and let the hose run on his open wound.

She began to back toward the house. "I'm going to get the first aid kit. You better be here when I get back, or I'll tell Mr. Merkle and—"

"I know, I know," he said with distaste. "I'll never work in this business again."

Breathlessly she ran inside, seized the first aid kit out of the downstairs bathroom cabinet, and sprinted back to him. He'd gone back to the garden, picked up his T-shirt, wet it, and now held it to his side and was turning off the water. He'd pulled out the biggest splinter, and blood still trickled down his ribs.

"I brought soap, too," she said. "Let me really clean those cuts."

"*I'll* do it," he said firmly, and took the bar from her. His wet fingers brushed her dry ones, and a spectacular jolt of awareness went through her.

She stood and watched as he soaped and rinsed his wounds, his face rigid with control. And for the first time, she let herself look at the tattoos on his body. There were bands of them around both upper arms, like bracelets of an exotic design. On top of his right shoulder, a crescent moon was etched in blue, a star inside its curve, and on the right a picture of the sun. Both the sun and moon had faces.

The skin of his chest was smooth and bronzed, with only a dusting of dark hair down his breastbone. He had well-developed pectoral muscles, and above each brownish nipple was a tattoo of a flying bird. They were identical and faced each other from opposite sides of his chest.

"Okay," he said. "Now give me some tape and let me get on with the job."

"I'll tape you," she said, trying to keep her eyes off the flying birds. "Some are in awkward spots. Especially the one on your ribs. That one's going to take some doing."

He sighed. His chest heaved, and the birds moved in unison.

"Come over by the pool and sit down. It'll be easier, and the light's better. I need to get the rest of those splinters out."

"Just do it here," he muttered.

"No," she countered. "You've actually lost a lot of blood. Come sit down for a minute. Do I have to *drag* you?"

She seized his hand, and he gave a snort of surprise. Still he followed her, at a maddening amble, as if she were making a fuss about nothing. He refused to sit on any of the furniture, but instead plopped down at the farthest edge of the concrete around the pool. She sat beside him and opened her kit.

"I don't know why you won't make yourself more comfortable," she grumbled.

He gave her an impatient look and showed his palm, the skin still red and damp with scratches from grabbing at the falling roses. "I'll slop up your nice, clean poolside."

He struck a dramatic pose and stared at his hand. In a surprisingly sonorous voice he said, "Will all great Neptune's ocean wash this blood clean from my hand? No, this my hand will rather the multitudinous seas incarnadine, making the green one red."

He paused and gave her a wry look. "And your white pool furniture corpuscle pink."

He could not have surprised her more if he had suddenly sprouted man-sized wings.

She stared at him, the antiseptic wipe in her hand forgotten. "That's from *Macbeth*," she breathed.

"Yeah?" he said, raising his brows questioning. "So what? Despite what you might think, I can actually read."

She felt the rebuke in his words, but she held his gaze. "I know you can read. I just didn't think you'd read Shakespeare."

"Last year, I had two study halls in a row," he said, almost defensively. "I'd get my stuff done and there was nothing else to read. It was the assigned play. I didn't want to read the algebra book, for God's sake."

He's proud, she thought. *He's smart and brave—and proud. But everybody's looked at him as if he's dirt.*

"Well," she murmured a bit ashamed of herself, "it's not the kind of thing I'd guess you'd memorize, that's all."

"I didn't memorize it on purpose," he said. "I just read it about a hundred times. It stuck in my mind."

"Oh." She gazed into his face, still stunning in spite of its scratches. She wondered what else was in that mind of his.

And he looked back, as if wondering the same thing about her.

That was the beginning of it for her. That was how it started. A boy fell down in the roses.

CHAPTER THREE

OKAY, KANE THOUGHT, his footsteps echoing in the empty hallway. The Halesboro Speedway was haunted.

It was haunted by its own former eminence. Down the hall that housed the offices—most now seemingly deserted—were photos and framed newspaper and magazine stories of the track in its heyday. It had been one of the toughest tracks in the nation, both a driver's dream and nightmare. A dream to win, a nightmare fighting for that win.

A high-banked oval, the track was one of the most abrasive on the circuit. The asphalt with its high sand content chewed up tires like a monster gnawing jerky. It was as demanding as tracks came, and its nickname, fully earned, was Hellsboro.

But a hard track had made for challenging races; drivers had fought out thrilling contests here, set unforgettable records. Halesboro saw one of the closest finishes in NASCAR history, a 1999 win by 0.0033 seconds—people still talked about it, a decade later.

The photos and the yellowing clippings brought back vivid images and high emotions. Memories hung in the air like ghostly smoke. Outside, Kane had seen the old statue of black granite, an imposing carving of a flame symbolizing "Hellsboro," and on the flame's granite and bronze pedestal were engraved the names of the track's greatest winners.

But if the nostalgia of greatness haunted the halls, so did the sense of glory so long past it was turning into the depressing sense of present weakness and future failure. What the hell was he getting himself into?

Kane found Clyde by the scoreboard next to the infield care center, and the two men shook hands with self-conscious awkwardness. The last time Kane had seen the older man, Clyde had been his mentor, teaching him and encouraging him to learn more. Clyde didn't give a damn that Kane didn't come from "respectable" people. Clyde had grown up poor himself, nothing handed to him; he was a self-made man who'd earned the respect he got.

Maybe Clyde had seen something of himself in the teen-age Kane, who'd volunteered as a crewman for local, more recreational races. Andrew J. Simmons gave small importance to those races. He provided what the community thought he should provide—a training ground for kids with racing talent.

Clyde saw the local races as something far more impor-tant, a low rung that a determined young man could use to climb higher. He might rise into the racing stratosphere if he had the guts, the brains and reflexes. Now Clyde looked at his protégé with something akin to shyness.

"You don't look like the kid that blew this place and didn't leave a forwarding address," Clyde told him, taking in the dark silk shirt, the tailored slacks, the expensive shoes. "But I've heard about you and what you been doin'. Good on you, boy."

Kane felt a pang of emotion looking at the aging man. Clyde's brown eyes still shone with alertness; his weathered face was kind. "I had good teachers," Kane said gruffly.

"Best teacher's the school of hard knocks," Clyde said, with a measuring sideways glance. "Want to see the track, the pits?"

"And the stands," Kane answered. "Yeah. All of it."

"It isn't what it was," Clyde warned him. "Life's like a big ol' seesaw. Some things go up—" he looked Kane over "—and some go down. You feelin' sentimental, or you got another reason to come back and look this over?"

I've got more than one reason, Kane thought, keeping all expression from his face. And he thought of an old proverb. "The heart has reasons that reason does not know." He kept those words from crossing his lips and ejected the idea from his mind. He was excellent at hiding what he thought and what he felt.

But Clyde, somehow, had always known him a little too well for Kane's own comfort. Clyde said. "She called me about you. Lori. You seen her, huh?"

"Yeah," Kane said tonelessly. "Sure."

"She's been through a lot," Clyde said. "Her daddy wasn't himself in his last years. Responsibility for this place wasn't supposed to fall on her. It was supposed to be her brother's concern. You heard what happened to him?"

Kane nodded without emotion. "Yeah. I read it in the papers."

A. J. Simmons, Jr., Second Lieutenant in the North Carolina National Guard, had died in Afghanistan four years ago.

Clyde shook his head. "The old man never got over it. A J dyin' did him in. Nobody but Lori to hold things together. She's done her best. Always has. Kept her chin up through the whole thing. But the odds against her? Look at that scoreboard."

Kane looked up. It was the same scoreboard that had stood there more than twenty years ago, and it had been old then.

"It can only show the first five positions in the race," Clyde muttered. "Shoulda replaced it years ago." He turned and gestured at the track. "And look at that asphalt. That asphalt needs serious work..."

Kane could see that, as well as the worn seating rising in tiers, the shoddiness that had set in. He saw the shot out night lights and all the signs of the Halesboro's aging infrastructure. They surrounded him like both a challenge and a rebuke.

He took in the changes time had brought, none of them good. But his mind only half registered them. What he saw more vividly was Lori herself, that first afternoon they'd talked.

Seeing her in that office made him feel as if he'd stepped into a time machine. He'd hurtled backward to that summer day they'd truly met. The memory came rushing back so strongly he still couldn't exorcise it.

HE'D SEEN HER the minute he'd popped the latch and opened the gate into her backyard.

He hadn't expected that. Oh, no.

She lay stretched on a white lounge chair by the pool, shaded by a big green-and-white umbrella. It was the biggest umbrella he'd ever seen, and it had a NASCAR logo on it. But even its shadow couldn't dull the red-gold of her hair heaped atop her head, or dim the white curve of her throat as she sat reading her book.

She barely glanced at him; his presence didn't even seem to register. She went back to perusing her book, and his heart knotted in his chest like a fist clenching so hard it hurt. He'd seen her at school before—a petite girl with a face so lovely it could commandeer his gaze and keep it if he didn't control himself. He was glad he was a master of self-control.

This girl was out of his league. Half the guys in school wanted her, and she could have her pick of them. The odd thing was she hadn't picked anybody. Even in his self-imposed distance from other students, he heard she went out. But not with anyone special.

He figured she was smart enough—he'd heard she was very smart indeed—to be saving herself for someone better than Halesboro could offer. She'd end up going to an expensive university and marrying a handsome boy with a daddy even richer than hers.

And her daddy was mighty rich. He owned and ran the speedway, and Kane knew he socialized with all those famous racing people. He imagined Lori at formal dinners in an impossibly fancy banquet room in her big house, being courted by handsome young drivers, guys who were up-and-coming heroes and would someday be millionaires.

So, to him, she seemed the most unattainable girl in school—and the most desirable. The maddening thing wasn't that she was desirable simply because she was pretty. Halesboro had pretty girls aplenty.

No. There was something different about Lori Simmons,

some indefinable thing that set her off from all the others. She never called attention to herself, yet somehow she commanded attention. She gave off a sense of individuality, a natural independence.

She carried more books than any other girl in school. He mostly hated school, but he liked books. And she didn't just carry her assigned textbooks. He'd see her sitting in study hall, her homework done—she seemed to get her homework done with lightning speed; she must never have to take it home—instead she'd be reading something he'd never heard of. That always made him feel curious…and inferior, a know-nothing.

What, for instance, was *Wuthering Heights?* She'd sat at the study table, reading it so intently she seemed to tune out the rest of the world. What did *wuthering* mean, anyway? It wasn't in the dictionary, because he looked it up, and it wasn't in the library because he'd looked there, too.

He hadn't expected to see her that afternoon he went to work in her father's backyard.

The whole time he was there, he kept stealing glances at her, but he never once caught her looking back. Why should she? She was like a princess who lived in a castle, and he was like the raggle-taggle gypsy in the song.

He made himself concentrate—almost ninety-seven percent—on pruning the roses. He was lucky to get this job from Old Man Merkle, and he intended to keep it. He wanted to do a good job, so Mrs. Simmons would want him back. "She's picky, that one," Merkle had said in disgust. "Can't ever please her."

He'd checked out two books on roses from the public library and spent Friday night reading about how to prune roses, for God's sake. Every other guy in town was out hooting and cruising and raising hell, and he was cramming his brain full with stuff like "growth nodes" and "nutrients in woody canes."

But three percent of the time he couldn't help himself, and he'd steal a look at the princess, who, as a princess should, ignored him. But his heart vaulted and stuck in his throat when she stood, shed her white gauzy blouse and lowered herself into the pool. That made concentration difficult.

Then she got out, the full sunshine on her gold-red hair and water streaming down her pale body, hidden only by the two green pieces of her bathing suit. That made concentration almost impossible.

But he had a lot of willpower—"stubborn as hell," his mother called him—and he did fine until he started to work on that central trellis. There was something wrong with the trellis itself, he sensed, and Merkle had let the vines overpower it.

He was half-convinced that the lattice work was rotten under all those vines, and that old man Merkle should have replaced it long—

Then the damn thing came down on top of him. A broken slat shot into his ribs, and he had his arms full of thorny roses about to crash into the dirt. Merkle would kill him.

He fought with all his strength to save the thing, and at last it seemed stabilized, and he realized his head and arms and throat stung with scratches, and his side was bleeding.

And while he still seemed half-smothered by roses, he looked between them and saw—oh, humiliation—that *now* she noticed him. Her mouth dropped open, and the book fell out of her hand. She didn't even seem to know it. Her attention was focused on him.

He felt like a perfect fool. He extricated himself and made for the shed to repair the damage from the broken trellis, but Lori Simmons was on him like a duck on a june bug. He was appalled. He felt like a clumsy peasant, and he did all he could to ward off her attempt to help him.

She was not a girl who could be warded off once she'd made up her mind. He didn't think the U.S. Marines could ward her off. And before he could help himself, he'd been captured.

He'd sat at the edge of the pool's concrete, and she actually seized his hand to examine it, and her touch made him hot, dizzy, confused, desirous and so desperate to impress her that he'd blurted out some lines of poetry, hardly knowing where they came from. He'd been trying to be a smart aleck, show her he wasn't like some poor yard dog who'd got a thorn in his paw.

And she'd kept hold of his hand and looked into his face as if she really saw him for the first time, and he found himself mumbling some nonsense about study hall, but all he could look at were her eyes, and all he could think of were her lips.

He felt as if he were tumbling into an alternate universe. She sat beside him, her bright hair dancing in the breeze. The emerald green of her damp bathing suit clung to her slender body, and her eyes were the same emerald green. And she looked at him as if he were *somebody.* Somebody special.

Her hands were on him, gentle and sure. She took a pair of tweezers and pulled the thorn from deep in his arm, and he could not allow himself to flinch in this girl's presence. She was dabbing his arms and then his chest with antiseptic.

Oh.

Good.

Lord.

She cleaned his side, used tweezers to pull out the remaining slivers—they were impressively long, and he was rather glad they were, and acted as if nothing hurt at all, like a knight trying to seem nonchalant about his wounds.

She poured antiseptic right into the gash. Yikes! He had to allow himself to clench his teeth a bit. "Did that hurt?" she asked, her voice so full of concern something inside him melted.

"It…um…smarted a bit," he admitted. "Nothing really."

"I'll put a bandage on it," she said, and took one from its wrapper. She held the edges of the cut together with small, steady fingers. Her fingertips made him forget that his side hurt, he was only conscious of her touch.

"Be sure to change that often," she said. "Promise."

"I will," he said gruffly. He wasn't used to anybody fussing over him like this.

People hurting you? He'd been there, plenty of times. But somebody who touched you gently, kindly, with the utmost deliberate care, bent on making you feel better, this was novel. And he liked it. He liked it a *lot*.

He tried to think of something smart to say and couldn't. He just let her keep doing what she was doing.

She wiped clean the scratch on his neck. "I don't think that needs a bandage," she said in almost a whisper. "Just let it get some air."

He could feel her breath on his throat. "Yeah," he managed to say.

She put her hand on his face and turned it so she could examine the long scratch next to his mouth. He stared straight ahead at a long row of gooseberry bushes.

She ran her fingers along the edge of the cut, so lightly it was like a moth exploring his skin. "It's deep," she said in the same hushed voice. "I'll clean it."

She dabbed the antiseptic on, and he found that he was having trouble breathing. He swallowed and stared at the gooseberry bushes so hard he almost saw them double.

She smelled like chlorine and menthol and camphor and other medicinal stuff—oh, better than roses any day. And three times her fingers brushed his lips, making him half-dizzy with longing for more.

But then she took her hand away, and he had an eerie sensation of incompleteness. "I think that's most of it," she said, searching his face for any other damage.

He searched hers, too, but not for flaws. It was just so hard to resist looking. She glanced downward and picked up his T-shirt, which was wet from sweat and blood and the hose.

She unfolded it and clucked her tongue softly. "I don't think this can be saved," she murmured.

He looked at the pathetic, ruined thing in her manicured hands. He started to take it from her. But she hung on.

"Oh," she said. "It's a NASCAR shirt. I didn't realize—"

She probably hadn't realized because it was so faded. He'd bought it at the Salvation Army.

She looked into his eyes and gave him an enquiring little smile. "You're a fan?"

He tried to act casual. "Well…yeah. Sure."

"Do you ever go to the speedway?" she asked.

"Uh, yes," he said with as much aplomb as he could. "I do, actually. From time to time."

He knew of a gap beneath the wall he could sneak under, and he'd done so many times. He didn't have money for tickets. He gave his mother some of his money, but he put the rest away, because someday soon he was going to take it and go far, far from here.

He took the shirt from her. "I'll just throw it away."

"Do you want another one? I could loan you one of my brother's."

"No," he said and swallowed again. "I might bleed on it. I'm comfortable."

But he wasn't. He usually felt fine shirtless, but he usually wasn't around a girl like this. He stole a glance at her body. Her bathing suit was damp, and on her chest he saw droplets of water, maybe from the pool or from perspiration.

He looked away quickly and saw her fallen book. He reached for it and looked at it. Then he looked at her in surprise.

"You're reading a comic book?" he said in disbelief.

Her expression grew defensive. "It's not a comic book. It's a graphic novel."

"It looks like a comic book to me," he said dubiously. "It's got a mouse on the cover."

"It's actually a very serious story," she said, defensively. "It's about war. And prejudice. And man's cruelty to man."

He looked at her in puzzlement. "And about mice?"

"All right," she said with a little shrug that made her bosom move first up, then down. "Mice, too."

"You're going to have to explain that to me," he said, studying how serious her expression had become.

And so she started to explain. And he listened, and he

understood what she was getting at, and she showed him some of the pictures, and he bent his head closer to hers.

"I'd loan it to you," she said. "But it's not mine. It's my aunt's."

He allowed himself a small smile. "You must have some weird aunt."

"Don't you know her? She teaches at school. Mrs. Attwater."

His heart gave another unexpected little buck. "Mrs. Attwater is your *aunt?*"

"Yes," she said. "What's wrong with that?"

Somehow, it just seemed too perfect to him. If she was going to be anybody in the world's niece, she should be Mrs. Attwater's.

"She's my favorite teacher," he said. That was true. He didn't add that it was the first time he'd ever had a favorite teacher, and he generally didn't have much use for teachers at all.

"I…I could ask her to loan it to you," Lori suggested.

Why was she looking at him like that? He was having trouble breathing again. "Naw. That's okay," he said. "Listen, thanks and all, but I better get back to work."

He squinted at the sky and was surprised to see it had become cloudy. When had that happened? Probably all the trees could have turned upside down and waved their roots in the air and he wouldn't have noticed.

"And you—" he looked her up and down cautiously "—you should get back under your umbrella. You can get more sunburned when it's cloudy, you know? Uh…" He felt it imperative to say something that sounded semi-intelligent. "Uh…the light's UV rays can come through clouds."

"I've learned that to my sorrow," she said with a rueful dimple playing in her cheek.

She looked at him curiously. "Could I ask you something personal?"

He felt even more self-conscious. "I guess. What?"

"You've got those tattoos," she said, nodding at his body. "What are those designs?"

"Oh." He cocked his head as if the answer had no importance. "They're mostly from the South Seas. Polynesia."

"Why the South Seas?"

"I want to go there someday. Doesn't everybody?"

"I never thought about it," she said, looking interested. "But what about those two birds on either side of your chest? Are they Polynesian?"

"No," he said and swallowed again. "They're some kind of seagulls, I guess."

"Do they mean something?"

He gave a short laugh. "When I get old, my chest'll get sunken. And they'll get closer and closer together."

She looked into his eyes more closely. "And then?"

"And then, when they get so close that it looks like they're going to crash into each other…"

"Yes?" she urged.

He laughed again. "Then I'll know that at last it's time for me to start behaving."

She looked at him warily, as if unsure whether to believe him. But he'd told her the truth. His mother, Brenda, had told him so many times that he was going to Hell if he didn't change his ways, he'd gotten the bird tattoos as a private sardonic joke to remind him when he should start repenting. He thought it was funny at the time. Lori didn't seem to think so.

"Oh" was all she said.

But then raindrops began to fall around them, making a plopping sound on the concrete, jarring the grass blades.

"Don't let your book get wet," he cautioned her. "Thanks again. I've got to get back to work."

"You can't work if it rains," she protested, but she hugged the book to her protectively.

"Sure I can. In this business, what's a little more mud?"

"But—"

"I mean it," he said. "I've done it before. I'll quit if it gets too bad."

The rain began to fall more steadily.

"Go on," he said. "Go on inside. I'll be fine."

"You're sure?" she asked with concern.

"I'm sure. You've taken care of me. Now take care of yourself."

She nodded. "'Bye," she said softly. "See you around."

"Yeah," he said, drinking her in. "See you around."

She turned, snatched up her flip-flops and ran toward the back door. He went into the shed into find stakes and twine.

When he came out, she was standing there, a little umbrella over her head. It had dogs and cats on it. She held a bright yellow plastic poncho out to him. It had a faded Halesboro Speedway logo on the front.

"Here," she said, thrusting it at him. "Take this. I don't want all that antiseptic washing off or those bandages coming loose."

"No," he protested. "I've got to work with those roses. It'll get torn."

"It's already torn. I was going to throw it out. I've got a new one. Take it. I mean it. Take it. Put it on."

He shook his head. "You are the bossiest little thing…"

"Yes, I am," she told him. "Please. Just put it on. You can throw it away when you get home."

"Thanks," he said, taking it from her.

"Put it on," she said.

He did.

"You're welcome," she told him, looking suddenly shy. Then she turned and fled back to the house.

He worked for forty minutes in the rain. He wore the poncho home. But he didn't throw it away.

He didn't believe he'd ever throw it away. He intended to keep it until the seagulls on his chest were ready to crash into each other. For as long as his heart kept beating.

"NOW," CLYDE WAS SAYING as they walked the track, "Back when we had NASCAR races, drivers complained this was a one-groove track. Hard to drive on, hard to pass, especially on Turn Four."

Kane studied it and nodded. "Transition to the front straightaway's too abrupt."

"Yup," agreed Clyde, "So Andy Simmons tried to patch it. Added about five feet of pavement at the bottom of the exit of the turn. Drivers said they couldn't tell a bit a difference."

"It's not the kind of problem you solve with a patch," Kane said. He could visualize a solution, but it would cost and cost big.

Clyde looked at him with narrowed eyes, but was too polite to ask any leading questions. He just nodded at the track and said, "She's a challenge, all right. 'Course, with faith, all things are possible."

Kane gave a small, bitter smile. "In this town, it always seemed it was *money* that made all things possible."

Clyde crossed his arms. "There's a limit to what money can buy. Come on. I'll walk you around the track, then show you pit road."

Kane fell in step beside him, but often he took his eyes from the aging asphalt to steal a glance up at the empty stands. There was seating for 60,000 spectators. He gazed up at the VIP suites and wondered if there'd been any use for them lately.

That long ago summer when he'd been seventeen, he'd volunteered to help Clyde as a cleanup man on Sundays, the big race day. He'd volunteered the day after he'd talked to Lori by the pool.

He knew he looked screwy, with his scratched face and arms, his long hair, but he'd talked earnestly to Clyde, swearing he'd do any job, no matter how menial or dirty. He just wanted to be around racing, he'd said; he'd do anything, and he'd do it for nothing.

Clyde must have seen that he meant it. And Kane worked hard; he made himself welcome, and Clyde finally appreciated him enough to pay him $3.85 an hour.

Kane could have made the same money more easily by washing dishes or frying burgers. But he wanted to be at the speedway, where from time to time he could look up at that center VIP suite, knowing that Lori was there.

He'd heard that she *had* to be there; her parents insisted on it. She and her brother could bring all the friends they wanted, but Sunday race time was *family* time.

So he'd pushed his broom, emptied the trash barrels and picked up the empties and other litter simply to be in her presence. He was certain she didn't even know he was there.

But that was all right. She would.

The song about the gypsy kept running through his head all the time, an old, old song about a man winning the heart of a lady.

That was precisely what Kane meant to do, impossible as it might seem—win the love of a lady.

CHAPTER FOUR

LORI COULD NOT BELIEVE this was happening. There were just a few cars parked on the west end of Main Street. But one of them was a black sports car.

It could only belong to Kane. Two junior high school girls strolled past it, eyeing it as suspiciously as if it were a flying saucer. She didn't blame them; it did seem utterly alien sitting in front of The Groove Café.

Lori parked the sputtering Mustang three spaces behind the sports car. Clyde had confirmed her worst fear this afternoon; her car's transmission was going out. She needed to replace it as soon as possible.

She glanced in the rearview mirror. She'd washed her hair, so that it fell in bright, clean waves to her shoulders. But she hadn't put on full makeup again. Let Kane see the freckles, the fine lines at the corners of her eyes, the faint ones starting to bracket her mouth.

Let him also see her green and white seersucker pants and matching blouse that were three years old and had been bought at the Value-Mart store in Asheville. Let him see her exactly as she was, and let him glory in how she'd changed.

She told herself she didn't care. Not a bit. But her heart still hammered as she walked up the three concrete stairs of the café and opened the door.

She saw him sitting in the dark green leatherette booth, and her pulses accelerated even harder. He'd changed clothes. He wore a white NASCAR T-shirt with a picture of Kent Grosso on it. It was an old T-shirt, faded.

He slid out of the booth and stood when she stepped inside. He was wearing jeans and canvas shoes. The jeans, too, were faded. The shoes looked expensive but well-worn, even a bit tattered.

My God, she thought, her breath thickening in her throat. He looks almost the way he did twenty years ago—just a little older and not as thin. Suddenly it was as if he'd never left town. Somehow she'd blinked, two decades had passed and here he was.

The cheekbones were just as high and aristocratic. The dark eyes still pierced her with their alertness and a sense of anything but aristocracy. In them was the gleam of a born rebel. His lips turned up slightly in a smile that both welcomed her and challenged her.

He hadn't gotten rid of his tattoos. Somehow, she found that embarrassing. He had enough money, obviously, why hadn't he had the things taken off?

"Ah, Ms. Garland," Kane now said with false enthusiasm. "How nice to see you again."

He seized her hand, gave it a gentlemanly shake and then gestured for her to sit down. "Lovely weather we're having," he said. "So nice to be up in the mountains again."

He was so patently insincere that she knew he was mocking her, and she wasn't sure why he bothered. He held all the winning cards, didn't he? He'd always had a talent for jibes, a gift for needling those who were pompous. Did he think *she* belonged in that category?

"Oh, act normal," she said under her breath. "People are looking."

His eyes widened as if she'd told him he'd just landed in Oz and was surrounded by hidden Munchkins. But he smiled more naturally and whispered back, "Let 'em."

"Fine," she said with a brisk nod. "Let 'em indeed."

For people were eyeing them, the café's few patrons and Clara, the heavyset waitress behind the counter, and the owner,

Otis Jr., sitting as usual in the front booth, so he could see what went on both outside and inside.

"So," Kane said, "this is what it's like. To be seen with you in public. I finally know, after all these years."

"And so do I," she said sweetly. "Hardly worth the wait, was it?"

"Depends on your vantage point, I'd say."

His expression was one of cocky self-satisfaction and made her want to throttle him.

Clara materialized by her side, setting down water glasses before them. "Hi, hon," she said to Lori. "You want a menu?"

"No. Just a glass of iced tea, please."

"You?" Clara asked Kane.

"Tell me," he said, "do you still make that hamburger steak with the fried onions and hash browns?"

"Specialty of the house," she said, studying him carefully. "And to drink?"

"Same as the lady," he said.

She nodded and lumbered off.

"I looked over the contract," Lori said. "I have it in my bag." She reached for her oversized white tote. "I had my lawyer review it."

"No, no," he said with a dismissive gesture. "Business later. It's been a long time since we've seen each other. We have a lot of catching up to do."

"Do we?" She met his gaze and held it.

But suddenly the derision in his eyes disappeared, and his face became so tightly controlled she couldn't read it. "I know you've had a hard time," he said quietly. "I'm sorry."

This took her aback. For a moment she could summon no words. But then she changed the tack of the conversation. "But you've had a very good run. Tell me about it. I didn't know for the longest time what happened to you—"

"Did you wonder?" he interrupted. He asked the words with no expression at all.

"Of course, I wondered," she said. "I wondered for years. And then I heard you were a…a lawyer."

He held up his hand as a signal to stop. "Yes. And I've heard every lawyer joke in the world, so spare me."

She studied him more closely. *This is the boy that I loved. This is a stranger. Who is this man, really?* "I never thought it was a joke. I was glad for you. And proud of you. S-so you obviously finished high school. Where? In Charlotte?"

"Yeah," he said in the same tone. "Went to Charlotte. Did odd jobs. Worked as a cleanup man at the Motorworks store and got my GED. Then took any kind of job I could to make it through college. And law school."

"You always were smart. Aileen said you were brilliant."

His face softened slightly at the mention of her aunt's name. "Aileen. How is she?"

"Fine, thank God," Lori said. Aileen was the only family she had left. "She still lives in that little cottage on Ingalls Street. She walks a mile a day, still has her garden. She drives over to the county seat and works one day a week as a volunteer at the pet shelter."

He nodded. "Good for her. I want to see her."

"And she'll want to see you," said Lori. "And she'll ask me all about you. So tell. After law school, what?"

He raised one eyebrow as if he himself didn't quite understand how it had all come about. "I was interested in contract law. I went to work as a consultant for a firm of sports agents in Atlanta. Then I went with an agency back in Charlotte. A kid from here got in touch with me. A basketball player."

She looked at him in surprise. "Roman McCandless? *You* worked with Roman McCandless?"

McCandless was the most famous person ever to come out of Halesboro. He was six feet ten inches tall, and some said the best small forward in decades. He was a great player, and Halesboro had renamed a street for him.

Kane allowed himself a crooked grin. "My first client. My agency was going to sell him short. Literally. I told him,

'Don't sign. it. You can do better.' He said, 'Can you help me?' And, all of a sudden, I was an agent."

"And one client led to another?"

"North Carolina produces good roundball players. I got a reputation for treating them right. Then a NASCAR driver asked me to represent him. I branched out."

"I don't think anybody here ever knew that you and Roman worked together," she mused.

"It's only in the movies that people know the names of sports agents," Kane said. "Besides, Rome's family left here. They went to Florida. They've both passed on now."

"I'm sorry to hear it," she said. "But you have NASCAR connections, too? Who?"

"The best known's probably Kent Grosso."

"Kent Grosso?" she cried. "The 2007 NASCAR Sprint Cup Series champion?"

"And Dean Grosso," he added.

"The 2008 champion?" she asked in disbelief.

"Yeah. Those wins helped pay for the sports car."

"The sports car," she said, with a little frown. "I think I ought to talk to you about that. I mean, isn't it sort of—"

"Over the top? Yeah. That's why I like it. What? You think it's ostentatious?"

"Actually, the word that came to mind is *gauche*. But *ostentatious* will do."

He gave a harsh sigh of frustration. "You're still sassy. Life hasn't knocked that out of you."

She wasn't so sure. She said nothing.

Clara came to the booth and thudded down two tall glasses of tea, then left.

Kane stared at his but didn't touch it. He said, "I heard about your mother. I'm sorry."

She took a deep, painful breath. Her mother had died of a heart attack ten years after Kane left town. There'd been no warning—none. That morning Kitty Simmons had played two sets of tennis. She came home, changed her clothes, sat down in the living room with the newspaper and died, her pen in hand, the newspaper crossword puzzle half-finished.

"It happened fast," Lori said. "The doctor said she didn't suffer. I'm just sorry nobody was with her. I don't know what happened to your mother after she left here. Is she all right?"

"Brenda? I've got no idea where she is or how she is," he said coldly.

"I'm sorry."

"Don't be," he said.

"You could hire someone to find her, couldn't you?"

"Why would I want to?"

Lori nodded and stared at the table top. He'd told her of the fights they had. The vicious things she'd say, her threats.

"Your little sister?" she asked.

"Stacy? Doing well. Very well. We're in touch." He paused. "And I read about your brother. In Afghanistan. Sorry."

She gave him a sharp look. Her brother's friends had held Kane while A.J. battered and bloodied his face for seeing Lori. He'd helped drive Kane out of Halesboro. How could Kane feel any sympathy for A.J.?

Again Kane showed the old, uncanny ability to read her thoughts. He said, "I'm sorry for *you*. War's hell."

"Yes, but he didn't die in combat," she said, her jaw tightening. "It was an accident. A stupid accident. A road collision with another armored vehicle. It never should have happened. But Daddy took it hard, and he was already ailing."

"So Clyde told me."

"A.J. was supposed to take over the speedway," she said. "Then he was gone. Daddy asked me to do it. But I wasn't trained for it like A.J. was."

"You were teaching," he said, and she wondered how he knew.

"Right. Trying to make high school kids like literature. I don't think I competed very well with video games or the Internet."

"I doubt that."

She shrugged and they were both silent a moment. She sipped her tea. He still hadn't touched his glass.

He sat back farther in his seat. "Your marriage to the boy hero didn't work out."

So he knew that, too. He must have stayed in touch with somebody in Halesboro, after all. Scott, the "boy hero" had been the homecoming king the year that Kane dropped out. She shook her head sadly. "No. It didn't work out."

"You had no kids." Again, he said it, didn't ask it.

"No children. It wasn't meant to be. Probably just as well." She ran her hand through her hair. "Let's talk about something else."

"What?" he asked, leaning his crossed arms on the table in front of him.

"Why you came here," she said, raising her chin. "Business. I can believe you studied contract law, all right. Your offer's a good one. I'll sign it. The speedway will be yours. And it stays a speedway."

"I agreed to it. It's in writing."

She smiled at him in sad puzzlement. "That means you'll try to save it. And, frankly, I'm not sure it can be saved. I need to tell you that. To be honest."

"Maybe you underestimate me," he said.

"Or maybe the time's come round for the phoenixes to rise out of their ashes," she said, almost flippantly. "The speedway. McCorkle Castle. It finally sold. Or have you heard that, too?"

"I've heard," he said. "Do you know who bought it?"

"Nobody seems to know." She looked at him, feeling a sudden chill of apprehension. "I hope it wasn't *you*."

He laughed. "What in hell would I do with a castle?"

"Sell tickets for people to see it?" she suggested. "So Halesboro has a tourist attraction besides the track?"

"Sorry," he said, "I've only got one small fortune to gamble. No castle."

Clara set his plate in front of him. The air was suddenly fragrant with the sizzling beef and the tang of onions and fried potatoes. Kane looked at Lori. "I wish you'd eat. I invited you here to eat."

"I'm not hungry," she said. Or if she was, she couldn't feel it. Perhaps the day's events had overloaded her brain, and her sensory system was out of whack. Except concerning Kane. Somehow, she was very aware of Kane, in a sensory and sensuous way.

He still looked good in a T-shirt and jeans. He looked marvelous. All right, he looked sexy. And his voice, after all these years, still did things to her. And so did the way he could look at her.

"You know what?" he said after half a dozen bites. "I'm not hungry, either. Let's go somewhere more private. You're right. It's like being on display here."

She'd only been half aware of it, but the café had filled up, mostly with people sipping their coffee or tea or soft drink. Most of them furtively watched her and Kane. They recognized him, but he was the other. The one who didn't belong. They were wary, suspicious. That was the curse of a small town for you.

"More private?" she asked doubtfully. "Where?"

"Let's go up to your Uncle June's," he said.

"The castle? We can't. I told you, it's been sold."

"We'll sneak onto the grounds like we used to. By the carriage house. Like old times."

No, no, no, her mind warned. "These are new times," she said. "The old times are over."

"I'm not so sure about that," he said.

HE LEFT ENOUGH MONEY on the table to pay the bill and leave a flamboyantly large tip. He knew he was showing off. But if people wanted to stare at him, he'd give them something to see.

Once outside the door, he thought of taking Lori's arm to guide her to his car, but her body language told him not to touch her. He understood why.

Once in the sports car, she said, "I'm not going on the

castle grounds. For one thing, they're posted. The place is under renovation. There's probably security up there. Somebody could call the police on us."

"Fine," he said, starting the car. He shouldn't try to take her there anyway. They'd had too many necking sections by or in the carriage house. He remembered them so clearly that his lips tingled, his throat tightened, and his body ached.

"But I just want to drive up that way and see it again," he said. "Just a little closer. It's been a long time."

He'd worked on the castle grounds that fateful summer he was seventeen. That was the weekday job for Old Man Merkle. Helping tend that gigantic yard. He felt he'd ridden that lawn tractor for hundreds of miles under the hot sun. But he checked gardening books out of the library and studied, and soon Merkle promoted him to tend the shade gardens, all ten of them.

Sometimes the owner of the place, Junior McCorkle himself, would often come outside, carrying a pair of gallon thermos jugs of iced tea for the workers and handing out salt tablets. Occasionally he even hung around and helped Kane pick slugs out of the hostas and knock Japanese beetles into jars of soapy water. Junior enjoyed waging war on the beetles and just passing the time of day.

Kane had liked the old guy a lot. He'd been surprised to learn that the man hadn't been Lori's uncle at all, only a family friend. "I read about Junior passing on," he said with atypical solemnity. "I was tempted to come back for the funeral. He was one of a kind. He had a fortune and a castle, but he never stopped being a good ol' boy."

"I know," Lori said. "He was Daddy's silent partner. When he died, he left his share of the speedway to Daddy."

"That sounds like Junior," Kane said, remembering. In the dusk, at the Bin Birnam's top, he could see the spires of the castle, bluish in the dimming light. He felt odd, disjointed in time, unsettled in his emotions. He hadn't expected it to be like this.

"This is the first time we've ever been in a car together," Lori said pensively. "I never imagined that it would be like this."

She didn't seem impressed by his fancy car. After all these years, he was perplexed that he still couldn't quite figure her out. "What *did* you imagine it'd be like?"

"I didn't try to imagine," she murmured. "The future seemed a long way off. I didn't think very far ahead."

He hadn't, either. He had a vague idea of being a success, of showing all of Halesboro what he really was and what he could accomplish. And he, in turn, would scorn the town that had once scorned him.

He didn't know how he'd do this. Being an agent? That had never occurred to him. What he'd thought about most that last year was Lori Simmons. He'd succeed, and he'd take her with him. He'd steal Halesboro's princess and take her where the lights were bright and the buildings were tall and the opportunities were limitless.

So naive. So stupid. So *young*. He'd come back rich, after all these years, and he found it gave him no satisfaction. He had the power to meddle with the destiny of this town, a fantasy he'd once cherished, but now that he was here, it seemed a petty goal.

And he'd expected to put Lori Simmons Garland in her place. Not to hurt her. He actually meant to help her—in his way. And he'd meant his way to do two things. First, she'd regret how she'd treated him, and she'd spend the rest of her life kicking herself for being such a shallow little twit back then.

Second, would exorcise her. Because she was his first love, and lost at that, and lost with maximum melodrama, he hadn't been able to get her out of his mind. Ever. She held part of him captive, and he was determined to be free.

He expected to find everything he remembered about her wrong or changed. Twenty-one years had passed, she'd married that asinine jock Scott Garland, and she'd never left Halesboro. Her fortunes had fallen and her wrongheaded marriage had failed.

He'd expected to find her bent down by fate, possibly— though he didn't wish it on her—broken. She would be middle-aged, and probably her red hair turning gray or cheaply dyed. She'd have gained weight, and that little hourglass figure would have turned as round as the clock in the town clock tower.

Wrinkles would line her too-fair skin, and she'd be nothing except a frumpy, provincial divorcee with a thickening waist. The spirit he once thought so high and frisky would be flat as day-old champagne. Her rebellious nature would now be duty-bound and conventional. He would see her, and he would be over her.

It wasn't working out that way. She didn't look twenty years older. She hardly looked *ten* years older. Her figure was even better. Her hair was still as bright, her eyes still sparking with life, and she was even prettier than when she'd been sixteen.

She was just as spirited and just as independent, full of nerve and verve, and she didn't seem bowled over by his new, improved, moneyed status. In fact, she seemed a bit disappointed in him.

And as if to prove his worst suspicions, she turned to him and said, "Why are you dressed like that? Trying to recapture your youth? What happened to the silk shirt? The fancy shoes—what are they, Gucci?"

He tried to keep a disgusted slant from his mouth. The shoes were actually Ferragamos, but he wasn't going to brag about that. "This," he said, gesturing at his T-shirt and jeans, "is how I usually dress on my own time."

"You were on your own time today," she pointed out. "Do you always dress up to tromp around a speedway?"

"I was making a *business* call," he retorted. "Business hours are over."

"But we were supposed to be going for a business supper," she reminded him. "So when do we talk business?"

They were passing the speedway, and on impulse, he pulled in and parked in the westernmost corner of its parking lot. He could look out and slightly up and see McCorkle Castle now, glowing silver under a rising three-quarter moon.

"I said we had some catching up to do," he said, switching off the car. He pointed at the castle. "I picked up a lot of slugs on that land. I drowned a lot of beetles. What happened when Junior died? I thought he was going to leave it to the town."

He undid his seat belt, but she kept hers fastened, as if it were some kind of device that protected her from him. "He was older than Daddy. Like Daddy, he started getting forgetful, a bit erratic. His stepdaughter got power of attorney."

He grimaced. "Cynthia, the Southern belle? I kind of remember her. She always looked like her mouth was full of vinegar."

"Cynthia got everything," Lori said. "But she didn't want the castle. Too much upkeep. So she put it up for sale. And it didn't sell for years. And the years weren't kind to it."

He nodded. He knew that the South was quick to reclaim whatever land humankind had wrested from it. The weeds grew quickly, the woods closed in, the warm damp entered timbers. Mortar and concrete cracked. And a structure, even a castle, could go to ruin.

"I'm glad somebody's saving it," she said, sounding truly grateful. She stared at the towers that rose against the darkening sky. "I hope somebody doesn't do something horrible with it."

He examined her profile, still, almost exactly as he remembered it. She'd kept that way of holding her head high, her chin up.

"Something horrible like what?" he asked.

"Oh, I don't know. I can think of all kinds of things. Making it into a fancy resort and building all sorts of touristy little units all around it. Cutting down trees and putting in golf courses and miniature golf courses."

She wrinkled her nose in distaste. "One swimming pool won't do. There'll have to be five—and kiddy pools. And they'll make the lake bigger and have speedboats and water skis and a Zoom Flume waterslide, and a phony beach, and a sports complex and—ugh!"

"What a pessimistic imagination you have," he marveled. "I never knew. What if somebody just wants it for a home?"

"Probably some rock star with a bunch of wild friends and hangers-on, getting hammered and climbing up on the battlements to shoot squirrels and deer and throwing wild parties…"

"Puritan," he teased. "Don't make up such scenarios. Wait and see what happens."

"Well," she fretted, "what if it's somebody who hates the speedway? You can hear it very clearly from up there. Uncle June didn't mind, because he loved racing, and, of course, he was pretty deaf, so the noise wouldn't have bothered him anyway…" Her voice trailed off.

He wanted to reach over, unfasten her seat belt and draw her to him, kiss that enchanting little nose and then her lips. His mind tumbled backward to the nights they'd met on the castle grounds, remembering how completely he'd lost himself in her kisses…how he felt his body couldn't get close enough to hers.

He hadn't broken her spell at all. He'd come back only to fall under it, almost as completely as before. She was still a princess. She was born to it.

And he was still only the gypsy rover. He was born to that.

But this time he wasn't going to try to win the lady. It could never be the same. Somehow he knew this. He had a keenly developed sense of survival, and it was sending him strong warning signals.

He settled back against his seat, his blood thudding in his ears, his body tingling with suppressed desire.

"Okay," he said. "I guess we're caught up. Let's talk business."

"Wait," she said, turning to him. "I've got a question for you."

The warning signals amped up, shrill yet silent. "What?"

The moonlight had turned her face into a poem of silver and shadows. "Didn't you ever marry?"

He went very still. "No," he said.

He could feel her eyes searching his face and he kept it blank, implacable.

"Ever get close?" she asked.

He felt her presence like a mesmerizing energy surrounding him, invading him.

"No." He said it very shortly.

"Why not?" she asked.

Because I never got over you, he thought. *But I should have. Long ago.*

He said, "Because there are too many beautiful women in the world for me to stick to just one."

She seemed to think about this. She didn't seem put off by it. She certainly didn't seem disappointed.

"Okay," she said. "Just curious. Now, let's talk business."

CHAPTER FIVE

OF COURSE, she thought. *His world is full of beautiful women. Young women. Eager to please and well-versed in the art of doing so.*

If he wanted to make her feel unglamorous and past her prime, he'd succeeded. Did he think she deserved it? She'd been high-handed enough with him once upon a time. But they'd been very young, and the statute of limitations should have run out.

She cast him her coolest glance.

"Well?" she said pointedly. "Talk."

He took a deep breath, one hand clamped on the steering wheel. "For one thing," he muttered, his voice tinged with disgust, "something needs to be done about this parking lot. It's full of grass. It's full of potholes. It's full of weeds."

"I'm all too aware of that. Next item."

"The track needs to be reconfigured," he said, not looking at her. "That exit off Turn Four is a problem. Your dad tried a quick fix, and it didn't work."

"I'm aware of that, too. He did what he could."

"It wasn't good enough."

She fought against bristling. She knew her father had increasingly made bad decisions, but she didn't want to hear Kane criticize him.

He irritated her again by seeming to know what she thought before she thought it. "It wasn't his fault," he said, "I know. But still a problem that's got to be fixed. That's first.

I'm going to have plans drawn up. And the whole track needs resurfacing."

"I know."

"I'd like it fast, really fast, but with multiple grooves. With a chance for really close finishes. But to keep rough asphalt on it. That's part of what made Hellsboro famous."

"Check," she said with a curt nod.

"I want the grandstand inspected, the whole shebang, a structural analysis, structural reliability assessments, condition survey." He gripped the steering wheel more tightly. "Electrical, plumbing, safety features from top to bottom. Landscape inspection, too. Retaining walls, drainage, all of it."

He reeled off the list almost mechanically, as if he'd thought about it a long time. "It needs a new night-lighting system—"

She knew all this, but his recital made her queasy with nervousness. She looked at him apprehensively. "Do you know how much all this is going to *cost?*"

"A lot," he said and shrugged. "That scoreboard's got to be replaced. Pit road still looks solid, but it needs to be modernized. The infield's a mess. The seating's going to have to be replaced. The VIP suites refurbished. And a new security system needs to be installed. The one you've got is obsolete."

Butterflies of financial panic swarmed in her stomach. A knot threatened to choke her throat. "Kane," she said, "are you sure you're not overreaching on this? I mean it's good to be confident, but…but…"

He turned and gave her his one-cornered, sardonic smile. "But pride goeth before a fall. Is that what you're thinking?"

"Daddy wanted to keep it a speedway. He didn't have delusions of making it a showplace. A few renovations and the place can be self-sustaining. You can keep the drivers' school. You can rent the track out for movies and TV. There's still a roster of races."

"Not enough," he said. "Because it'll be the races that bring the fans back." He leaned nearer, looking at her more closely. "Good grief, you're all fidgety. What's wrong?"

"Don't you think I'd get more races if I could?" she challenged. "You act like this is *Field of Dreams* or something. If you rebuild it, they will come. It's not going to be easy."

He leaned a bit nearer still. She could feel the warmth of his body, smell the scent of his aftershave. "I was never much interested in what was easy. Most things worth having are hard to get."

A velvety suggestiveness had crept into his tone. He was too near, and too many of her old feelings came flooding back—the excitement, the attraction, the fascination and the sense of the forbidden.

She edged away from him in the seat, closer to the rolled-down window. "You always did fizz with energy," he said softly. "Especially when you got wound up. Let's go someplace and walk around."

"Suits me," she said. She yearned for open air, not this sense of being confined so closely with him. She was too conscious of him, all her senses too heightened and prickly.

"How about the park, go to the old footbridge?" he asked.

"Fine." Though they both knew the park and the bridge, they'd never been there together. It was too far from Lori's home and too public in those days. It held no memories of him. It was neutral ground.

He drove to the little park at the east edge of town and parked. "Wow," he said, as he pulled up in its gravel lot. "It looks a lot smaller than I remember."

In the headlights, it didn't seem like much—only a few square blocks of trees with an ancient footpath winding its way into the shadows.

He turned off the engine, killed the lights. His was the only car in the lot.

"Nobody much comes here any longer," she said. "After you left, Uncle June donated a bigger park to the town, on the opposite side. It has two ball diamonds and a playground and picnic tables. All that's left here is scenery. And a couple of benches. This is where Aunt Aileen comes when she takes her walks."

He got out and started toward her door, but she didn't wait for him. Swiftly she unfastened her seat belt and opened her door. He was already there at her side.

The moon was bright enough that they should be able to make their way to the bridge without trouble. She headed for the path, and he kept stride with her, his thumbs hooked into the back pockets of his jeans.

"Sometime I'd like to take a long walk with Aileen," he said. "Yeah. I'd like that."

She always believed in you, thought Lori. *She did before anyone else did. She always saw the potential in you. Even when you were the poor kid with the tattoos and long hair and that attitude that the rest of us didn't even exist.*

He looked up, squinting at the overhanging branches of the black gum and mountain ash trees. "They've grown," he said. "I remember the colors in the fall. Old Man Merkle told me his father planted these trees. Over a hundred years ago, I bet."

She nodded and looked at the shadows play on the path. "I still want to know how you think you're going to get more races here, Kane. The town's not what it was. Uncle June's gone, and there aren't any more tours of the castle grounds. People told Daddy a long time ago that Halesboro needed more attractions to draw the crowds in. That was one of its problems from the beginning."

"There are lots of ways to draw crowds," he said. "And when the crowds start showing up again, the races'll be easier to get. Especially when the facility's improved."

A mockingbird caroled its almost unbearably sweet song to the night air, such a beautiful sound it made something in Lori's chest hurt. She remembered lying in Kane's young, strong arms, listening to the mockingbirds sing at Uncle June's.

Often Kane and she went to the little brook that ran downhill from McCorkle Castle's carriage house. The water came tumbling from higher up the mountain in a narrow, splashing waterfall. It was like a magic spot, with small ferns, and they would lie there, talking and kissing…and sometimes going further than they should—but never as far as he wanted.

She'd been shy and frightened by anything beyond a few intimate caresses. She realized now how difficult it must have been for him, how he wished for far more than she'd dared to give. She'd sometimes felt sinful and sometimes felt prudish. But she still remembered those kisses. Oh, my, yes.

But if he recalled those nights, he didn't speak of them. He said, "You want to know how I'll get people to start coming back? I've got things planned. Appearances. Events. Promotions. Exhibits. Displays. Much, much more spectacle before the races."

She stopped and looked at him aghast. "*Stunts?* You're talking *stunts?* My father had no patience with things like that. To him it was about the racing, not some…some sideshow."

He, too, had stopped. "It's about the racing, all right. But we have to get people to come see it. And if it takes a little hoopla, babe, then we give 'em hoopla."

"We?" she flung back. "What's this 'we' stuff? If you want to hang by your heels from a hot air balloon —"

He cocked his head sarcastically. "I thought you read the contract carefully. You know what the offer is. You work for me to bring this track back to life. You work for me one year. Remember?"

He'd addled her so badly that she hadn't remembered. Hardly two straight thoughts in a row had made it through her head since he'd walked into her office that morning. She almost sputtered in frustration.

He bent nearer. "Or maybe now you don't want to sign the contract. You'd rather Devlin buys Hellsboro, knocks it down and plows it under. Would you rather do that?"

Confusion and anger so roiled her that she couldn't speak. But he, of course, could.

"Look yonder in the moonlight, princess. It's the bridge. Look at it hard."

What sort of deviltry was he up to now? As if in defiance,

she glared at the old bridge arching over the gurgling brook. It was the same brook that fell down the mountain's slope, so near the carriage house. The bridge was built of the same silvery gray limestone as the carriage house, as McCorkle Castle itself.

He moved nearer to her still. "What's a bridge for, Lori? What's its purpose? Why do you use one?"

I'd like to use this one to throw you off of, she thought, in exasperation, but she couldn't let him see how he'd rattled her.

She drew back a bit and said, coolly as she could. "A bridge connects things."

"Very good," he replied. "You cross it to get from one spot to another. And the bridge that has to be crossed is change, Lori. And lots of it. On one side of that bridge is Halesboro dying," he said, holding out his right hand, palm up. "On the other side, with luck and hard work—and here's the hard part for you—adaptability, is Halesboro living. Now. Are we going to cross it? Or aren't we?"

She listened to the splashing of the brook. She remembered the two of them, long ago, beside this brook. They were young lovers then, very naive ones, really. What had become of those two innocents?

She squared her shoulders. She turned and walked to the center of the bridge. "I'm here," she said, turning to face him. "Is that what you want?"

"It's exactly what I want," he said. "I'll walk you to the other side."

If he wanted to dish it out, she thought, she'd show him she could take it. He came to her and nodded her to go with him to other side. Then she stopped again, listening to the flow and rush of the water.

He gazed down at her. "You're not happy with my plans," he said.

"It doesn't matter if I'm happy. I'm about to be your employee. The hired help."

"Yes," he said, raising his hand and bringing his fingertips near her cheek. "Just like I used to be at your place. The hired help."

For a heart-stopping moment, she thought he was going to touch her. But he didn't. His hand lowered. He glanced up at the sky again. "I'll take you back to your car," he said.

She realized that she'd been holding her breath. She let it out, slowly, silently in relief. And with the slightest tinge of disappointment.

HE DROVE HER BACK to Main Street. They hardly spoke.

This time he was out of the sports car and opening her door for her almost as soon as she had her seat belt undone. He nearly offered his hand to help her out, but he realized she'd take it in hers as if she were forcing herself to clasp a toad.

He walked her to her car, an aging Mustang of an improbably bright blue. "Thank you for the tea," she said as she got in.

"You're welcome," he answered. He wished she'd eaten something; she hadn't even finished the tea. She was probably starving. Maybe that's why she seemed a bit shaky.

Or maybe it was because he'd acted like a lunkhead. He'd been phony and condescending when he'd greeted her. He'd made sure he'd called all the shots all evening long. He'd gotten her exactly where he'd wanted her, and he'd kept her there, cornered. It was exactly the way he planned it. And it made him feel like a bully.

But he said, "I'll come by your office tomorrow, same time." He didn't ask permission. He simply told her, as if she had no say in it. She nodded with a sort of aristocratic stoicism. He watched as she drove off, the old car making weird noises. Its transmission was going out, he could tell.

He was tempted to follow her home to see if she'd make it okay. But no, that would be like stalking. He got into his car, which suddenly struck him as exactly the sort of a car an arrogant jerk would drive if he were coming back to show off in the old home town that had held him in such contempt.

He'd wanted to talk to her on the way back. He wanted

especially to know about the marriage, how she felt about it ending. He'd had a detective in Charlotte check her out. He knew about the deaths in her family, the problems her father's illness had caused. He knew she'd filed for divorce from Scott Garland four years ago on the grounds of irreconcilable differences, but he didn't know precisely what differences.

Had he come here to save her, or to punish her, or both? He'd wanted to find her not at all as he remembered her—only a small-town woman with no hold over him. But it wasn't playing out that way, and he had no one to blame except himself.

He drove back to the Halesboro Luxury Motel, which was not luxurious and never had been. But it was the best that the town had to offer these days. He opened his suitcase, took out a pint of gin and poured himself a double shot in a plastic glass. He didn't bother with ice. He wanted something to deaden his feelings and do it fast.

But he couldn't stop thinking about her. Even her freckles—she hadn't bothered to cover them tonight—filled him with odd nostalgia. He hadn't come back to Halesboro without a lot of homework—including hiring a private investigator, Fenneman, to check out Lori.

Fenneman said she no longer lived in the house she'd shared with Scott Garland; she'd sold it and lived on Lark Street, the other side of town. The location was ironically close to where Kane, his mother and sister had lived. Even a town as small as Halesboro had its wrong side, the place where the losers and the luckless dwelt.

Kane told himself maybe Lark Street had changed for the better. Be realistic, he told himself cynically. *Nothing* in Halesboro had changed for the better—except his mother was gone, completely disappeared.

But he had to know about Lori. He looked up her address again in Fenneman's notes. He could see the neighborhood in his mind's eye.

With a jolt he realized she lived on the same block that Rome McCandless had lived as a kid—Rome, his first client.

When Kane had left Halesboro, McCandless was hardly more than a toddler. He was so tall and gangly for his age that other kids tormented him and adults sniggered at him. He had hair as orange as a carrot and the biggest feet Kane had ever seen on a child.

He seemed destined to grow up to be every bit as much an outsider as Kane, but fate dealt Rome a wild card. He would grow into his feet, his tall body would shoot even taller, and he would have perfect control over it.

Sports had a place for a kid like that, and that place was the basketball court. Rome became the state's outstanding high school basketball player, then its outstanding college player, then a pro with Kane as his agent.

Rome McCandless, child geek, had become "the Roman Candle," sports hero, and ultimately a very wealthy hero. Kane and McCandless, boys from the wrong side of Halesboro, helped each other make fortunes.

Now Lori, once the town's princess, was reduced to living on Rome's old block, not far from where Kane himself had lived. Time had been like a Ferris wheel, moving those at the bottom to the top and vice versa.

But how unlikely that the three of them were bound together by this obscure neighborhood, unknown to the world outside Halesboro. It was ironic. And eerie.

LORI TRIED not to visit the past too often and then to be selective. She made herself remember all the good things about her parents, none of their flaws. What good did it do to list grievances against the dead? Anything they'd done that had hurt her they'd done out of love, or what they believed was love.

Her parents, of course, had wanted a perfect daughter who would grow into a perfect lady. She would be a gracious hostess, a skilled household manager and a strong yet ornamental pillar of the community. She would marry one of her own kind, and she would live among her own kind, and she would think like her own kind of people thought.

Neither of her parents had expected disobedience or non-conformity of any kind. But then, they hadn't expected Kane Ledger, either.

Both her parents were horrified by her rebellion when they discovered it, and both were grateful that it was cut so short—it lasted only months that had been, her father thought, mercifully secret. Shamefully secretive and devious, her mother had accused.

But Lori still wondered, how else could it have been except secret?

Two Saturdays after she and Kane first talked, her mother mentioned that Mr. Merkle was again sending over someone to tend the roses. Instinctively, Lori was certain that someone would be Kane.

She schemed to stay home again and station herself poolside. Sinfully, she wished her green swimsuit was skimpier, her skin less freckled, her chest larger, her hips more curvy.

She put up her hair again, studiously making it look unstudied. Makeup would seem phony by the pool, so she allowed herself only lip gloss. She stationed herself under the green and white NASCAR umbrella again, and tried to read the book she'd borrowed from Aileen.

At exactly ten o'clock, Kane came through the back gate again. This time they gave each other curt, cursory nods and immediately began to pretend the other wasn't there.

But she watched him, how she watched him. He wore another pair of tight, faded, low-slung jeans. His T-shirt was plain, gray, and the cloth, even from a distance, looked thin with wear. It quickly darkened with sweat, but he waited until he was nearly drenched to take it off.

Her heart quickened and her breath stuck in her throat. She thought he was the most beautiful boy she'd ever seen. His brown body wasn't heavy with muscles, as her football playing brother's was, but it had a lean perfection of form.

His tattoos no longer looked barbaric to her; they looked

exotic. They somehow fit him and went with his long dark hair. His hair hung to his shoulders and gleamed blue-black in the sunshine. This time he hadn't tied it back, but he pulled out an old blue bandana, folded it the long way, and tied it around his head for a sweatband. It made him look like a pirate.

Once she caught him stealing a glance at her, and when their eyes met, a tingle ran through her stomach and quivered down clear to her thighs.

He was far enough away that she couldn't see any signs of his scratches, but he had a flesh-colored Band-Aid that looked pale against his tanned side. Noon passed, the heat felt blistering, and she took a quick dip in the pool.

She went back to her lounge chair and read until her stomach growled. Surely it was one o'clock by now, she thought. And he hadn't stopped for lunch. From time to time, he took a swig of water from an old plastic bottle with the label half peeled off.

Finally, she could stand it no longer. She went into the house and came out with a tray she set on the white table that supported the umbrella. She'd brought a pitcher of lemonade and a plate of cheese and crackers— a big plate.

She took a deep breath, and then marched with determination to the rose garden. "Hey," she said. "You didn't take a lunch break."

"I didn't bring a lunch," he said, barely looking up. "I'd rather work."

"Mr. Merkle takes a lunch break," she said silkily. "A half hour. And we still pay him for his time. It's like an employee right or something."

He eyed her suspiciously. She'd forgotten how dark those eyes were, and how expressive. What they expressed was suspicion. "I never heard of that," he said.

"Well, it's true," she said, hoping it was. "Come have a lemonade and some crackers."

He squinted at her in disbelief. "What?"

"Yes," she told him. "The heat's terrible, you're not eating and you could pass out."

"I never passed out in my life," he said indignantly.

"Besides, I want to ask you about something."

The suspicion glittered in his gaze again. "What?" he repeated.

"Come sit down. I'll tell you then. Otherwise I'll have you go home early. I'll tell Daddy I was worried about you."

She turned, knowing he would follow her. And he did, although she could feel intense reluctance radiating from him. She pulled up a smaller chair beside the lounge and made sure it was in the shadow of the umbrella. "Please sit," she said.

"You're uppity," he accused, but he sat.

"You're intractable," she said. She said it as a test, to see if he knew what she meant.

He did. "That," he said with irony, "is the pot calling the kettle black."

She smiled inwardly. Yes, she was being stubborn and difficult. So was he.

She poured two glasses of lemonade and slid one toward him. She piled crackers on a paper plate and put a handful of cheddar cheese cubes beside them. She set the plate in front of him and filled her own.

He hesitated, then took a cracker and a cheese cube and popped both into his mouth. He ate with apparent hunger. He did the same thing again. Then he regarded her with one dark eyebrow cocked. "So what do you want to ask me?"

She nibbled a cracker with a daintiness that would have made her mother proud. "You got all cut up last time," she said. "How are you?"

He held out his bare arm. Traces of the scratches were faint. "Fine. I heal fast."

"You must," she said softly. The long shallow cut along his throat was barely visible. But the one beside his mouth was going to leave a scar, she could tell.

He reached for another cracker. Between bites, he surprised her by saying, "You were right about the graphic novel. It's not a comic. It's serious. I liked it."

"You read it?" she asked in amazement.

"Yeah," he said, reaching for more food. "Sometimes I hitch-hike over to Asheville. I found it in a used bookstore there."

"Hitchhiking's dangerous," she countered.

"I can take care of myself," he muttered, then took a large swallow of lemonade. He licked his lips. They were perfect male lips, she decided. Strong, firmly cut, neither too thin nor too full. With a shock, she realized he was staring at her mouth, as well.

They both straightened up and looked away. "I better get back to work," he said. "Thanks." He stood and walked, straight-backed, toward the garden again.

He was still working at four-thirty, when she heard the phone ringing from the kitchen. She ran to answer it.

Her mother was calling from a service station outside of Charlotte. The car had broken down, and she and Lori's father and A.J. wouldn't be home for another two hours.

Two hours, she thought, drifting back outside. She sat again in the lounge chair, partly reading her book, but mostly watching him.

An hour later, when the sun was starting to ride down the sky, she saw him strip off his gloves and stuff them into his back pocket. He must be making ready to quit. But then she heard him laugh and whoop. She looked up sharply, straight at him, no subterfuge.

He'd caught something, some kind of animal, and it seemed to delight him.

Telling herself she was merely curious, she rose and strolled to his side. "What do you have?" she asked.

He crouched, his hand covering something. "Littlest frog I ever saw," he said.

"Really?" She knelt beside him. He smelled of earth and roses. "Let me see."

"You'll have to look fast," he warned her. "He'll probably hop away."

"I will," she said, and the breeze ruffled through the garden until the scent of flowers half-intoxicated her. She felt slightly dizzy, as if she were too close to him.

He raised his bare hand from the grass. There sat a tiny frog, brilliant green, a perfect little thing that looked as if it had been carved from a living jewel.

She caught her breath. It was a lovely little creature with small golden eyes. It seemed to look back at her. It blinked.

"I thought he'd split," Kane said. "Maybe he likes you."

She smiled and kept looking at the gem-like frog. She was suddenly afraid to look at Kane. She found herself speechless.

Kane said, "Want to kiss a frog? Turn him into a prince?"

For some reason, that embarrassed her, made her heart hammer strangely and her voice go shaky. "No," she said.

A moment of silence hung heavily between them. He leaned closer. "Yes, you do," he said, and laid his hand on her neck, drawing her nearer. "You have the power. I've known it from the first."

His mouth lowered to hers. She put her hands on his bare shoulders and kissed him back. In that kiss, she felt that she had both lost herself—and found herself.

CHAPTER SIX

KANE FINISHED the gin and fell into an uneasy asleep. His dreams were erratic, and images of Lori and him, both young again, drifted in and out of his mind. Yet these dream people, while both young, also seemed their true age, too, and at the same time ageless, beyond the touch of time.

Although the images were disjointed and herky-jerky, Lori seemed to hold them together in some order far stronger than logic. Her—and the feeling he'd had for her then.

Before her, he'd been a loner, sworn never to be dependent on anybody. And after it was over with her, he became more of a loner than ever. He "made love" to women. But he didn't love them. He'd loved once, and it had hurt like hell. It was enough to almost kill a man.

He woke up wondering why he was back in Halesboro, why he was getting himself tangled up again with the girl who'd betrayed him years ago, and he was no longer sure.

Shaving that morning, he looked in the mirror and saw a man with startlingly regular features and unhappy eyes. He'd told her he'd meet her again this morning, and he would. And then he needed to go back to Charlotte.

And he needed to keep as much distance as he could from this place. And from her.

As for the speedway, he'd find somebody else to battle its multitude of woes. What another guy from this region had once said was all too right: "You can't go home again."

LORI HADN'T slept well, either. The rude-sounding shrill of the telephone woke her. She answered sleepily, but her aunt Aileen's voice immediately jolted her into wakefulness. "Lori, why didn't you *call* me?"

Aileen was in her seventies now, but there was no tremor of age in her voice. It was strong, feisty and sure of itself, just like its owner. She gave Lori no chance to answer.

Aileen said, "I heard Kane Ledger's back. Is it true?"

"Y-yes," Lori stammered. "It's true."

"Ha!" Aileen said triumphantly. "He came back because of you. I knew it as soon as I heard he was here."

Lori blushed. She caught a look at herself in the bedroom mirror. Her face was creased from being pressed into the pillow. Tousled hair hung in her sleep-drugged eyes. Her old white nightgown hung down, wrinkled and limp. It looked like the shabby garment of a down-on-its-luck ghost.

Who'd come back because of me? she wondered, looking at her wan image. "He's not here for me," she protested.

"Then why is he here?"

"I don't know," Lori stated with emphasis.

"I think he wants to impress you, show you how successful he's become," Aileen said in her husky voice. "And the town. Are you seeing him again today?"

"He's supposed to drop by the speedway," Lori muttered, exhausted. She'd had a night filled with dreams mostly about Kane, disturbing ones she didn't want to admit to anyone, even herself.

"Ask him to give me a call," said Aileen. "I'd love to hear from him, see him. Maybe he'd come for a visit."

"He asked about you. He said he wanted to get in touch."

"Then tell him I'd be delighted." She paused, as if for dramatic effect. "But now, about you. Have you asked him the big question about the speedway?"

Lori's body stiffened with wariness. "What big question?"

"You know what. He's supposed to have connections.

Could he help you get a NASCAR-sanctioned race again at Halesboro?"

Lori gave a short, mirthless laugh. "I don't think so. I'd say that it's next to impossible."

"And I'd say, my dear, that there are some men who don't know the meaning of the word *impossible*."

Lori's muscles stiffened. "Maybe some men," she said, "have to learn it the hard way."

LORI WENT to the speedway early, the Mustang acting up all the way. It labored to take off and then shifted roughly, clunking into gear. The ominous noises multiplied and grew even more ominous, and a rancid odor began to float up from underneath the floorboards.

She told Clyde when she reached the speedway. He shook his head and said he and the mechanic from the driving school should get started on it today. The thing might break down on her at any time.

She thanked him and patted him on the shoulder, keeping up a facade of stoic good cheer. But when she got to her office, she locked the door, turned off her cell phone and pulled the plugs on the two phones that sat on the desk. She felt a primal need to be alone.

She'd agreed verbally to Kane's offer; she'd made up her mind she had to take it. She couldn't live with accepting the Devlin bid.

But she hadn't yet signed Kane's document. She wanted to be alone, no one looking on, when she did that. She opened the leather folder and read all the offer's paperwork again. Then she simply stared at the document for a long time.

At last, she took her father's Waterford pen from its holder and numbly, her hand moving like that of an automaton, she signed and dated all of the lines of her agreement. She would give it to Kane, and soon they'd be in the title office, signing over the final transfer, him handing her the check.

She signed the last line and put back the pen and sat, no

longer really seeing anything before her. The end had truly begun. She'd wondered what to wear to the speedway today when she handed over the papers.

She'd toyed with the idea of wearing the dark dress she'd worn to her father's funeral but dismissed it as melodramatic and self-pitying. So she'd dressed as she usually did on an ordinary summer day—plain green cotton shorts and a green and white Halesboro Speedway T-shirt.

She started going about her tasks, working on another publicity release for the Stang Fest, getting the payroll checks ready and, finally, starting to put the books in some kind of final order.

At ten sharp, a knock rattled her door, and the sound pierced her heart like a nail being driven through it. Kane was here, as hellishly punctual as he was yesterday.

She sprang out of her chair and unlocked the door. He stood there, casually, one hip cocked. He was in jeans again, and this time a blue cambric shirt with the sleeves rolled up to the forearms. They were seemingly ordinary clothes, but he looked extraordinarily handsome and at ease in them.

His expression was so blasé. "May I come in?"

"Certainly." She gestured at the empty guest chair.

He sauntered in and sat, crossing his ankle over his knee. "I can't stay long. I've got an engineer and an architect coming up from Charlotte. I need to show them everything. You got an extra set of keys?"

She opened the desk drawer and extracted a large key ring. It had been her father's backup set and still had his silver fob hanging from it with his engraved initials, AJS. She thrust it at Kane and he took it casually, letting the keys jingle. Perhaps their tinkling sounded lighthearted to him. It didn't to her.

How would Andrew Jackson Simmons feel? she wondered bitterly. He'd come to despise Kane, the common laborer with the gall to try to corrupt his daughter. What would he think if he knew now that Kane held not only the keys to the speedway, but to Andrew's very lifework and legacy?

She forbade herself to think of it—yet. "Clyde can help show you around," she said.

"Fine. I'll have to spend all day with these guys. They need to get back to Charlotte by seven. Then I need to talk to you some more. Meet me at the café again. Seven-thirty's a good time. The rush'll be over by then."

They both realized that he wasn't asking her, he was telling her.

"Sure," she said with a toss of her head. "By the way, what about this office? Will you want it? It's always been the owner's. It's the biggest. I'll move down the hall."

He glanced indifferently around the room, its chipped paint, its old awards, old clippings, old photos. "If you don't mind," he shrugged. "But none of that stuff. That can go. Well, except the desk. It'd be a nice desk if it was refinished."

Her heart clenched painfully. This desk had been in her family for years. But she wouldn't ask Kane for any favors, not a single one.

"Certainly. I'll clear everything else out. When do you want to move in?"

"I don't intend to actually move in," he said. "It'll just be handy to have a place when I drop by from time to time."

"Of course," she said with false cheer.

A silence weighed between them, and she felt its heaviness, bearing down, swinging the balance of power forever, from her past to his future.

She tried to disguise any such feeling. "Oh. Aileen phoned this morning. She said she hoped to see you."

He smiled, his eyes on her tightly controlled lips. "I'll do that. Maybe she and I can have breakfast tomorrow. I have to get back to Charlotte by noon."

"Oh, right," Lori said. "You do have a business to take care of."

"No," he corrected, one corner of his mouth turning up. "Now I have two businesses." He held up two fingers so they resembled a victory sign. "The agency—and Halesboro."

"Yes," she said, resenting what that victory sign implied. "You're a busy man. Don't let me keep you. I'll give Clyde a call and tell him to be on the lookout for you and your... consultants."

He stood, but didn't move away; he just looked down at her. "Aren't you forgetting something?"

"Am I?" she asked.

"The offer. You signed it?"

He embarrassed her because he'd clearly rattled her. But she only gave a little laugh. "The offer. Of course. Here it is. Everything in order, I hope."

She handed him the leather folder, and he took it from her, his fingers almost, but not quite, touching hers. "Thanks," he said. "It's official now. And I'll see you tonight. Do you want this door closed again?"

"Yes. Please." She used all her control to keep her voice steady. "That would be lovely."

"Fine," he said. With the folder under his arm, the key ring in his hand, he stepped out, easing the door shut behind him.

She sat very straight in her chair, listening as the sound of his confident footsteps faded away. The speedway was his now. She put her elbows on the old desk, her face in her hands, and she cried like a child.

KANE ARRIVED at The Groove Café at exactly seven-thirty. She wasn't there yet. A few patrons lingered, most of them nursing their drinks, and he recognized some of them, and he knew some of them recognized him.

Their eyes followed him as he crossed the room, and they didn't smile, although two gave him a curt nod. He nodded back, just as curtly. Only Otis Jr. spoke, saying, "Hello. Take a seat, any seat." They hadn't much liked him when he was poor. And they seemed to distrust him and perhaps resent him now that he was rich.

He took the booth farthest in the back corner next to the jukebox. Clara came out of the kitchen and heavily set down a glass of water. She alone seemed friendly. Being tipped well obviously brought out her congenial side. She welcomed him back and asked if he was expecting anyone else. He saw a slight but sly glint come into her eyes when he answered yes.

He asked for ginger ale and nursed it. Lori came, five minutes late. She still wore her green shorts and green and white speedway T. The customers watched her, too, but most of them also greeted her, asked her how she was. She smiled, she nodded, she greeted them in return. She belonged here as surely as he did not.

She sat down, tossing her red-gold hair and pushing it back from her brow. "Sorry I'm late. Clyde gave me a ride. My car won't be fixed until tomorrow."

"Now that you've sold the place, you ought to get a better one," Kane told her. "That one's at the stage where everything's going to have to be replaced."

"I don't want a new one," she said. "I like the one I have."

"Any particular reason?" he asked, conscious that people watched them from the corners of their eyes. He took a sip of his drink.

"It was my brother's," she said matter-of-factly. "He left it with me when he went to war."

The drink seemed to stick sideways in his throat. He wished he'd kept his stupid mouth shut. For years, he'd despised A.J. for a lout and a muscle-bound coward. But A.J. was dead now, and Lori, in the complicated way of families, might not have liked her brother, but she'd loved him.

"Sorry," Kane said.

"You couldn't have known," she said, then quickly changed the subject. "Clyde said you and 'those city fellers' have got some fancy ideas about the speedway."

"Fancy to Clyde, maybe," he said. "Pretty basic, really. Changes are needed. And I hope Halesboro can change, too."

"Change back to what it was?" she asked. "No. I think that Halesboro's gone forever."

He nodded, feeling an odd nostalgia for a place that had

never welcomed him, that still didn't seem to welcome him. "This," he said, with a gesture indicating the café, "seems the one thing that hasn't changed."

Clara, putting down the menus and a water glass for Lori, had overheard him. "Otis is too cheap to change," she said sotto voce. "The same music's on the jukebox as twenty years ago. Oldest jukebox in the state, I bet. Still plays 45's."

Kane gave her a disbelieving smile. "Go on."

"I'll prove it," Clara said. The jukebox stood next to their booth. She took three quarters from her apron pocket and began to drop them in and punch buttons.

A moment later, Kane heard Randy Travis's voice, as he'd heard it here two decades ago.

The song was "Always and Forever," and when he'd been seventeen, he'd thought of Lori every time he heard it.

Sometimes he heard it when he was in the kitchen, up to his elbows in dishwater and she was sitting in one of these booths with her girlfriends. He could see her when he passed the porthole-like windows in the kitchen doors.

He was so conscious of her out there that he ached, and he knew she was conscious of him, as well. Back then, the world seemed suffused by incandescent romance.

He was a would-be Romeo, scraping plates and scouring silverware. And she'd been his Juliet, dipping her French fries in ketchup and drinking her cherry-lemon-lime cola. After all this time, it should seem merely ridiculous.

But now she looked at him as if she remembered, too, and didn't find it ridiculous at all. He didn't, either. He found it touching and painful. And he also felt as if part of him had been missing since those days. Did she feel the same?

Impossible, he told himself sternly.

"See?" Clara said, "Just like old times. Same as ever. Know what you want?"

"Hamburger steak, medium," Kane muttered.

"The patty melt," Lori said, staring at the menu as if she hadn't seen it at least five thousand times. "And iced tea, please."

"Gotcha." Clara plodded off, and Randy Travis sang on, despite the scratches on the record.

"So," Kane said wryly, "this place is in some island in the time-space continuum. It really hasn't changed. But a lot has. What happened to the Bostwick Hotel?"

"Closed three years ago," Lori said, tracing a line down the condensation on her water glass. "Not enough business. It's been for sale, but the Bostwicks still own it."

"The Ming Toy Restaurant? The racing teams said it was the best Chinese food in the state."

"Moved to Asheville. They cater to the college crowd now."

"The Military Theater?" he asked. Once they'd been bold enough to meet in the darkest corner of its balcony and had necked all through *Who Framed Roger Rabbit.*

"People go to the multiplexes in Asheville or Henderson."

He took another sip of his drink. "What about the textile mills?"

She shook her head. "Still empty. Uncle June's step-daughter owns them. She'd sell them for next to nothing, but nobody seems to want to buy a hundred-year-old textile mill."

"Those buildings were like fortresses," he said. "They'll be standing when everything else falls."

She smiled pensively. "I suppose they will."

"What about the old racing crowd?" he asked. "You ever see any of them? Drivers? Teams? Lightning Kinsky? Rolly Munson? Flash Gorton?"

"You know," she said, meeting his eyes squarely for the first time, "almost all of them came to Daddy's funeral. And afterwards, we all sat around and talked about the old days. I still hear from a lot of them at Christmas."

She paused. "They knew, by the grapevine, that Daddy wasn't quite himself for the last few years he had. But he didn't get really…you know…in bad shape until nearly the end. I guess the first sign was when he became paranoid. He—imagined things. I tried to reason with him. A lot of people did. He wouldn't listen."

"You couldn't step in? Get power of attorney? A conservatorship?"

"I thought about it. I tried to talk to A.J. about it. He wouldn't consider it. He said everything would be fine once he got home again. But he didn't come home. And that did something to Daddy. And then Daddy was gone, too."

He resisted the urge to put his hand over hers. "He never should have gotten so bitter about NASCAR. They had no grudge against him."

"He was always sure he was right. Even when he was wrong. NASCAR never had a vendetta against him. But what's done is done."

"Sometimes what's done can be undone," Kane said. "It's time for Halesboro and NASCAR to start over."

But her face told him she didn't believe him. Above all else, he wanted to change that expression, to see that she had faith in him the way she once did—before…

Back then, more than once she'd told him, "I think you could do anything you put your mind to. Anything." But the girl who'd said that was gone, and a more wary and realistic woman had taken her place. Did he really still care what she thought? It would be so much more satisfying not to.

"I can't *promise* anything," he said.

"I know that," she replied, but she held her chin up, just as she used to.

They were saved from saying any more by Clara, who plunked down a plate before each of them. "Enjoy," she said, which was what she always said to everyone.

CLARA MUST BE in a nostalgic mood. Or a sadistic one, Lori thought unhappily. She feigned a hearty appetite, but the jukebox unnerved her and made her feel that although she sat there, thirty-seven years old, she was simultaneously only sixteen.

Now the Pet Shop Boys sang "Always on My Mind." The sound brought back, all too vividly, when she'd loved Kane. And lost him.

But she had to act as if she didn't remember that time at all, that it was unimportant and forgotten. Instead she talked shop with him: races and tracks, drivers and teams, owners and sponsors. But the conversation seemed to take place in some ghostly sphere where the present didn't seem nearly as vivid as the past, and long-dormant emotions came surging back to haunt her.

Lori found herself in an eerie time warp, where Kane was at once a boy of seventeen who was her soul mate, but also a grown man she really didn't know and couldn't understand. For years she'd supposed that if she met him again, she'd wonder what she'd ever seen in him, laugh at herself for having once found him attractive.

But he still cast a spell over her that was extremely physical—yet went far beyond the physical. He was mysterious, and he hadn't lost his air of being a loner, quietly yet fiercely independent.

She hesitated to ask him anything too personal, but there was one question she couldn't help raising. Raising her eyes to meet his dark gaze, she said, "I never imagined you as an *agent*. An agent's a kind of salesman. He has to schmooze and compromise. It's hard to imagine you doing either."

For a moment, disdain flickered in his gaze, and she knew she'd offended him. But his expression quickly turned cool and neutral. When he spoke, his voice was calm.

"My job's to take care of my clients. The most important thing I have to do is be trustworthy. You've been around sports all your life. You've seen what can happen to a talented athlete. Suddenly everybody wants a piece of him."

She nodded because she *had* seen it. She remembered a young driver called Hawk Roberts, who seemed destined to be both a champion and a star. But he let his father manage his career, and the father was ruled by greed and pride.

His decisions changed Hawk from a rising star to a falling one. Five years later, nobody seemed to know what became of Hawk, where he was or even if he was still alive. "A flash in the pan," her father had said. Clyde would mutter, "What a waste. What a shame."

Kane seemed to know how she felt, and a frown line appeared between his eyebrows. "A gifted kid can make the right moves and stay a contender his whole career. Or he can make the wrong moves and permanently louse up his life. I've got a duty not to be a yes-man to somebody like that. And a duty to tell him the truth even when he doesn't want to hear it.

"Athletes learn fast that the world's full of people who'd love to use them, get at the money and exploit the fame. A smart athlete won't trust everybody he meets. Just the opposite. So an agent has to *earn* that trust. By talking straight and playing fair."

Lori said, "That's how you got Kent Grosso for a client?"

"Yeah," he said. "Kent's at the top right now. He's getting all kinds of offers. It'd be tempting for him to say yes to everything. But he shouldn't. His day has only twenty-four hours, his week only seven days. For his own good, he's got to be selective."

She lifted her chin. "And you help him do the selecting?"

"I tell him what I think. And I think about what I tell him. If he wanted to, he could devote himself to raking in all the fast bucks that he can. But in the long run, grabbing fast bucks can burn a person out. Kent's got a family, a new wife, and he wants a future brighter than being some old miser who sold his soul."

"You make being an agent sound like a noble calling," she said dubiously.

"It's a job," he countered. "It can be done badly. It can be done well. I've tried to do it well."

"And it hasn't exactly made you poor," she pointed out.

"Money buys some things. It doesn't buy everything."

"It bought you the speedway. Does that make you happy?" she challenged.

"Happy?" He looked her up and down. "Maybe it will. Maybe it won't. We'll just have to see, won't we?"

"Not 'we,'" she corrected. "You. Because it's going to be yours. It won't be my concern any longer."

He shook his head and gave her a cryptic smile. "It'll always be your concern because it's part of you. You've been connected to it your whole life. It's part of your family, your past, your very identity. And it'll be 'we' because you'll be working for me. Remember?"

She pushed her plate away. She couldn't finish her meal; she'd lost her appetite. "I remember. And I'll use that time to put even more emotional distance between me and what used to be. I don't intend to wallow in the past. The speedway's future is in your hands now."

He, too, pushed away his plate without finishing the last few bites. He crossed his arms and leaned his elbows on the table. When he spoke, his tone was edged with mockery. "And do you hope that I succeed? Or fail?"

She shrugged as casually as she could. "I hope you succeed, of course. For my father's sake. The speedway meant the world to him."

He gave her a measuring look. "I'm not walking into this blindly, you know. I've done my research. And I've got plans."

"Good."

"Don't you want to know those plans?"

She crossed her own arms. "I figure you'll tell me if you think I should know."

"I love it when you pretend to be demure," he said. "But I'll give you credit. You've done a lot of things to keep money coming in. But there's one thing you left undone. You don't have enough NASCAR drivers or teams testing at the track. There's money there. And a certain prestige."

"We have a couple, Will Branch, Trey Sanford," she countered.

"Yes, but we need more higher-profile drivers. I've talked to Dean Grosso. He likes the idea of the Cargill-Grosso team testing here. It's a tough track. It challenges cars and challenges drivers. It's only two hours from Charlotte and since the ban on testing at all NASCAR-sanctioned tracks, teams need other tracks. Halesboro's an ideal alternative. Dean's willing to try it."

This news didn't merely surprise her, it came close to astonishing her. Dean Grosso, Kent's father, was at least fifty and had been a top driver, close to legendary. He'd also just become owner of one of the most exciting teams in NASCAR. If he chose to test even a few times at Halesboro, the publicity for the speedway would be sensational.

"Dean Grosso?" she said in disbelief. "He'd have his team test *here?* Including Kent? A NASCAR Sprint Cup Series champion, just like his dad?"

"Including Kent and Roberto Castillo. Dean and his wife, Patsy, said they'd agree to attend a barbecue if we held one at the speedway. Dean and Kent would both be willing to meet fans and sign autographs."

She struggled to control her rising excitement. "That'd be a moneymaker and a public relations coup to have such famous drivers. How did you arrange this all so fast?"

"I've helped the Grossos over the years. They're willing to help me in return. So are some of the other drivers I represent. Justin Murphy, for one."

"But you *just* bought the track. You talked this over with them beforehand?"

"It came up. We talked about it. Dean's excited. He has fond memories of Halesboro. He always finished in the top ten when he raced here. Three times he finished first."

"And you?" she asked. "Will you keep on being an agent? Or not?"

His expression grew wry. "Got to keep the day job, babe. It'll take a steady flow of cash to get this place up and running again."

In spite of her elation over the prospect of testing, she frowned. "You know, this 'agent' business is changing things. It could turn NASCAR into something like the NFL or pro basketball or—"

He reached over and gently laid his finger against her lips. "Shh. How many times do I have to tell you that you can't fight change? It runs through everything like a life force. The town's changed. The speedway's changed. You and I have changed."

He drew back his hand. Her mouth tingled and her cheeks burned, for she knew everyone in the café had probably seen him touch her that way.

"Let's not get all philosophical," she managed to return. "Right now I'm coping with an awful lot of change in my life. I'd like something that...abides."

He gave her an odd look, as if trying to decode her words. "What's that mean?"

"Oh, it doesn't mean anything," she said in frustration. "It's been a long day, that's all. I need to go home. To think. And get some rest."

"Your car's still working?" he asked, raising one eyebrow.

She was too addled to even think of lying. "I...I...Clyde brought me here. Goblins ate my transmission. I'll walk home. It's nice out, and I could use some fresh air."

"I'll drive you," he said.

"No. Really. It's not that far. And I *like* to walk."

"Then I'll go with you. A gentleman doesn't let a lady walk in the dark alone...unprotected."

Lori felt too emotionally drained to argue—and she remembered that he could argue like the very devil if he chose to. Her body was full of restless tingles, and she yearned to move, to outpace her nervousness.

Kane paid, left a tip, opened the door and stayed close to her as they stepped into the evening. Dusk was thickening and the streetlights shone. A gentle mountain breeze blew, cooling away the day's heat.

Kane automatically set off in the direction of the house where she'd grown up. Did he think she was living there again? Did he really know how the debts had cost her almost everything, her parents' home and her own, as well?

He'd find out soon enough, she thought. And the little house she rented was not many blocks beyond the big house she'd once taken for granted. Kane didn't try to take her arm, and she was grateful.

She stole a peek at his shadowy profile. He *did* talk about change too glibly for her taste. But he was right when he said he'd changed. In their teens, he'd usually looked like a half-wild boy with his shabby clothes, his shaggy hair and tattoos. But even back then, he had a slender elegance to him, the natural grace of a beautiful young animal. He still had it.

When they came to the house where her family had lived, Kane surprised her by not slowing, not taking the sidewalk that led to the front porch. The house stood in the moonlight like a gleaming ghost, but he passed it without mentioning it, not even seeming to notice it.

He knows, she thought. And he did seem to be heading straight for where she lived now, on the edge of his old neighborhood. In her bones, she felt the presence of her own old home, tall, white, and spacious—and lost to her forever. She supposed she'd always miss it.

She remembered lounging by the pool, not guessing how privileged she'd been. And, of course, she could not help remembering Kane, the hired help, sweating in the garden, his bare chest and back and shoulders gleaming in the sunlight.

Memories came back, unbidden but stronger than ever. How he'd kissed her the first time and how, when she stole out by night to meet him by the carriage house and the brook, he'd take her in those strong arms and kiss her again and again. The tree frogs sang down from the darkness. Everything was perfect—until, spoiled and willful, she'd betrayed him.

Although he was silent as they walked, she wondered if he, too, was thinking back to those days and those nights. Did he relish that they'd traded places? That now she was the poor one, he the one with money and influence?

He turned down another side street without her prompting. Her heart beat faster and her throat tightened. *He knows exactly where I live. He said he'd done his research. Had it included her?*

"We passed where Roman lived," he said. "Did you notice? Do you remember him back when he was actually little?"

"I can remember his mother pushing him in a stroller," she replied. "This long, skinny toddler with hair like fire. And I remember when he was in fourth grade, he was already taller than I was—and I was a senior in high school."

He gave a short, cheerless laugh. "And I was pushing a broom in Charlotte in the daytime. Nights I waited tables at a pizza place."

He paused at the edge of her yard and looked at her little house. A cloud had covered the moon, and the house's off-white paint looked drab and gray.

"This is it, right?" he asked, no emotion in his voice. "Where you live now?"

"This is it. Thanks for keeping me company. I'll be fine now. Good night."

"I'll walk you to the door," he said, and he touched her elbow to show her he wasn't leaving until he saw that she was safely inside.

The contact, brief and perfunctory as it was, made her oddly giddy, as if she really were sixteen again. And from somewhere, a tree frog started to sing. Lori damned its beady little eyes. It seemed that wherever they went tonight, the old music came back to haunt her.

She speeded her pace, wanting to get inside as fast as possible. But he stayed close to her side, and together they ascended the three concrete steps to the small porch. She already had her keys in hand.

"Well," she managed to say, thrusting the key into the lock. "Home at last. Thanks again. I'll see you tomorrow?"

She wouldn't even mention asking him in; it was a dangerous idea. Besides, her landlady lived across the street and always kept a careful and suspicious eye on Lori.

"No," Kane said in a low voice. "I have to get back to Charlotte. I'll have breakfast with Aileen, then leave."

"Oh," she said, which was the best substitute for a response she could think of. She wished the tree frog would get severe laryngitis and shut up. But it caroled on, and now another answered it—were these mating calls?

Don't even think of it, she warned herself, and she realized at the same instance that Kane had eased uncomfortably close to her. His nearness made her skin prickle and set off unwanted tickles in her stomach.

"So it's not just good night," he said, almost whispering. "It's goodbye. But I'll be in touch. And I'll see you again before the Cargill-Grosso tests."

"Oh," she repeated. "Yes. Well. Fine. Thanks."

"Thank you," he said. "I probably won't be back for the title signing. I'll appoint a proxy."

"Oh. Okay…"

Her hand was on the doorknob; she twisted it and the door creaked, opening inward. She started to step inside, eager for escape.

"And Lori?" he said.

"Yes?"

"Don't worry. I'll take care of your speedway. I promise you."

She nodded, feeling helpless.

"Sleep tight," he said, and stepped backward. Then he turned, and in a blink, it seemed, he was striding back down her walk. He didn't turn to look at her again.

She slipped inside, turning on the light. She felt both relieved and strangely empty now that he was gone.

He hadn't tried to kiss her. Thank heaven. Or should she be disappointed? Did he still resent her? Perhaps no longer felt any desire for her and was glad of it? He probably thought she was too provincial, too prickly, and—she had to face it—too old.

She should be glad. Very glad. It made things much simpler and promised a kind of security.

As if to emphasize that security, she locked the door from the inside. She told herself to enjoy the solitude. And the safety. Yes, he was leaving, and she could again tamp down all those unsettling and sensual memories of him.

But even though the door and all the windows were shut, she could still hear, from the lush Carolina night surrounding her, the serenade of the tree frogs courting in the darkness.

CHAPTER SEVEN

"I GOT BAD NEWS for you," Clyde told Lori the next morning. "Replacing that transmission won't be cheap. The lowest price that Eddie and I could figure is eight hundred dollars."

Lori pressed her lips together so she wouldn't swear. But after the closing, she'd have money again.

"I can put it on my credit card, I guess," she said reluctantly. She'd fought to keep her credit card debt to a minimum. She'd ridden A.J.'s Vespa to the speedway this morning. She had helmet hair and rumpled clothes, but at least she had wheels.

"Fine," said Clyde. "And Kane's gone back to Charlotte?"

She nodded, nearly sure of what Clyde would say next. And she was right.

He looked her in the eyes. "It's gonna be Kane buying this place, isn't it? And not Devlin."

"It's not a done deal yet," she said evasively. *When I sign over the title it will be a done deal.*

"I hope it gets done," Clyde offered. "Give the old place a fightin' chance. Devlin gets this property, and Halesboro's doomed. Kane's a smart guy. Always was. Sharp as a tack."

Lori gave a half-hearted nod. Was Kane also a good man? An honest one? A realistic one? The day of the independent speedway was almost over. He might *think* he could revive the track, but could he actually do it?

"Yes," she admitted. "He was always smart."

"And a hard worker," added Clyde. "Even your daddy said that. 'That kid's tireless and efficient, Never wastes a move, and he learns quick. He could go far.' That's what he said."

Lori found herself gritting her teeth. Her father had thought that way—once. Until he found out that Kane was secretly seeing Lori. Didn't Clyde remember how her father's admiration had turned to disgust?

Or was Clyde slyly reminding her that once Andrew Jackson Simmons had thought Kane was a young man of high promise. And he had, until things suddenly became more personal.

As a worker, Kane was a prize. But as a potential suitor for Lori? That was different. Her father quickly adopted a double standard. Then he saw Kane as an insolent piece of trash.

"I'd better get down to work," Lori said, cutting the conversation short. "I'll see you later. I need to have some things moved out of the main office. I'm moving down the hall."

Clyde looked at her curiously. But she forced a bland smile and left without explanation.

AT TEN O'CLOCK, a woman called, saying that she was Kane's secretary and she had some information for Lori and a list of requests. Her name was Susan Haversham, and she sounded young, sexy and sure of herself.

Madly, Lori scribbled down what the woman told her. The Grosso-Cargill testing would begin next month. The tests would last two days. Dean and Kent Grosso and Kent's team would attend an open-to-the-public barbecue.

Lori's job was to arrange for the barbecue, publicize it locally, order posters for the teams to autograph, as well as contact vendors who'd bring souvenir caps, T-shirts and other merchandise for fans.

The list of Things To Do grew longer, and Lori started to feel overwhelmed. She'd never been part of a project so large. And she still had to start composing a letter to her employees about Kane's buying the speedway.

Lori knew that rumors were certainly already circulating about the sale and that people who worked at the speedway would be nervous about keeping their jobs. Kane had said that all of them would get a six-week grace period and a professional evaluation.

"And," Susan said, "Mr. Ledger's lawyer will call to give you more details about the closing. It should take place in about thirty days. Mr. Ledger says you're not using a Realtor?"

I couldn't afford to, Lori thought. But her friend Liz had been generous with advice.

"He says you may want to have a lawyer with you at the closing. I'll send you some information about inspections, fees, deeds, interim interest, PMI, transfer taxes…"

Lori resisted a strong urge to scream or whimper. She wrote even faster and thanked heaven for Liz. Susan of the Sultry Voice might as well be speaking in ancient Greek.

KANE'S CONDO was a penthouse suite atop a forty-story tower in uptown Charlotte. He'd paid a ridiculous amount of money for it, and now he supposed he should sell it. It was worth twice what the speedway was, and it had been an extravagance.

It had been fun to own, but the novelty had quickly worn off. A decorator had recommended a lot of fancy furnishings that weren't his style. So he kept his old furniture, a motley collection of stuff that was comfortable and that he was used to and that was probably still giving the decorator screaming nightmares.

Now he sat on his rat-gray sofa, drinking beer from a can. He guessed you could take the boy out of the rental house, but you couldn't take the rental house out of the boy. He liked his small luxuries, but the large ones had come to bore him.

He remembered how disdainfully Lori had looked at his sports car. As if he drove it to show off. Face it: she was right. He'd wanted to roll into town and impress the hell out of everybody. He'd wanted to generate envy. Hey, look everybody, the bad boy made it big time. Much, much better than any of you did.

He'd trade the car down for something less flashy. He liked cars, and he talked about them with the NASCAR people he knew, Dean and Kent Grosso, Justin Murphy, Sid Cochran, all of them and the guys on their teams. Maybe he'd buy a real stock car, a regular production model.

He thought of Lori, still driving her brother's car. Kane had no love for A.J., for he'd been a bully and snob. But that Lori would keep the old Mustang touched him. Being touched was a dangerous feeling, and he tried to block it.

He finished the beer, crumpled the can, went to the kitchen and threw it into the recycling bin. And he found himself, on the way back, pulling an old Halesboro High yearbook from his shelves.

He'd picked up the book at a flea market, opened it, and there was Lori's junior portrait. She was smiling her great smile. Her head was tilted, her chin up, her face lovely.

He was thirty-two years old when he found the book, but his heart had quaked and he felt dizzy, weak in his knees. He should have slammed the thing shut, because he knew what else it contained, but instead, like a fool, he'd bought it. And sometimes, like a really dim-witted fool, he'd open it and look at the pictures of her. Tonight, he couldn't help doing it again.

He sat on the worn gray sofa and started paging through it: Lori, the prettiest girl in the choir, the most desirable girl in swim club, even though her mother made her wear that super-modest tank suit, the smartest girl in the forensic club, the candid shot of her in study hall, showing her perfect profile as she gazed dreamily out a window.

And the other candid shot that still made him feel sick, her at the spring prom with Scott Garland, who'd been homecoming king. She was in Garland's arms, looking up at him almost impassively. Garland stared back, his expression adoring and possessive.

That spring, Kane, tired of hiding in the shadows, was starting to wonder if Lori was ashamed of him. He had actually asked her to that dance. They loved each other; why not be open about it? He'd got a suit at the Salvation Army. He'd trimmed his hair shorter. He'd learned to dance from

Irma, a middle-aged waitress at the Piney Woods Café. Everybody on the staff teased him that he must have a girl.

He was acting completely out of character, but he was tired of hiding their relationship. He asked Lori to go. She refused. She said her father wouldn't let her and that he'd get suspicious. She said her mother would have a fit. And when he asked if she was ashamed of him, she got mad and said she was just being sensible.

He accused her of being too frightened to face her parents' shock and her friends' ridicule. She got angrier still and what she said next cut his heart in two as painfully as if she'd wielded a cleaver.

She'd already been invited to the prom by Scott Garland. And she said she'd told Scott yes. Why? Scott's mother had told her mother that he was asking Lori. Her mother and father and A.J. encouraged her to accept and were suspicious she hadn't said yes immediately. She couldn't refuse, she needed to throw her parents off track. She couldn't go with Kane because…well…she just couldn't, and he should know that. And besides that, she *wanted* to go to the prom.

His princess had become imperious. She was willful and defensive, insisting she'd done the right thing and that she'd been going to break it to him gently. This was the perfect way to defuse her parents' concern about her never dating. And she was worried that her brother, A.J., a senior, suspected something.

"At school, you shouldn't look at me the way you do," she complained.

"At school," Kane countered, "you might recognize that I exist. You act like I'm not even there."

She refused to listen to him. She was used to having her way, and she intended to do as she pleased. They parted in anger.

The next day at school, he slipped a note to her as she passed. She stuck it in her algebra book. A.J. saw, and before she could stop him, Kane watched as he snatched it out and read it.

Kane had written, "I love you, and you love me. Just don't *go* to the damn dance. Meet me tonight at the carriage house."

A.J. threw Lori a look of contempt, ripped the note in half and stuffed it in his pocket. Lori looked horrified, knowing he would tell their parents.

Kane didn't see her the rest of the day. After school, he went to work a five-hour shift washing dishes at the Piney Woods Café. He was taking a short cut up a back alley to get home and change clothes, when he realized a car was following him.

"Hey, Ledger, stop!" He recognized the voice: A.J.'s.

Kane kept walking. "Hey, Ledger. I got the note you slipped my sister. You gonna talk to me, man to man? Or you gonna run off like a chicken?"

Kane knew then that he wasn't going to run even if A.J. had a baseball bat and intended to crack open his skull. He turned and faced the car. It moved slowly toward him and stopped, only twelve inches away. A.J. got out. And so did two of his football teammates. They beat him half-senseless.

But he remembered the messages they'd delivered with their blows.

"Stay away from my sister, trash boy."

"Stay away from her, punk."

"Go back to the gutter where you belong."

"Go away…"

"Stay away…"

Finally A.J. stood over him and growled, "It's over between you and her. I had a talk with her. She won't be seeing you again. And I told my folks. They'll ground her. Until prom night when she goes out with Scott. I mean it is *so* over for you, scumbag."

They left him lying in the gravel, his mouth full of blood. He got up and limped home. He'd fought back and hard. He'd landed some good punches, but he couldn't fight off three. His face was battered, but no teeth broken and only one black eye. His body hurt from being kicked. He cleaned himself up as best he could.

He looked at himself in the mirror and repeated A.J.'s words. "It's over."

Maybe Lori was even grateful. Maybe she wanted to rejoin her own kind. Maybe she was destined for somebody like Scott Garland, and always had been. And Kane was nothing but a fool.

But A.J. was right. It *was* over. Until he'd fallen for Lori, he couldn't wait to leave Halesboro. Well, there was no time like the present. He was sick of the town, the people, his mother and her drunkenness and her ham-fisted boyfriend. He was going to split, and nobody could stop him.

His mother, Brenda, tried. She screamed at him, his little half-sister, Stacy, cried; the boyfriend hit Stacy, Kane hit the boyfriend, Brenda, hysterical, called the police, and Kane simply left, made his way back to the carriage house, and slept there till morning.

As soon as the bank opened, he got his money out and planned to hitchhike out of town. If nobody gave him a ride, he'd walk to Charlotte.

And that's what he did, walk to Charlotte, not looking back. Now he gazed a long time at Lori's yearbook photo and closed the book. He tried not to think back, just as he hadn't looked back. But he didn't have a lot of success.

AILEEN HAD INVITED Lori over for supper. They sat at the table, Lori nervous, certain that Aileen was not going to beat around the bush. She'd quickly bring up the subject of Kane.

She waited only until they sat down at the table. "What a strange day," Aileen said, filling their wineglasses. "Breakfast with Kane Ledger. Supper with you. He's really buying the speedway. True?"

"True," Lori said.

"So he saved your behind, did he?" Aileen was outspoken and thought for herself. Her brother, Lori's father, always warned Lori not to take after her so much.

"Yes," Lori admitted. "He saved my tushy. I don't know why, but why care?"

"Hmmph," Aileen returned, the hint of sarcasm in her

voice. "But tell me. Does he really think he can turn the speedway around?"

"He seems to."

Aileen passed her the lasagna. "Well, I suppose if it can be done, he'll do it. Did I ever tell you he had the highest IQ of any student I ever taught?"

"You've told me," Lori said. *Too often,* she thought.

"I know it was because of you."

"I know that you know."

"And that A.J. and two of his friends beat the hell out of him," Aileen said.

"Yes. A.J. told me. He wanted me to know they hurt him."

"But I don't think for a minute that they scared him out of town."

Lori agreed. Kane would never run out of fear. He'd left because of her. She said, "I was crazy about him. But I treated him like dirt at the end. It was getting harder and harder to hide that we were seeing each other. It was getting harder and harder not to…uh…"

"'Go all the way' was the quaint phrase we used in my day."

"Yes," Lori said with a sigh. "I was *terrified* of getting pregnant."

"Wise girl."

"I mean, I was tempted—"

"Normal girl."

"But I wasn't ready, and we both knew we couldn't be seen together in public. And he thought I was ashamed of him. And the bad thing is, in a way I *was* ashamed. He was so different from everybody else. I liked that in him, but it scared me, too. He wasn't afraid to be different. But I was."

"He marched to a different drummer," Aileen said. "High school isn't the greatest place for a nonconformist. In fact, it's usually living hell."

"I meant to tell him about going out with Scott. That my parents were starting to suspect something. And I really *did* want to go to the prom. I'd given up all the things that other girls did. I never thought that Kane would ask me. And yet—"

Her voice trailed off. Aileen gave her a knowing look. "Having a secret love stopped being quite so exciting. You were missing out on things. You wanted it both ways."

Lori nodded, feeling ashamed. "Yes, I did. And I was used to getting what I wanted. I thought Kane should understand if he cared for me."

"But you were thinking more about your own feelings than his."

"Yes. And maybe I was trying to put some distance between us. Things were getting so intense, it was getting scary. Sometimes I wanted to be like other people again."

Aileen reached over and patted Lori's arm. "You were very young, my dear."

"And spoiled," Lori admitted. "I didn't mean to hurt him that way. And then what A.J. did, that was terrible. I didn't speak to him for months."

"It *was* terrible. But what's done is done. And I did suspect something was going on between you and Kane—from the way he'd look at you. You acted as if you didn't dare look back. So what did it feel like, seeing him after all these years?"

"Strange, that's all," said Lori.

This was a lie. The old attraction had flared up as if it had never died. As a boy, he'd radiated a sense of danger, of the forbidden. As a man, he seemed far more dangerous. Lori feared that now he could hurt her as badly, or worse, than she had ever hurt him.

She shrugged and tried to seem cheerfully unconcerned. "How did it feel for you to see him again? To see how well he's done for himself?"

"He was sweet," Aileen said. "He thanked me for believing in him when he hardly believed in himself. I told him it was easy. He had a certain spark, that undefinable something. It was a blow when he left. But now he's back."

Now he's back, thought Lori. *The question is whether he's literally back with a vengeance.*

KANE CALLED HER at the speedway the next morning. She wished her heart didn't beat so fast and so hard at the sound of his voice.

He'd always spoken softly in a velvety voice and without a trace of a Southern accent. "Lori, it's Kane. I've got the Cargill-Grosso team lined up for testing on the 1st and 2nd of July. On the evening of July 1st, we'll have the barbecue. Kent will be there, and so will Dean. Roberto Castillo can't attend, but he'll donate autographed photos. Since the event's so close to the 4th, I thought we'd have fireworks in the infield. Also a blue-grass group to play. Take down these numbers, will you?"

She snatched up her pen and began to write down numbers and notes.

"Some bunting, too," he said. "And red and white balloons for the kids. Get in touch with this company…I may have some special Halesboro T-shirts made. Gotta check prices. Also, in ads and press releases, emphasize that kids under twelve get in free."

"Free?" Lori said in disbelief. "We haven't done that in years. We couldn't afford to."

"We can't afford not to," he countered. "We want our image to be like NASCAR—family-friendly. Free passes for kids give families a price break. On races, too."

"Races, too!" she exclaimed.

"Think of young families on a tight budget. You want to appeal to them, be their best buy. It's that or have empty seats. Also, free tickets for the press. We want coverage, and we want their goodwill."

"You're going to lose money on this," she warned.

"Not in the long run. Also, I'm thinking of changing the name to Ledger's Halesboro Speedway."

Lori winced. She resented the idea, his appropriating the Halesboro racing heritage that her father had built. Tonelessly, she said, "It's your decision."

"I have to think about it," he said. "Also thinking of have a special two-hundred-lap memorial race named in your father's honor."

Honor her father? Now she felt as if she were on a carnival ride that spun too swiftly. From resentment, she whirled into feeling deeply touched. "He'd like that. He'd love that."

"He was decent to me. But I probably fell from grace big-time."

"Yes. But he'd still be proud to have a race named for him."

"Good. Now, for the next weekend after the Fourth, I'll make reservations for you to go to the Illinois NASCAR Sprint Cup Series race with me. I want you there. And at the one in Pennsylvania early next month."

Her mood took another 180 degree turn. He might be able to give her orders at the office, but could he take her weekends, too, demanding she travel hundreds of miles? How high-handed did he intend to get?

"Why do I need to go to Illinois? Or to Pocono?"

"I'm meeting some NASCAR people there. I want to run some ideas by them. And for you to talk about the Halesboro's place in racing history and the fans' affection. We double-team them."

"I can't afford it," she said. "I've got debts."

"I'll pay for it. It's a business expense."

"People will talk," she said uneasily.

"Who cares?" he said, a sudden edge in his voice. Did he remember that her cowardice had helped wreck their relationship? She could be seen at a dance with the homecoming king, but not Kane, the rebel who didn't fit in.

She closed her eyes, took a deep breath. "If you insist. What counts is the speedway."

"Remember that," he almost purred. "The speedway. You keep your word to your father. And, with luck, I make a bundle."

"And that's what this is about, isn't it? You're sure you can beat the odds and make a lot of money. And show everybody in Halesboro that you're top gun."

"What else would it be about?" he asked. He laughed, and something in that laugh came close to frightening her.

BY THE END OF THE DAY, Lori slumped in exhaustion over her desk. She'd spent all day talking to a seemingly endless string of people. Party suppliers. Vendors. The printer who did the Kent and Dean Grosso posters. The manager of the Bluegrass String Band, an up-and-coming folk-country group. Catering companies. The Magic Dragon Fireworks Company.

A desultory rain drummed at her window. Her head spun with names, instructions, recommendations, estimates, prices and enough details to boggle her mind for days. Clyde stopped by just as she was straightening her cluttered desk.

"You're working late," he said.

"Kane Ledger has big plans. I take care of the grunt work."

"Want a ride home?" Clyde asked, leaning against her door frame. "It's wet out there."

"I'd love one," she said with feeling.

"I should've asked sooner. I had a list of stuff to do, too. There's a feller coming to give an estimate on replacing the scoreboard. Another company to make recommendations on cleaning up pit road. And an expert to eyeball the track surface. That Kane, he thinks of everything, doesn't he?"

"He certainly does," she agreed with a sigh.

"Kinda wanted to talk to you, too," Clyde said. "I've heard tell of some funny things happenin' around town."

"Funny things?" she echoed.

"Tell you when I pick you up. Meet me in the lot in five minutes?"

Five minutes later, she reached the parking lot, her umbrella up, her book bag filled with paperwork. Clyde's truck pulled up, he helped her load the Vespa into the back, and she got into the passenger's seat. As he started the engine, she turned to him.

"So what's happening in town?"

"Nobody yet knows who bought Junior McCorkle's castle," Clyde said, tilting the bill of his cap up. "And nobody knows much what's going on. It's mysterious. Now the same lawyer phoned up Liz and made an offer on the old Military Theater. He's representin' somebody. But who? Nobody knows."

Lori frowned quizzically. "The Military Theater? It's been closed for *years*. What would anybody want with it?"

"I don't know," Clyde said. "Most little town picture shows closed years ago. People go to the video store or drive over to Henderson or Asheville to a multiplex."

"Do you think it's the same person who bought the castle?"

"Maybe. Maybe not. But they asked Liz about other properties. Like the old hotel."

"The Bostwick? It closed when track attendance fell—that was over four years ago. I mean it was a beautiful building once, but it's been empty so long."

"Yup. Take some major fixin' up. But this caller was interested in pretty near all property for sale 'round Halesboro. No offer. Just a heckuva lot of *askin'*."

Lori's brow creased in puzzlement. "Why the sudden interest? What's up? Is there something about Halesboro we don't know? Are we going to become some kind of hot spot?"

"Not that I've heard." Clyde shrugged. "About all we got here these days is a lot of scenery."

"And a lot of outsiders suddenly interested in real estate," mused Lori. "Including the Devlin Corporation. I wonder if Kane knows anything about this. Knows but isn't telling."

A SPORTS AGENT must not only understand sports, he must understand money—how it moved, where it moved and why.

This meant Kane not only understood key sports like NASCAR, he'd developed a sixth sense about business. Maybe it was that he was naturally competitive. Maybe it was because he'd grown up poor as dirt, and, now that he was rich, he intended to stay that way.

Kent Grosso joked that if a dollar crinkled in Seattle, Kane heard it in Charlotte and his ears would perk up like a fox's.

That wasn't true. Kane didn't bother trying to hear dollars crinkle. Instead, he tried to anticipate trends, to hear the earliest promising rumors, to sniff them on the wind, to see the writing on the wall when it was still only the faintest of preliminary pencil marks.

There were things that he hadn't yet told most of his clients and that he certainly hadn't told Lori. She was already nervous about his wheeling and dealing. But wheeling and dealing were what he did.

She liked the old ways best, sticking to tradition. What he had in mind were new ways that blew tradition to hell. But at this point, what she didn't know wouldn't hurt her.

CHAPTER EIGHT

"SOMETHING'S up," said Liz Bitcon. "Real estate's been in a slump for years in this town. Now I'm getting queries about all sorts of property. Most come through different law firms in Charlotte. But some are from as far away as Missouri—and New Jersey, believe it or not."

Liz and Lori sat in Lori's office having coffee. The pungent scent of fresh paint wafted from farther down the hall.

Lori blinked in surprise. "Missouri? New Jersey? I heard that somebody was asking about the hotel and the Military Theater…"

Liz, a tall woman with a spill of ash-blond curls, leaned closer. "Listen," she said in a low voice. "Please don't repeat this. But one call was about the old mill buildings."

Lori blinked even harder. "Uncle June's mills? They've been empty for years! Who'd want them? And why?"

"You tell me," Liz said earnestly. "I mean they were built very well. But to make them into anything else would take a fortune. I don't know if this is connected to Junior's castle or not. And I still don't know who bought *that*."

"You have no idea?"

"None. Officially, the purchaser is an organization called Smith-Smith, Inc. of Charlotte. It's got no address, no phone, only a post office box and answering service. I've searched all over the Internet, but I can't find out who's behind it. It could be anybody."

"Smith-Smith?" Lori frowned. "It'd be hard to be vaguer. Do you think it's legit?"

"My worst nightmare is it's some kind of shell corporation that could be a cover-up." Liz rolled her eyes heavenward. "I pray not."

"But the castle's going to stay a residence? At least that's what I heard."

"There are workmen coming and going, but nobody's talking about what they're doing to the place."

"How could they not talk?" Lori demanded.

Liz shrugged. "Most of them are specialists and come here, stay on the grounds until their part's done, then they go back to where they came from. They're using the carriage house as a sort of combined bunkhouse and eating place."

Lori tried not to flinch at the words *carriage house*. They brought unwanted memories surging back: being in Kane's arms, hungrily kissing and being kissed, and the touching that had both excited and frightened her. But Lori's expression must have betrayed her.

Liz gave her a sharp look. "You never really got over him, did you? Kane, I mean."

"It was puppy love, and it didn't last long," Lori said, but a blush heated her cheeks. Liz, who'd been her friend since kindergarten, had been the first to guess that she and Kane were infatuated. And Liz kept the secret, but, trying to be kind, kept warning Lori against him. "He's the kind of guy who can go wrong," she'd said. "It's written all over him."

Now Liz gave her a long, serious look. "Most people think Kane's back because he resents Halesboro, that he's trying to prove he's a very big deal. And you know what people are saying about you two, don't you?"

Lori tensed. "Nobody's said anything—to my face."

"Half the town thinks he came back because he still wants you."

"That's not true," Lori protested, not letting herself think such a thing.

"The other half thinks he's going to even the score with you. You hurt him. And, if you let him, he'll hurt you back."

She put her hand atop Lori's. "We've been friends for over thirty years. I do *not* want to see you harmed—not your emotions or your reputation."

Liz withdrew her hand, reached into her big canvas tote and pulled out a copy of Charlotte's most influential paper, folded to a page in the sports section. "Seen today's news?"

She offered it to Lori, who took it with a frisson of apprehension.

Liz said. "This may help fill in the blanks about what's happening here."

Lori gazed at a black-and-white photo that showed Kane, wearing a suit and tie, sitting at a table with an older man and a young woman, an extremely beautiful brunette in a low-cut dress. Lori swallowed hard and read the picture's cut line.

"Sports agent Kane Ledger (right) dines with business magnate D. B. Horning and his daughter Zoey at Barrington's."

The article beneath carried the headline New NASCAR Sponsor In The Offing?

Charlotte sports agent Kane Ledger was spotted having an intent supper conversation at Barrington's with D. B. Horning, the flamboyant Missouri entrepreneur.

Is Ledger angling for a new sponsor for his sometimes problematic NASCAR driver Justin Murphy? Or is Horning interested in sponsoring another of Ledger's charges?

Horning's daughter Zoey, a former Miss Missouri, seems to listen with interest. She is currently vice-president of real estate development and acquisitions at the Horning organization.

"There could be a connection," Liz said. "First, I got a query from a law firm in Missouri. That's where Horning's from. Second, he brought his daughter, who specializes in real estate development and acquisition. These people may not be talking about a NASCAR sponsorship at all. They may be talking about Halesboro."

The suggestion unsettled Lori, but she found herself concentrating more on the photo, the way Zoey Horning was looking at Kane. It seemed she found *him* more interesting than the conversation. A beauty queen with a seductive gaze and sensual lips, she was clearly pleased by what she saw.

Kane stared back at the young woman with the sort of smile that suggested he and she shared a secret, perhaps an intimate one. A humiliating dart of jealousy penetrated Lori's heart.

This was the kind of woman Kane could have now. She looked to be no more than twenty-four or twenty-five, she was exquisitely groomed, and an impressive double string of pearls hung from her neck and nestled in her even more impressive cleavage.

"Of course," Liz said with a dismissive wave, "it may mean nothing at all. But when I go back to my office, I'm going to do an Internet search for D. B. Horning. I never heard of him before, and I want to know if there's any reason he'd be interested in Halesboro."

She drank the last of her coffee, then picked up her tote and stood. "I need to get back. Keep the paper. And let me know if you learn anything, okay?"

"Sure," Lori said, trying not to look at the picture again. "Thanks for stopping by. And if anybody's interested in pricing even more Halesboro property, keep me posted, will you?"

"Will do. And take it easy, friend. You've been on an emotional roller coaster these last weeks. Save some time for yourself for a change."

"Sounds good," Lori said, forcing a smile.

"Ciao, kiddo."

"Right. See you later." As soon as Liz closed the door behind her, Lori snatched up the paper again and studied the photo of Horning, Zoey and Kane. Was the picture the real reason that

Liz had brought the paper? To show Lori that some kind of un-disguised chemistry flowed between Zoey and Kane?

Her friend's words echoed ominously in her mind: "I do *not* want to see you harmed." And if she allowed herself to care for him again, he had the power to humiliate her far worse than she had him.

Right. Letting an old crush reclaim her was the stupidest thing she could do. She needed to lock herself in a small, dull cage, safe from her own feelings.

LIZ PHONED LORI an hour later. "This is getting weirder and weirder," she said, sounding stunned. "A Realtor just called me for prices on three more empty buildings. The old Spellman Drugstore, Stoner's Photography and MacIntyre's Sewing Supplies."

"What?" Lori asked, feeling as if she were Alice falling down the rabbit hole. "A Realtor from Missouri? Or New Jersey?"

"Neither," Liz said dryly. "Las Vegas."

Lori's mind whirled giddily. "Why would anybody in Vegas want three deserted shops in a town where they roll up the sidewalks at night? Something's going on, all right. But I'll bet Kane knows what."

"And *that's* why he bought the speedway," Liz said, her voice edged with suspicion. "He has some kind of information, but he's not sharing it. Outside forces might be trying to buy up this town. That somebody plans on changing this place big-time."

Lori's stomach went queasy. "But they won't change it back to what it was, not the town we knew."

"What it was didn't work," Liz reminded her. "That was one of the strikes against the speedway. Except for the castle, it was the only attraction here."

"I don't want to see this town become a tourist trap," Lori said with conviction. "I'm going to call Kane and *demand* to know what's going on."

"At least I might get some real estate commissions," Liz said wistfully.

"Do you want a bunch of strangers buying our home town from under us?"

"Better that than watching it dry up and blow away."

But Lori had visions of her old family home turned into an upscale bed and breakfast for yuppies. Of somebody putting a pitch-and-putt golf course on one of the old horse farms. The empty shops on Main Street would become boutiques full of designer clothes and overpriced knickknacks.

Or a horse farm could turn into an amusement park, garish with Ferris wheels and screaming roller coasters, and cheap carnival games. Main Street could become a strip of T-shirt shops and fast food franchises and stores full of cheesy souvenirs.

"I'm going to call Kane right *now,*" she told Liz. And she meant it.

SUSAN HAVERSHAM RAPPED at Kane's doorframe, her expression uneasy. "That Garland woman's calling from Halesboro," she said. "She wants to talk to you right now. She sounds unhappy. As in *dangerously* unhappy."

Susan, tall and imperious, wasn't used to people that she couldn't chill into submission. She considered Kane to be the king of the office, but she was the viceroy, the captain of the guards and, above all, the gatekeeper. Kane stifled a smile, wondering what the little redhead had said to shake the usually unshakeable Susan.

"Put her call through," he told her. "I'll take it."

Susan gave a huff of disapproval and stomped back to her desk. Kane's desk phone buzzed, and he let it buzz five times, just for the sport of it. Then he picked it up.

"Ledger Agency. This is Kane Ledger."

"And this is Lori Garland," she said, clearly in high dudgeon. "Some strange stuff is happening up here. Concerning real estate. Lots of it. And I think you know why. You haven't been telling me the whole story." She paused ominously, then accused, "I think you have *insider's knowledge*—and are acting on it."

He gave a short laugh. "Doing that's illegal in stock trading. Not in buying property."

"What's going on? Liz got queries today about the hotel, the pharmacy, the photographer's studio and the sewing store."

He frowned. He'd expected a query on the old Ming Toy Restaurant, as well. Why hadn't *that* happened?

"Good for Liz," he said pleasantly. "I imagine that her business had been slow for a while. Now she's getting nibbles. You should be happy for her."

"Yesterday somebody wanted to know about the mills. The mills! Why's Halesboro so popular lately? What do these people know that we don't? What do you know that you aren't telling me?"

"I don't know anything for certain," he hedged. "I don't have a crystal ball. But there are places where old mill buildings have sold. Happened up in Manchester, New Hampshire, a while back. Converted them into offices, stores, restaurants...great success story."

"Don't tell me about New Hampshire when I asked you about Halesboro," she retorted.

He couldn't hold back a wry smile. She was still independent—and feisty. He'd expected his return to Halesboro would have humbled her a little. No. Not her.

"The economy's in flux," he said vaguely. "Sometimes certain investments seem hot—but aren't. And vice versa. Right now, speculators can buy low in Halesboro. Is it a smart buy? Time will tell."

"You paid full price for the speedway. Did you know things would be happening in Halesboro? You're foxy about money. Is there going to be a boom here?"

He laughed again. "Foxy? No. Lucky? Yes. A boom? In this economy, a boom can go bust overnight."

"You're foxy," she persisted. "You started out with nothing and ended up rich."

His smile died. He could have said *And your family started out with a fortune and ended up with next to nothing.* He knew about money because he'd learned the hard way. Until the last five years, she'd never had to worry. When it came to business, she was a rookie. But rookie or not, she was still as dauntless as she'd been at sixteen.

"You keep saying the speedway will succeed. Why are you sure?" she challenged. "Are you involved in *making* something happen? Are you right in the middle of it?"

She was good, he had to admit. She should have been nearly down and out, but she was still so bright, so bold. Was it her old arrogance, that of the pampered princess? Or was it simply that she had a character that wouldn't, that *couldn't* bow easily to circumstance?

He pictured her, sitting in her office, probably, her golden-red hair tied back in a pony tail, her green eyes full of spirit, and her chin set at a stubborn angle. He chose his words carefully. "I don't want to talk about it. Not now. Maybe when I come up there for the testing and the barbecue."

"That's still weeks away," she countered. "I want to know *now.*"

"Now's not the right time. You're going to have to trust me."

"Trust you," she repeated tonelessly.

"Right. Things might come to pass that help the town, the track, the whole county. *Might.* Or might not. I don't have happy memories of Halesboro—"

Except for bittersweet ones of you. In my memory, I can still taste your mouth. Still feel your body so close to mine it made me crazy.

"—but," he said, "Halesboro changed my life. It's part of me. It's fallen on hard times, and I don't want it to fall on worse. After all, I've sunk a lot of money into the place. And I'll sink more. I want it to prosper, not to wither up and die."

"Prosper at the price of what?" she asked. "Its traditions? Its character? Everything it used to be?"

"We'll talk about it when I'm there. Until then, just trust me."

The darker side of his nature made him add, "Once upon a time you did. Or seemed to. I've got to go now. Take care, babe."

When he hung up, his emotions simmered in conflict. How did he feel about her?

Sometimes his emotions seemed to change from minute to minute. They veered back and forth, barely under control. But again he promised himself that he'd get her out of his mind; it was just going to take more effort than he'd thought.

He glanced at his watch. It was true he had to leave. He had to meet Zoey Horning. She was the kind of woman he should be thinking about, not Lori. Hadn't he learned his lesson? He should have. Lori had carved it into his heart, and it felt as if she'd done it with a piece of jagged glass.

A WEEK LATER, Liz and Lori sat in The Groove Café, having supper. Liz's husband, Glen, was out of town for a real estate conference, their son was staying overnight with a friend, and Liz was relishing an evening of freedom—and gossipy chitchat.

"Kane's been seeing more of that Zoey Horning," Liz said. "I found a Charlotte society blog on the Internet. It even said they'd gone apartment-hunting together."

Lori's heart constricted and her stomach knotted. She despised herself for letting such turmoil sweep her and struggled to hide her feelings.

"Oh," she said primly. "And did you find out who these Horning people are? If they might have something to do with Halesboro?"

"I am practically the queen of surfing the Internet," Liz said with a grin. "Yes, Horning's heir to the Horning Outlets Center empire. His only heir is Zoey. She's got a Master's of Business Administration from Harvard. Graduated magna cum laude."

Lori swallowed hard. *Harvard? Magna cum laude? The heiress of a fortune? And a beautiful young woman, as well?* She remembered the photo of Kane and the striking brunette in the paper. Lori had a degree in education from UNC Wilmington, a very good school—but not nearly as famous as

Harvard. She might have once been princess of Halesboro, but Zoey was a *real* princess of both finance and society.

Lori swallowed again and asked, "What's Horning Outlets Center?"

"Exactly what it sounds like. Discount malls. Big ones. Successful ones. All across the country. Upscale ones and 'value-centered' ones. Last year, Horning Outlets pulled in 132 million shoppers."

The number made Lori feel dizzy. "You think they might put a mall here?"

"I'm thinking that the old mill buildings would be perfect for an enclosed mall. Cheaper than building one up from the ground. And it'd give Halesboro what it didn't have before. An attraction *besides* the speedway. Maybe your friend Kane is putting together a smart deal. Maybe you really should trust him. On business, at least."

Lori pushed her plate away, her sandwich only half-eaten. She heard the hidden warning in Liz's words. Trust Kane to bring money into the town. Trust him with finance, but not her heart. Not when he was squiring around a woman like Zoey Horning.

"What about the rest of it?" Lori asked. "Those other properties? Do you think they tie in somehow with the Horning malls?"

"I have some theories," said Liz. "But that's all they are at this point. Didn't Kane say he'd tell you more when the Cargill-Grosso team came here to test?"

"Yes. But—"

"Ask him straight out. Don't let him dodge questions. You can do it. I know you can."

Lori smiled wanly. "If he gets a Horning mall established here, what else might he set up? Come on, what's your theory?"

"Only a theory," Liz said with a shrug. "I always wanted to be a detective. But playing detective can lead to wild speculation. You're better off getting facts from him instead of fantasies from me."

Lori bent lower over the table to get closer to Liz. In a

whisper she asked, "You think he could put a bigger deal together than just getting Horning here?"

Liz tossed her head, her expression cynical. "His whole *job* is putting deals together, sugar. He handles people worth millions—like Kent Grosso. And even richer—Roman McCandless."

Lori said nothing, only wondered how a giant mall would affect Halesboro. Could it succeed? Could it help draw people to the speedway? If it did succeed, would it radically change the town?"

Liz studied her friend's face. "Maybe Kane could pull off a huge deal. Your Aunt Aileen always said he was smart. He was *your* boyfriend. Just how smart do you think he is?"

Lori shrugged to signal she didn't know the answer. But she thought, *He's probably way too smart for me. He's not only got the speedway and me in his power. He might have the whole future of Halesboro under his control.*

And, she wondered, what did he want from Halesboro, the town that had been so cruel to him? Did he want to change it forever, wipe out what it had once been and turn it into an entity that owed him everything, and where everyone would have to scrape and bow to him?

"Don't look so pensive," Liz said. "You've sold the track. You're going to be in the clear. I might sell some expensive property. And if I do, you know what? Glen and I might make a decent living, finally. If Halesboro changes? Terrific. Because either it does or it dies a long, slow death. And so does your father's speedway. You can look on Kane as a hero or a villain. It's your choice."

And what, wondered Lori, if he's both a hero and a villain? What then?

AT LAST IT WAS the week of the Fourth of July. Lori felt drowned in details—she had to increase security at the speedway, have the shrubs around the speedway tended, rent a tent in case of rain, rent picnic tables and benches, contract to have party lights hung, negotiate with the fireworks display designer, scrounge prizes for a ticket stub drawing, confirm the musicians, order small floral centerpieces.

The barbecue itself brought on a deluge of decisions. Kane didn't want a posh catered affair that would seem uncomfortably formal. "Down-home and friendly and Southern," he said.

Lori checked out restaurants in the region that prepared and served food for special occasions. She finally settled on This Little Piggy Bar-B-Que in Asheville, which didn't sound elegant, but was revered by worshippers of spare ribs. She ordered red, white and blue paper plates, cups and napkins, even toothpicks. The minutiae of it all was staggering.

Kane had sunk even more time and money into the track. The lights were repaired, the scoreboard replaced, the track more expertly repaired until it could be resurfaced. He had people working to modernize pit road, and the parking lot and infield had been cleaned up. The expenditure must have come at a mind-boggling price—and there was more work to come.

But the advanced ticket sales amazed her. Kane was right: Kent and Dean Grosso attracted crowds, and both men were bringing the cars they'd driven to win the NASCAR Sprint Cup championship. Oh, yes, there was plenty to draw in not only NASCAR devotees, but racing fans in general.

By the time the Cargill-Grosso Racing team hauler and motor home pulled in on the morning of the first, Lori's heart beat like a jackhammer, and her stomach danced nervously. Would everything work out? What had she forgotten? What might go wrong?

Dean Grosso remembered Lori and gave her a hug. So did his wife, the down-to-earth Patsy. Patsy wore crisply pressed jeans and a pale blue polo shirt that complemented her eyes. She seemed as unaffected and friendly as ever, but her face looked thinner and her expression strained.

Under Dean's affability, Lori could see a change in him, a sort of anxiety, and she knew what troubled the couple. Someone had kidnapped their infant daughter Gina—three decades ago. Later, authorities confirmed that baby Gina had died. Dean and Patsy struggled to accept the tragedy and soldier on. But if they ever talked about their lost child, it wasn't to outsiders. Many people on the NASCAR circuit didn't even know of the kidnapping.

Recently, persistent rumors arose that Gina was *not* dead, but living somewhere under a different name, probably not knowing her true parentage. Now Dean and Patsy hoped to find her—but if they didn't? It would be like ripping open a wound that never really healed, like losing their daughter a second time.

Lori put her hand on Patsy's shoulder. "I heard the stories about Gina. I hope with all my heart that you find her and can reunite."

Patsy said softly, "Thank you." But clearly she didn't want to talk about Gina. "Oh," she said, "there's Kent. I have something I forgot to tell him. Excuse me…"

And then she was gone. Lori, saddened, turned to Dean. "I'm sorry," she told him, shaking her head. "I shouldn't have said anything. I'll apologize to her."

Dean chucked her under her chin. "No. She understands. People are just trying to be kind. They feel compelled to say something. Otherwise, it's like trying to ignore the elephant in the room. That's one of the reasons I was glad to get involved with Halesboro again. It gives me less time to think— and worry. Patsy, too. This is one of her favorite tracks."

"It's very generous of you to support it," Lori said.

Dean tried to smile, but his dark eyes stayed serious. "I remember your daddy well. And you, such a little thing with so much energy. But I'm doing it for Kane, too. He's worked hard on our behalf. A good man, Kane. He'll be along in another hour or so. Had to drop a friend off at the airport."

"Oh," Lori said, trying to disguise the sudden emotion which shook her. She knew who that "friend" must be. Zoey Horning.

Liz, now enthralled by the Charlotte gossip blog, had said that Zoey was flying back to Missouri today to help her parents celebrate their anniversary. Lori imagined Kane taking the girl in his arms and kissing her goodbye. She knew what his lips tasted like. She knew how his kisses could intoxicate.

She couldn't wait for him to arrive, and paradoxically, she wished he wouldn't come at all. And she tried hard not to think of his mouth on the lush ripeness of Zoey Horning's.

FIFTY-EIGHT MINUTES LATER, a new silver-colored sedan pulled up in the parking lot, and Kane got out, wearing low-slung jeans, a red shirt open at the collar, black sunglasses, and black cowboy boots.

Lori tried to rip her gaze away and concentrate on spotting the party supply truck, which was late. But he'd caught her looking and flashed her a devilish grin. He walked up to her and took off his sunglasses. The breeze ruffled his dark hair so that for a moment, he almost resembled the tousle-haired boy he'd once been.

What right did he have to be so handsome, so well-built and self-possessed? She thought of her ex-husband, Scott. The same age as Kane, he now had a potbelly, a receding hairline and bifocals. The gene pool was neither fair nor democratic.

"Lori," Kane said softly. "How's it going?"

"I guess we'll see tonight," she tossed back. "What happened to the sports car? Or is this your second car?"

"I traded in the other one. The new one's an American-made sedan. It seemed more appropriate. But I've leased a different sports car. It tends to impress clients."

He studied her face. "You look radiant. Fresh and natural. I like it when your freckles show. You don't even have on any lipstick."

"You do," she said, staring coolly at his cheek. It bore the jewel-red print of a mouth.

"Oops," he said, "thought I got it all off." He pulled out a handkerchief. "Show me where it is. I can't see."

Reluctantly she raised her hand and touched her index finger to his face, just below his right cheekbone. And what amazing cheekbones he had. She'd loved them once. Quickly she snatched her finger back and pressed her lips tightly together. If she had no lipstick on, it was because she'd chewed it off from nervousness.

He smiled as he wiped his face. "Did I get it off?"

"Not quite," she said, her tone clipped.

He handed her the kerchief. "Get it for me. You can see it."

She felt resentful and embarrassed, but she scrubbed at his cheek hard, harder than she had to. She'd wiped lipstick off him before. But back then it had been hers.

"Here," she said, tossing the cloth back to him. "I suppose that kissy-print is from Zoey Horning."

He arched a brow and allowed himself a one-cornered smile. "You know Zoey?"

She could have bitten off her tongue. "No. It's just that the two of you've been mentioned a lot lately in the Charlotte gossip blogs."

His expression changed to one of disbelief. "You *read* that garbage? You used to be so picky about what you read."

"*I* don't read it," she countered defensively. "Liz does. People around here take an interest in you, now that you've come back. You know what a small town's like."

"Indeed, I do." His voice was silky. "That's why I live in the city."

She ached to ask him if the rumors of his romance were true, but she wouldn't give him the satisfaction. "Go ahead and go inside. You don't want to miss the testing, do you?"

"Of course not. That's why I'm here early. You coming in, too? See how your former track does under Kent's tires?"

"No thanks. I'm watching for a truck."

"A truck of what?" he said, a teasing look in his brown eyes.

She remembered that look well, and it came close to discombobulating her. "Festive paper dinnerware with matching festive paper napkins and gloriously tasteful balloons. The most glamorous plastic knives and forks."

"Ah, Lori." He sighed. "When you die, they better chisel

a warning on your tombstone: 'Back Off. She's Probably As Spunky As Ever.'"

He turned and started toward the main entrance. She put her hands on her hips and called after him. "Kane? You said you'd tell me more about what you know about the sudden interest in real estate up here. When?"

He stopped and glanced over his shoulder. "Tonight. After the barbecue. When we're alone." He had the nerve to wink at her. Then turning his back to her again, he sauntered off and disappeared inside.

Alone, she thought, anxiety tumbling through her. *What did he mean—alone?*

CHAPTER NINE

THE EVENING was a smash hit. For the first time in years, the Halesboro Speedway sprang to life again, throbbing with the sense of excitement.

At the barbecue after the autograph session, Kent Grosso gave a short, funny speech and Dean a longer, heartfelt one of his memories of the track. The Bluegrass String Band played the Appalachian music most people had known all their lives, sometimes happy, sometimes haunting.

The food from This Little Piggy was proclaimed ambrosial: the ribs were succulent, the chicken savory and the sandwiches scrumptious. The baked beans were stupendously good, the coleslaw luscious.

When it was over and the Grossos retired to Kent's motor home, the last guest gone home, Lori felt the bone-deep exhaustion of a hostess whose party has been a success, such a success that it had given the illusion of being effortless. Few people realized how much planning and labor it had taken.

Now, with the parking lot mostly empty again, Lori sat alone on a bench, looking up at the stars. The night seemed so peaceful that the chatter and the laughter of the crowd now seemed like a quickly fading dream.

She knew she was supposed to meet with Kane in his office, but she wasn't ready to face him. She needed a breathing space, a time, at last, to be alone.

A touch on her shoulder jolted her from her solitude. She whirled around to stare up at Kane. He had a bottle of wine in the crook of his left arm, and two glasses dangling from his left hand. "I thought you'd be out here somewhere," he murmured. "And I got tired of waiting for you."

"Just needed to catch my breath," she murmured. She stared off again into the night.

He sat down beside her. She supposed he didn't need to be invited; it was his track now, the parking lot *his* parking lot, the bench *his* bench.

He showed her the bottle. "I brought some cabernet sauvignon reserve. You could probably use a drink."

"That's expensive stuff," she said softly.

"You earned it. The whole 'festive' affair? You slammed it out of the park."

She smiled. "You really think so?"

"Absolutely," he said, starting to pour a glass. "Got everything right. Including the tone. Downhome, but still kind of upscale. Folksy, but first-rate. Here."

He handed her a glass and filled another. "It must have been tough to pull off. But you did it. I drink to your greatness." He tapped his glass against hers.

They each took a sip. It was excellent wine, subtle and complex. "My greatness," she echoed wryly.

"You know the town, you understand the kind of people drawn here tonight. I expected you to do well, but you exceeded expectations."

"My mother was a good hostess," she said. She tried not to fidget. His praise made her tingle with restlessness.

"She probably hated me, right?"

Lori didn't have the strength to lie. "Well, yes."

Her mother Kitty had once come home early from a practice at the track and found them talking in the garden. She gave them a disapproving look, but said nothing. Still, her appearance chilled them both and made them try hard to seem casual.

When A.J. broke the news about Kane and Lori, Kitty slapped Lori across the face. It was the first and only time she ever did it, but she was appalled and furious. "You told me you were just being nice to that…creature. And I believed you because you always went around adopting baby birds that fell out of the nest or abandoned puppies or stray kittens."

Kitty had started to cry then. "You deceived me. I thought you just felt sorry for him. I didn't want to imagine you'd feel anything else for such a lowlife. He's a guttersnipe, a hooligan, a long-haired piece of riffraff—"

In tears, Lori ran upstairs and locked herself in her room, feeling she had betrayed everyone, including herself. It took her years to comprehend that her mother barely understood sexual feelings because she'd had none herself. She'd been taught that such feelings were evil, and she believed that sex was a wife's duty; she told Lori this when Lori got engaged to Scott.

But now Kane acted as if the past held no pain. "Your father probably hated me, too, right?"

She nodded but wouldn't look him in the eye. "He liked you. He said you were a good worker. He had no notion that… that…"

"That I'd *aspire* to you?" he asked, giving the word a sarcastic flip. "That you'd stoop to someone as lowly as I was?"

"He wasn't happy about it," she said. That was a masterpiece of understatement. He'd watched her suspiciously until she got married. She'd lost his trust; she guessed, in a way, she was still trying to deserve it again. But Kane hadn't been "lowly"—she'd been the flawed one, betraying everyone, even herself.

"The hired help should keep in its place," he said, out of the corner of his mouth. He looked her up and down. "So tell me. What went wrong between you and Scott, the all-American boy?"

What went wrong is that he wasn't you, she thought, still not looking at Kane. She said, "I kept dating him because my folks liked him. When I went to the same college as he did, it seemed natural to keep going with him. And we sort of drifted into marriage. And then we drifted out. We were supposed to have everything in common, but really there was nothing."

"I heard he's in Raleigh now."

She took two sips of wine, wishing it would steel her; she didn't like talking about Scott. "He went to work for his older brother. His brother owns a golf course there. That was the love of Scott's life. Golf. He worked at the insurance company for years, the head of auditing. But there was less and less to audit. When his brother offered him the job, he was ecstatic. I didn't want to move. A.J. was gone, and Daddy was starting to fail. So Scott and I agreed there wasn't anything left that resembled a real marriage."

"So he ran away to the golf course?"

"Yes. And also with a nineteen-year-old waitress from Spartanburg. I thought he'd been spending a lot of time at night on the computer. He was trolling for women."

Kane's eyes narrowed as if disbelief. "He married this chick?"

She nodded. "And divorced her a year later. Then he married again. A college girl who worked in the golf shop at the course. I hear he's happy at last."

"I always suspected he was a jerk," Kane said in disgust. "Now I know it."

His statement made her nervous. "Very gallant of you," she said and took another drink. "But enough about me. Tell me why people are suddenly interested in Halesboro real estate. Hardly anybody buys property here."

"*I* did. So did the guy on the hill."

He nodded toward the mountain where Uncle June's castle stood. The construction company had installed lights to discourage anyone who was tempted to become a thief in the night. The trees around the castle gave the edges of the light a greenish glow, and in the center the pale stone towers shone.

The sight, with Kane here so close beside her, made her remember how intense their romance had been, more than half a lifetime ago. "Do you know who bought it?" she challenged. "I suspect if anybody knows besides the buyer, you would."

He shrugged. "The first rule of real estate is there's a buyer for every property."

"Sometimes a buyer takes a long time coming. Who *did* buy it?"

"How would I know that? You should ask Liz, right?"

"Liz can't figure it out. And if you won't talk about the castle, explain all the other queries about the other properties. It's time for you to lay your cards on the table."

He gave a sigh of resignation and put his arm along the back of the bench. It was so near her shoulders that her spine prickled with awareness. He said, "Sometimes things just seem ready to fit together. Like the planets align or something."

"Are the planets aligning so that the Hornings intend to buy the mill buildings?"

He gave her a smile that was too intimate, too seductive. "You always were such a *smart* girl."

"Not me. Liz, the detective."

"Smart to have a detective for a friend. Now this is confidential, all right? I mean it. The future of the speedway could depend on keeping this quiet for the time being."

"My lips are sealed."

He gazed at her lips with interest. "All right. The Hornings were in Charlotte. I'd met them before. And I volunteered to show them around. Zoey wanted to see Halesboro…"

Lori tensed. "Because you'd lived here?"

"Whatever," he said with another vague shrug. "So Papa Horning, D.B., noticed the mill buildings right off. And that the speedway was for sale. He saw that this was a beautiful spot, and we started kicking ideas around. One thing led to another. D.B.'s most profitable property is in Branson, Missouri."

Kane paused and with his free hand refilled her glass and his. His other hand accidentally touched the skin of her shoulder, bared by her green tank top. She sucked in her breath as if a live wire had brushed her, shooting electricity through her system. She quickly took another sip of wine.

"Ever been to Branson?" he asked, leaning just a bit closer. His hand was so near her shoulder that she could feel the heat radiating from it, a highly distracting sensation.

"Um. Yes. One long weekend." Scott and his brother had wanted to try out some of the Branson golf courses. They let their wives fend for themselves. And, of course, the first place that she and her sister-in-law had gone was the outlet mall.

"Branson was once a sleepy little town. Not much going on," Kane said. "But then certain elements came together. The only tourist attraction was a cave outside the city limits. A speculator bought the cave and built a theme park. He put on a musical show."

The cry of a hoot owl drifted down to them, and sounded very near. Kane looked up and smiled. "Wow. That brings back memories. Remember when we'd hear the hoot owl up at Uncle June's?"

He leaned nearer so that his forehead nearly touched hers. "You w-were saying?" she stammered. "He put on a music show? Yes?"

"It was a success. More music came to Branson. A theater opened on its main strip. And then another, and another. Today there are over fifty theaters and a hundred live shows. The town had two attractions, the theme park and the music shows.

"A third element came—the malls. Now Branson had three things that drew people, the park, the shows, and the shopping—"

"Wait a minute," she interrupted. "You're not saying—"

"I think you know what I'm saying. The Horning family owns the biggest outlet mall in the town. And D.B. knows the family who owns the theme park, the Tomlinsons. Like D.B., they've got similar parks in other locations."

"I see where you're going," Lori said, alarm rising. "There are three caves around here. Even one on Uncle June's property."

"Tomlinson knows how to use a cave as a draw," he said. "And he's interested. Plus, both the Hornings and Tomlinson know Karl deKooning. He owns one of the biggest theaters in Branson. He'd like to expand, especially if he could get in on the ground floor somewhere."

"The Military Theater!" Lori exclaimed. "Is he the one interested in the Military?"

"I can't comment on that," he said. "But let's say it's not beyond imagination."

"What else is going on?" she demanded. "What about the shops, the pharmacy? And what else? There are plenty of empty stores on Main Street."

"Exactly," he said. "Bargains at the mall, but more unusual stuff on Main Street. Centered around the themes of the mountain traditions, crafts, racing, and—"

"Stop!" she ordered. "You're overloading me with information. And I don't like all of it. Business is sagging here, and people are anxious to sell. But to be taken over, to become some sort of commercial playground, that's really going too far. I've seen—"

"Excuse me, I'm trying to explain—"

"You're trying to rationalize."

"Your lips are supposed to be sealed."

"Only about telling other people what—"

He leaned nearer still, and his hand grasped her shoulder. "I'll have to seal them for you."

His mouth was on hers, insistent and searching. She felt an instant of shock mixed with outrage, but it transformed into the strangest sensation—as if, after years of wandering alone, she'd finally come home.

KANE HADN'T MEANT to do this, but it had just…happened. Her lips had always fit perfectly against his; he used to marvel at it. Now he marveled again and kissed her more deeply. She didn't resist. For a moment she responded, kissing him back with shy hunger.

Then, suddenly she pulled away, turning her head so she wouldn't have to look at him. She pushed his hand away and stared off into the distance, in the direction of Uncle June's castle.

"We can't go back to what was," she said, a quaver in her

voice. "And I don't want to go back. It's past. It's been over for years."

Has it? It doesn't feel over. But he couldn't say that, couldn't make himself vulnerable again. Grudgingly, he drew back from her and stared at her profile, her chin up, nose in the air. She crossed her arms and tapped her foot.

Did she think she was still a princess and he was her court fool? "Sorry," he said. "Just wondered if it would be the same. It wasn't, was it?"

"Thank heaven we broke up. I never knew you could be so arrogant," she retorted.

"You're so damned stubborn you wouldn't let me finish a sentence. Why argue when matters are out of your hands? If Horning wants to buy the mills, he'll buy them. Likewise, Tomlinson and land for the theme park. Or would you rather the town and the speedway curl up and die?"

She turned and tossed him a challenging glance. "Malls and music and a theme park? That's supposed to help the speedway?"

"The track was the one main reason that outsiders came to Halesboro. If this works, and the track's renovated, NASCAR might rethink things. Put in a NASCAR Nationwide, NASCAR Camping World Truck, or NASCAR Whelen All-American Series race or another race from one of NASCAR's other developmental series. Because people will *want* to come to Halesboro. They'll come by the busload."

"At this moment, it's all pie in the sky," she sniffed.

"Your track needs NASCAR," he pointed out. "Not just for a race or a couple of races. For the prestige. NASCAR's the crème de la crème of auto racing. With more attractions at Halesboro, more people come, and more seats are filled. It's good business."

She didn't look happy, and she didn't look convinced.

"You saw how people flocked here to see Dean and Kent Grosso? NASCAR's a magic word for racing fans. It can't be denied."

"I'm not denying it," she said, putting her wineglass on the ground. "I'm just tired. I need to go home."

He set aside his own glass. "I'll walk you to your car."

They both rose and walked toward the Mustang. He could think of nothing to say. He still regretted the kiss. Had it confused her as much as it did him? *Impossible,* he thought. Old desires and new conflicts swam through him.

She unlocked the car, and he opened the door for her. "Thanks for all your work," he said. "You did a sensational job. Really."

She gave him a wan smile. "Thanks. You did a sensational job yourself. Getting the Grossos here, coming up with the ideas, the autographing, the barbecue and fireworks."

Her praise touched him. He wanted to take her in his arms again and just hold her close, very close, for a long time.

He didn't touch her. He closed the door, and when she drove off, he went back to the bench and picked up the wine bottle and the glasses.

He stared off at the mountain and the pale spires and towers of Uncle June's castle. *I shouldn't have come back here,* he thought. It made him remember what it felt like to be a lonely boy who'd lost everything.

Well, he'd set this scheme in motion. He would see it through. And Halesboro and Lori would owe everything to him, the town's most prodigal son. They would owe him whether they liked it or not. Whether they liked *him* or not.

THE NEXT MORNING, Kane pulled into the speedway's parking lot and saw a sight that made his skin crawl with apprehension. Two Halesboro police cars and a state police cruiser were parked near the entrance.

He got out, frowning in concern, when Lori came running toward him. "Kane!" she cried. "I've been waiting for you."

She came so fast that she almost bumped into him, and he reached out to steady her, grasping her by the upper arms. "What's wrong? What's with the police cars?"

"Something terrible's happened," she said, looking up at him, blinking back tears. "Kent's motor home and hauler were vandalized, the tires slashed, brake fluid splashed on the motor home."

Kane swore. "How'd that happen? You said you had extra security people."

"I *did*," she said, looking desperate and frightened. "They all claim they didn't see a thing."

"Show me," he said. Without thinking he seized her hand, but she didn't flinch, only hurried toward the entrance, leading him.

In the infield, he stared at the motor home, surrounded by the Grossos, Kent's team, track workers, as well as the security men, and three policemen.

"Oh, bloody hell," Kane said in disgust. He took the lead and walked over to Kent and Dean, who both looked stunned by disbelief and anger. Kent's wife, Tanya, clung to his arm, tears in her eyes. Patsy Grosso kept shaking her head in dismay.

Kent had one of the handsomest motor homes on the circuit, only two years old, repainted last winter in a rich café au lait color. It had cost him a fortune, Tanya had decorated it and he loved it. Now it seemed to crouch crookedly on its deflated tires, and the café au lait on the driver's side looked as if it had been laced with streaks of sour milk.

The hauler, too, had mangled tires and runny patches of ruined paint. Kane heard one of Kent's crewman say, "Somebody's got a vendetta against us. Somebody's out for Kent."

That was paranoid, Kane thought. Kent was one of the best-liked drivers in the business. He didn't get caught up in feuds and rivalries. Who could dislike him enough to sneak into the speedway and do this?

Lori tugged her hand free from Kane's and moved from his side. He missed her touch immediately.

Old Morrie, the night maintenance man, said to Clyde, "People used to say there was a jinx on this track. That's why it went downhill. It was built on a Cherokee burial ground—"

"That's nothing but superstition," Lori snapped. "My father

couldn't believe people latched on to that silly story. He was here when they broke ground and bulldozed the place. *Nobody* was buried here."

Kane turned to the state policeman. "What's the story? When did this happen?"

"Probably sometime early this morning, while it was still dark," the man said. "But none of the security people admit seeing anything. Or noticing anything until the shift changed at seven."

"Good grief," Kane said in frustration. "Not see how these vehicles are listing? Not see the paint damage? Were they *blind*?"

"Blind or catching a few winks," said the officer. "But it doesn't make sense. Unless it was an inside job."

"Inside job? Who'd want it done?"

"Ms. Garland said you outbid some developers for this place at the last minute. Stole it right from under their noses. That so?"

"I didn't steal it. I made a better offer."

Clyde spoke up. "This ain't the first time there's been vandalism here. Somebody kept shooting out the lights. Spray painted the walls. We need to *really* tighten security, is what."

The officer kept his attention on Kane. "Ms. Garland said the developers wanted to put condos here. Did they ever contact you about the property?"

"No," Kane answered. "And if they wanted to strike back, why do it in such a blatant, stupid way?"

"It had to be an inside job," Clyde put in. "You can't sneak into this place. No way."

"I used to sneak in all the time when I was a kid," Kane retorted. "And I can show you where. This place is old and in disrepair. I bet now there's a half a dozen ways to get in."

"Is it possible that one or more of the guests at the barbecue could have slipped off and hidden until everyone was gone?" asked the officer.

"I suppose," Kane said. "Damn!"

Lori's cell phone rang. She flipped it open and put it to her ear. Then she put her hand over it and said, sotto voce, "Word's out. It's the Asheville paper calling."

"Let me talk to them," said Kane.

He put himself in damage control mode. But he knew the story would spread. It would probably be all over the Internet racing sites by noon.

Kent pulled Tanya to his chest and held her. Dean muttered a few swear words. Patsy stared at the six security men with suspicion.

"IT'S MY FAULT," Lori said, shamefaced. She stood with Kane in the parking lot.

Kane leaned against her car and locked his hands behind his head. The muscles under his pale blue polo shirt rippled, and she had too good a view of his biceps. She struggled to pay no attention to them. He was a handsome devil, even more handsome than in high school.

He said, "It's not your fault. It's the security company's. How did somebody get past them and do all that damage? Either the guards were incompetent, or the cop was right. It was an inside job—and a good chance it was a guard who did it."

"It's my fault," she repeated, running a hand over her tousled hair. "I hired them. I've used that company before. But our security system isn't what it should be. I should have thought. I should have checked out who they were sending and double-checked to see if it was enough."

He gave her a sideways glance that was almost sympathetic. "No. Blame me. I gave you too much to do. I should have brought in a firm I knew. We're lucky that nothing worse happened."

She shook her head in misery. "I can't believe everybody in the motor home slept through it."

"The tires weren't actually slashed clear through," he told her. "The leakage was slow. The brake fluid looked poured on, not splashed. Somebody knew what he was doing."

"I can't get over the sheer *meanness* of it," Lori said sadly.

"Buck up. It's meanness that can be undone. Kent's got comprehensive insurance. It covers vandalism. Come on, he doesn't blame you. I'm responsible for this track now, remember? He came up here partly as a favor to *me*."

"This is hardly good publicity for you, then. Or for the track."

"Try to subscribe to the idea that there's no such thing as bad publicity."

She frowned and tilted her head. "You don't suppose this was aimed at you, do you? Somebody trying to sabotage you?"

He looked at her and, maddeningly, seemed amused. "Me? Who could dislike me? I'm not your typical blood-sucking leech of an agent. I am *beloved*."

He'd done it. He'd made her smile. He looked so innocent and righteous, she had to.

"Aha," he said, pleased. "Saw your dimple. Good. I've missed it. How about tonight I buy you supper, and then I need to hit the road and get back to Charlotte."

Her smile faded. "I don't know…"

"I owe it to you. You got everybody fed last night. Tonight you shouldn't have to lift a finger. We'll go someplace nice for a change."

"No," she said. "That'd just be more driving for you. We can go to The Groove."

"I like to drive and I've got a different car. We'll zip over to Asheville and back. I'm tired of being stared at in The Groove. Aren't you?"

She had to agree. Few people would recognize them in Asheville. And although she'd vowed not to get any more involved with him, the vandalism had shaken her badly. It would be good to get away, if only for a few hours. "Okay," she said, only half-reluctantly.

He opened the Mustang door for her, but suddenly a tall, dark man appeared. "Kane Ledger," the man said in a take-command voice. "And this, I take it, is your new partner, Lori Garland."

Lori eyed the man, who stared back, a slightly cocky sneer on his lips. "Lucas Haines," Kane said, clearly unimpressed.

"I didn't recognize you without your trench coat. This is Ms. Garland, my assistant. Lori, this is Lucas Haines, New York homicide detective. What brings you here, Lucas? We're fresh out of corpses up here, far as I know."

Lucas's mouth took on a smug twist. "But you've got trouble. I heard about the vandalism. I wanted to talk to you—and the Grossos and the team."

"The Grossos are on their way back to Mooresville. You'll have to settle for me. What happened? The department boot you down to property damage cases?"

"No, Ledger. There's been a murder, remember? Alan Cargill."

Kane's nostrils flared at the ridiculousness of it. Alan Cargill, former owner of Cargill racing, had been stabbed to death the night of the NASCAR Awards Banquet. Nearly seven months later, the case was still unsolved, and Lucas had proved beyond a doubt that he wasn't super cop.

"What's Halesboro got to do with Alan Cargill?" Kane demanded. He noticed that Lori, still standing by the car, looked worried.

Lucas shifted, putting his hands on his hips. His light jacket fell apart enough to show his shoulder holster. He said, "Brent Sanford used to be Cargill's driver—and your client. Brent Sanford got kicked off the Cargill team for sabotage. The word is he's bitter."

"Of course, he's bitter," Kane shot back. "He was innocent. Contaminating somebody's fuel tank? That's not his style. He's a competitive guy. But not a cheater."

"But Brent never thought Cargill—or you—defended him enough. His career was over."

Anger rose in Kane. "We did everything we could to help him. He knows that. Any man who says different is a liar. And his career *was* over, but not because of us. Rules were violated, and nobody could prove his innocence. It's a dirty shame, but it happened. And what's it got to do with me?"

Lucas gave him a knowing smile. "Four years ago, Brent

Sanford committed sabotage. Cargill, who fired him, was just murdered. Who bought Cargill's team? The father of Kent Grosso—the guy whose car Brent tampered with. Now it happens again, vandalism against Kent. At *your* speedway. And you're one of the guys that Brent thought hung him out to dry."

Lucas paused for drama. "Seen your old client Brent Sanford lately? Was he invited to your little party last night?"

Kane took a step forward and got in Lucas's face. "I haven't seen him. But we still talk. He never thought I 'hung him out to dry.' And once more, dammit, he was innocent. He lost his NASCAR career over something he didn't do."

He grabbed Lucas's lapel. "There's a difference between sabotage and vandalism. Look it up in your Dick Tracy Crime-stoppers book. You're grasping at straws."

"I have technical questions," Lucas practically barked.

"Then talk to the police. They've got the technical answers. Maybe they'll pull you out of the Land of Oz and back into reality."

He ignored Lucas and helped Lori into her car. "I'll pick you up for supper in a couple of hours. We'll sort this out. If this bozo comes after you, just tell him, 'No comment.' All right?"

She nodded and started her car.

Kane turned back to Lucas. "Leave her alone. I'm the owner now. You got sensible questions, you ask me—or the police. And stop trying to hang every crime that happens on Brent Sanford. Haven't you guys done enough to him? You couldn't convict him, but you smeared him out of the business."

He got in his own car and floored it. He left Lucas standing there, his face hard with anger.

THAT EVENING, Kane took Lori to the Chinese restaurant, Ming Toy's, which had moved from Halesboro to Asheville. The décor was more opulent and more oriental than it used to be, but the food was still excellent.

They got the subject of Lucas Haines out of the way fast

"Do you need to be concerned?" Lori asked.

He shook his head. "Lucas is trying to tie two NASCAR cases together. To make things neat. First, the sabotage to Kent's car four years ago. But it isn't neat. Brent was a suspect all right, but there was only the thinnest circumstantial evidence against him. He walked, but his reputation was tarnished for good.

"Now there's Cargill's murder. Lucas wants to tie it all up in a bow—with the knot around Brent. Lucas is so frustrated he spins crazy stories to connect everything. He's obsessed. Forget about him."

Lori agreed gratefully. She and he both took care to speak of neutral subjects. Whatever happened to so-and-so? Had she ever traveled? (Not much. Scott devoted his vacation time to visiting golf courses throughout the South.) Had he? (A lot. All over the U.S. Some of Europe and China, as well. And, of course, the South Pacific that had called to him so strongly all those years ago.)

She felt provincial and unsophisticated listening to his tales of globe-trotting. She supposed that he and Zoey could talk about Paris and London. Lori'd been born in Halesboro, lived her whole life in Halesboro, and the most exotic place she'd ever been was in California, Carmel-by-the-Sea, where Scott played golf and she spent a lot of time watching the sea otters and wishing she were as free and playful as they were.

"If it's not too personal," Kane asked suddenly, "how come you and Scott never had kids?"

"It just didn't happen. He blamed me. He wouldn't get tested himself. But I did. I was all right, but that infuriated him, and he wouldn't accept it. I think that's when the adultery started. He wanted to prove he was…you know."

He'd wanted to prove he was a stud, she thought. She wanted to change the subject. She wanted to ask him about apartment hunting with Zoey Horning, but she couldn't bring herself to do it. She glanced at her watch. "It's getting late. We should be going. You've got to get back to Charlotte."

He nodded, almost reluctantly. "Yeah. I guess I do." He

paused. "You know, this is the first time we ever really *went* somewhere nice together. Someday maybe I'll take you some-place where I didn't wash dishes."

WHEN THEY REACHED HALESBORO, he turned down her street and pulled into her drive. "Well," she said, "here we are. Thanks for supper. Tell Kent that I'm sorry about his motor home and hauler."

"I'll walk you to your door," Kane said. "And no, I won't tell him. You told him twelve times already."

He walked her up the stairs, and although the night was warm, she shivered, far too aware of his nearness. She had out her keys and made her voice sound chipper. "Again, thanks. I suppose I'll see you in Illinois next weekend?"

"Yes. You will. I booked us at the same hotel. For conve-nience."

"Oh." She hadn't thought about that, hadn't let herself think of it.

He put his hands on her shoulders, bent and kissed her on the forehead. "Again, you did a great job last night. You were wonderful."

It was a chaste kiss, almost brotherly, but she felt as if a star danced and twinkled where his lips had touched her.

"Good night," he said. "I'll phone you tomorrow."

And then he was gone, down the stairs and getting into his car. Quickly, unsettled and too excited, she unlocked her door and went inside. She realized she'd wanted more than that fleeting and restrained kiss. Paradoxically, she also wished it hadn't happened at all.

CHAPTER TEN

THE SOUNDS OF CONSTRUCTION echoed through Halesboro from the distance. Work on the castle had stepped up, and the renovations at the track began in earnest. Seats were torn out and replaced, the outside of the building was sandblasted, the sidewalks torn up and repoured.

A new fence was installed, better drainage put in, new retaining walls built, and safety barriers erected. The restroom space was expanded and improved, a new lighting system installed, the speakers relocated and construction started on a sound wall.

It was almost too much for Lori to keep up with. Besides the flurry of details, she fretted about going to Illinois with Kane and staying at the same hotel that weekend.

But before she knew it, it was Saturday morning, and she and Kane flew from Charlotte to Chicago's O'Hare Airport—first-class, no less. I remember—now—*this is how the other half lives,* she thought, bemused.

She'd never been in O'Hare before; it was huge and daunting, but Kane knew his way perfectly. He had a car reserved, a surprisingly modest one, and expertly navigated his way westward.

"Our rooms are in Homewood," he said. "That'll start us out in the morning closer to the airport than if we stay here. I'm sorry we can't see more of Chicago. But it'll be interesting to see this race. Ever been to this speedway before?"

She had to admit she hadn't.

He told her they'd watch the race from a corporate suite

and rattled off the amenities: free parking, catered meals, bar, stadium seats above the suites and a plasma screen television for those who'd like to stay inside and stay cool. "And garage and pit road tours. Do you want to take one? I think I've seen enough garages and pit roads to last me a while."

"Same here," she agreed. "Besides, seeing theirs will just make Halesboro's look worse." She paused. "If we're going to a suite, whose suite is it?"

He told her and her jaw dropped. "He's a corporate executive with…with NASCAR, isn't he?" she asked.

"Yeah. He's retiring this fall, but he's known for his judgment."

"I won't be able to say a word to him," Lori wailed. "I'll be completely tongue-tied."

"Just be yourself. Don't worry about talking. He'll ask you questions. Good ones. He's a canny guy."

"And how did *you* get invited to his suite?"

"I know him through the Grossos. He says he watches me. That I've got an eye for talent."

She sank weakly back against the seat. "I should have gone out and bought a better outfit." She wore a bargain pant suit she'd bought on the Internet, sage green and crinkly so that it wouldn't show wrinkles.

"You look fine," Kane said and gave her an approving glance. "That green brings out your eye color. And he's a down-home sort of guy. He doesn't like things that are all gussied up. People, either. He'll wear a suit, but after two laps he'll have the tie off, after seven he'll have the coat off, and I'll bet you ten bucks he'll be wearing fancy suspenders. Relax."

LORI HAD SEEN crowds at the Charlotte speedway, and the throngs of people here at the Illinois track seemed just as thick. The flatness of Illinois had struck her, and the speedway rose up like a huge flying saucer, dwarfing the highway and cars that led to it, towering over its lots and the fields beyond.

Once parked, they joined the crowd, and Kane took her arm

to steer her through the teeming human traffic. "Looks sold out." Kane spoke loudly to be heard over the noise of the crowd.

Lori nodded. This was a relatively new speedway. A fast track, its layout encouraged drivers to pass, and the banking made passing a challenge.

Soon Kane and Lori were out of the main crowd and inside the white corporate suite. He introduced her to Charles Channing, the head of Charlotte's CapCity Credit Card, a major supporter and sponsor of motor racing.

Channing slapped Kane on the back, and vigorously shook Lori's hand. "You're Andrew Jackson Simmons's girl?" he said almost gleefully. "I enjoyed many a race at Halesboro. I remember the first time Dean Grosso won there."

"I do, too," Lori said with a smile. She'd been twelve years old. And from that point on, she didn't have to worry about talking, because people joined the conversation, and it became a memoryfest about Halesboro's glory days.

Kane went his own way until the race started, apparently talking business. And Lori talked to a portly older man with a twinkle in his eye. It was the NASCAR executive who was about to retire. He was a charmer, and Kane was right: he asked questions about the Halesboro track and its place in North Carolina's racing tradition. She was relieved, for she could happily expand on that subject for a long time.

To her surprise, he listened intently and urged her to tell him more.

The man glanced at Kane, talking earnestly with Charles Channing. Kane had donned the jacket to his black suit, but no tie. Although his collar was unbuttoned; he managed somehow, to look both more stylish and more relaxed than any man in the room.

Her NASCAR companion tilted his head toward Kane. "And now Halesboro's in the hands of that rascal?" he asked with a smile.

She nodded, unsure how to respond.

"Now *that*," he said with a cherubic smile, "is going to be one interesting combination. Yes, ma'am. One *very* interesting combination."

THE RACE STARTED, and the track's quirkiness tested the drivers repeatedly on the infamous and seductive Turn Two. They attempted more passing than usual; some attempts succeeded, some didn't, and some became hair's breadth escapes from major danger. Lori saw Kane blanch when Justin Murphy just missed a wall.

In a last minute move, Kent Grosso edged out another of Kane's clients, Sid Cochran, for second place. Cochran took third, and Justin Murphy was number nine in the top ten. Lori shot Kane a furtive glance of admiration. Three of the drivers he represented in the top ten? He was good, all right.

Chitchat and drinks took place after the race was over, and Charles Channing, the credit card mogul, invited Kane and Lori to his hotel in Joliet for a drink. Kane gave Lori a knowing look and accepted for both of them.

Harrah's Joliet, Illinois, Hotel and Casino was one of the more imposing hotels in the city, and Channing confessed that although he didn't gamble much, he did play   and win—at blackjack. "I know how to play it, and I know how to win," he said. "I always go home with more money than I came with."

"A solid business philosophy," Kane said, as a waiter led them to their table. He put his hand on the small of Lori's back and she could feel the heat through her shirt.

"Now you," Channing said to Kane, "just may know how to play a different kind of game—the speedway game. There're rumors in the air lately. If what they hint is true, I'd like to talk to you sometime. Not here, but soon in Charlotte."

The waiter drew out Lori's chair, and Kane had to pull his hand away from her. He sat next to her, his knees almost touching hers

He and Channing sat, and Kane said, "You can talk in

front of Ms. Garland. She's my assistant at Halesboro. And a good one."

Channing gave her a polite smile. "I'm sure you are, Ms. Garland. You know that track and that town—and their problems. But I don't want to say too much yet. I have a plan of my own that I'm working on, and I think we can help each other."

His words sent Lori's mind speeding. What could Channing's credit card empire do for Halesboro? And vice versa? A glimmer of possibilities began to shine more strongly, hypnotically strong. But she said nothing, only listened to the men. They spoke in an almost coded language. On the surface it seemed bland and vague. But under that surface, Lori sensed a good deal was being said.

Kane stopped himself after one glass of wine, saying he and Lori needed to get back to Homewood and check in. Lori felt her cheeks redden, wondering if Channing thought they'd share a room. But Kane didn't mention sleeping arrangements.

Lori stood, leaving her wine spritzer half-full. The three shook hands, and Channing promised to phone Kane during the next week. Kane touched her back again as they left the restaurant. Lori's body shivered a bit, but she didn't shake off his hand.

"So," she said in the car, "was this a good day?"

"For me?" he asked. "Yes. When three clients finish in the top ten, that's a really good day."

He paused and stared at the road. The sky was starting to fade into evening. "For Halesboro Speedway? I think so. The guy from NASCAR was friendly. He expressed interest, cautious interest, but still he's watching the situation closely. I can tell."

She couldn't help smiling. "You're a good observer. And you were exactly right. After two laps, he pulled his tie off. After seven, he took off the coat. *And* he was wearing suspenders. Embroidered ones."

"And was I right about him being easy to talk to? He asked you a lot of questions?"

"Yes. He knows the speedway's history better than half the people in Halesboro do. I was impressed."

They were silent for a moment. At last Lori said, "Does Charles Channing know what you're up to? I mean, all this talk about the outlet mall and other things?"

"He talks as if he does."

"But he talks almost in riddles."

"You have to read the lines between the riddles," Kane said. "I think he's got a pretty good idea of what's going on. And he sees an opportunity, especially if NASCAR gives us a sanctioned race."

"And if you got that race?" she asked. "What would that mean to Channing?"

"It could mean several things. Some kind of sponsorship, maybe of the track itself. That'd help us. Maybe buy ads on any races televised there. Maybe use NASCAR drivers as spokesmen— or even have testimonials from guests. It could be powerful."

Lori pondered this. "But how? And why?"

"Be patient," he said. "Please. There are things I haven't told you yet, and I can't. Because *I'm* not supposed to know them. And I can't take a chance of that information being leaked."

Affronted, she raised her chin. "You don't trust me? I'd never betray a confidence."

The glance he slid her way was cool, almost cold. "You and I tried to keep something secret once before. It didn't work out so well. Or maybe you don't remember."

Her face burned and she was glad for the falling darkness. Oh, she remembered, all right. And why had their secret come to light? Because of her, her immaturity, because she'd been headstrong and spoiled.

She stared out the passenger window, knowing how selfishly she'd acted toward him. It hurt to say the words, but she said them. "I'm sorry about what happened back then. I'd give anything to go back in time and change how I treated you. But

I can't go back. I can only tell you that a day doesn't go by that I don't regret it. All I can do is apologize—inadequately."

"Apologize?" he repeated, his voice tinged by mockery. "Don't apologize, babe. You set me free. From Halesboro and everything connected to it."

That was an insult, and it hurt, for she'd sincerely tried to be contrite. She squared her jaw and asked, "If I set you free, why'd you come back?"

She saw his hand tighten on the wheel. At last he gave her a condescending look. "Don't bother your pretty head about why. Just figure out the common denominator between Charles Channing, the Hornings, the theme park and everything else going on."

"There's a common denominator?"

"Absolutely."

An uneasy silence fell between them. When they pulled up to their hotel, he turned to her. "You apologized. I wasn't very gracious. I acted like a kid. I'm sorry. Thinking of Halesboro does that to me. My feelings are mixed. It's like I have unfinished business there."

He got out, opened the door for her and offered his hand to help her out. She stood beside the car, staring up at him in the moonlight. "I don't understand your 'unfinished business.' Is it to help Halesboro? Or get even with it?"

He let go of her hand, his face stony. "A little of both," he said. "A little of both."

HE GOT THEIR SUITCASES and checked into the hotel. Their rooms were across the hall from each other. She wished he had booked ones on different floors, at least. As usual, he seemed to know what she thought.

"Afraid the mayor of Halesboro and the morals squad are going to find out we slept *near* each other?" he asked in the elevator. "With only two locked doors and a couple of dead bolts between us?"

His mood was changeable tonight. Changeable and tricky.

"Halesboro has a far-ranging morals squad," she said, un-smiling. "The arrangements could have been a bit more, well, discreet."

She slid her key card into the door and turned the knob. But the door stayed shut. She was nervous, and it was showing. *Damn!* Through gritted teeth, she said, "I hate these things. Whatever happened to good, old-fashioned keys?"

He came to her side and took the card from her. "Still jumpy about your reputation? About having your name linked to mine? Still resenting change, in any form? Ah, Lori. There. Your door's open. Go inside and lock and bolt it."

"I will," she vowed, and reached for the handle of her wheeled carry-on.

But he turned to her, putting his hands on either side of her face. "Again, I'm sorry. You're like Halesboro. You bring out mixed feelings. Thanks for coming with me. I'll be knocking on your door at seven. We've got an early flight."

Once again he bent and kissed her on the forehead. He gave her a look she couldn't fathom. "See you in the morning," he said.

She seized her bag and hurried inside. There she sat down on the edge of the double bed and put her face in her hands. What was that chaste kiss supposed to signify? It made it seem as if he were kissing his grandmother or some child he was putting to bed.

She brought out mixed feelings in him? Did he equate her with all of Halesboro and waver between wanting to help her or to hurt her? Did he know her emotions about him were every bit as confused as his about the town?

Sleep was elusive and restless. The next morning, she was ready long before he knocked on her door. On the way to the airport, Kane seemed lost in his own thoughts, and Lori was happy not to talk, simply to stare out at the flat landscape that was so foreign to her. She'd never realized that the mountains and foothills surrounding Halesboro gave her a feeling of shelter and security.

At the airport he bought a copy of a Chicago newspaper and immediately turned to the sports section. "Aha," he said a moment later. "It's happened. It's official."

They were seated in the boarding area, and she gave him a curious look. He showed her the page and said, "Sid Cochran's buying his own team. He won't sign again to race for Niday Motorsports."

Lori blinked in surprise. "I'd heard rumors, and that they didn't want to let him go. He's a fabulous driver."

"I heard it could happen this weekend," Kane said. "It's been a long time coming, but I knew it would happen."

"This is going to hurt Fulcrum Racing," Lori said solemnly. "He's their top driver."

"The owner's no fool. He's got a guy lined up. I know that, too."

"Replace Sid Cochran?" Lori asked. "With who? Wait! That kid who's only eighteen? The one there's so much buzz about?"

He flashed a one-sided smile. "The very one. Davy Welber."

"You're sure?"

"Ninety-nine percent sure. Fulcrum's owner, Roger, has been calling me about him for weeks."

"Calling you?" she said. "You mean you're—"

"Davy's agent," Kane said with satisfaction. "Kent Grosso introduced us. Kent says Davy's the Next Big Thing."

"Aren't you afraid he'll peak too young?" Lori asked in concern. "And he *is* young for all that pressure."

"He's eighteen going on forty-eight. He's got his head on straight. No ego problem. He's friendly, natural, easy with people. And he's a good-looking boy. A great athlete and a PR dream."

"I've seen his picture," Lori said excitedly. "He's going to be a heartthrob." She paused. "Do you think he'd ever come to Halesboro?"

"If Fulcrum and Davy agree to test there. If he wants to do anything beyond that, it'll be because he volunteers. I'm in business of making these guys money. I can't exploit them. Dean and Kent *offered* to put in appearances. And it was good of them."

"Very good," she said softly. *And there must be a great deal of good in you, she thought, to inspire such loyalty. And to attract a rising star like Davy Welber.*

But she said nothing. Too often she glimpsed another side of him, a darker side. He turned back to his newspaper and she to her paperback book.

When they landed in Charlotte, he walked her to her car. This time when they parted, he shook her hand, which was better than being kissed on the forehead as if she were two or a hundred and two.

"I'll be in touch and see you soon," he muttered. "It's going to be a busy month."

Fulcrum Racing had agreed to test twice at Halesboro. And there was the Culpepper Furniture 500 coming up and a local race, as well.

"Yes," she answered. "Busy."

"I'll call."

"Yes. Please do. And thanks for everything. I hope we did some good."

"I do, too."

She got into her car and watched him walk away. Was it her imagination, or did his tall figure really seem to give off a solitary aura? It wasn't loneliness, but rather a kind of iso lation, that of a man who was at heart a loner, who was always somehow set apart from others and always would be.

THE FIRST OFFICIAL RACE with Kane as Halesboro's owner went off perfectly, with far better attendance than usual. His innovations had worked. The pre-race activities—a parade of antique cars and an old-time music show—helped draw in the crowds. The kids attended free and seniors got a discount. Large soft drinks came with the offer of free refills. Twenty-five lucky fans got a free gas card in a ticket stub drawing.

In the scramble of events, Kane and Lori had no time to talk about anything except the speedway and the race. He had to go back to Charlotte that night, but he'd call her in the morning about testing. Niday Racing had signed on for testing next week, and Fast Max was ready to make a deal.

Lori's head spun after the race. This morning Liz had said that an offer had come from the Missouri law firm, a bid on the mills. The Hornings were going to do it, and Lori couldn't believe it. Junior McCorkle's stepdaughter would surely take the offer. It was the only one ever made.

On Tuesday, Fulcrum Racing rolled into town. Justin Murphy and Cork Kerry were good enough to hold autograph sessions after the test. Justin was good-looking and a fan favorite, and Cork, though no beauty, was a legend in his last season of racing. The spectators turned out, all right, and they got to have their photos taken with both drivers by the black stone flame in front of the speedway.

But trouble struck again. The next morning when Lori drove into the speedway parking lot, again she saw Halesboro's two cruisers and a state patrol car. Instinctively she knew why they were there, and she felt as if someone had punched her in the stomach.

Clyde met Lori at the entrance and told her the vandals had struck again—and done far worse damage: more tires stabbed, and this time the vehicles had been defaced with spray paint— lots of it, insulting to both sponsors and drivers. Obscene words had been burned into the infield grass with bleach.

She rushed to the track. Kane was already there, his face taut with anger.

Justin and Cork were both men with tempers. Cork was shouting at Kane, demanding what the hell kind of place was this? What had security been doing? This had happened once before. Why in hell had Kane let it happen again? What kind of incompetent fool was he?

Morrie, the maintenance man, muttered again about a jinx

until Kane threatened to fire him. Jimmy Pilgram, Morrie's teenage assistant looked frightened and asked if the track would shut down. It couldn't—he needed this job desperately. His mother was too sick to work, and he was her sole support.

Justin Murphy looked as if he wanted to punch Kane, and Kane looked as if he might punch back. To cool him down, Lori dragged him into his office.

He couldn't sit down, he paced. "I put on new security guards, but they all swore they'd seen nothing. Nothing!

"I told the state police I want every one of those security people to take a lie detector test. Every damned one. This is going beyond vandalism—way beyond."

"Kane," Lori said, "I think maybe there *is* a vendetta against the track. Or you. Or both."

He hit the top of the filing cabinet with his fist. "What am I going to have to do? Erect *gun towers?* Station guys with Uzis around the perimeter of the place?"

"Calm down," she stated. "Did you hear what I said? Somebody's specifically targeting this track. Who? Do you have enemies?"

He glared at her. "I've got people who don't like me. Sure. It goes with the business. But not to this extent."

"What about Devlin Development?" she asked. "Is it possible? That maybe they want this land bad enough to try to drive you off it?"

"We talked about that before. Why use such ham-handed tactics? Man, I was lucky to get Fulcrum Racing here, and this is their reward."

"Then cool them down. They both blow up fast, but it's a tempest in a teapot, and then it'll be over. Go out, apologize, and promise to pay for the repairs yourself. It's only a gesture, but at least this won't drive up their insurance rates."

He swore. "You know what? I'm going to have to put in a full electronic surveillance system. I should have done it first thing. But damn! It'll cost a fortune."

"*Tell* them you'll have it done," she said firmly. "*Tell* them you shouldn't have put it off. And that you're sorry that this had to happen to them to wake *you* up."

He gave her a long look. "I hate like the very devil to admit this, but…you're right. I'm also going to offer a reward to anybody who'll give info that'll lead to the arrest of whoever's doing this."

He took a moment to cool down. "Had breakfast?" he asked.

"No. I brought an energy bar. Thought I'd have that and some coffee."

"I'll take you out," he said. "I owe you."

She nodded and managed a smile. He tried to smile back but didn't quite manage. He turned and left.

She went to her own desk and got out the phone book. She was going to call a lawn maintenance company to replace the burned grass. Then she'd phone the speedway in Charlotte and get the name of the best blasted security system business in the South.

SHE SUGGESTED that instead of going to The Groove, they go to her house. It might be humble, but it was a refuge. "I'm not in the mood to be stared at," she told him.

"Me, either," he said.

Later, sitting at her kitchen table, he said, "Thanks for calling about the grass. I'll phone Vigil-Corps as soon as we get back."

"I never saw you mad before," she said, opening the refrigerator.

"I usually don't *get* mad. I was mostly angry at myself."

She frowned as she cracked eggs into a bowl. "You know, it's funny. Before you came, we had trouble with vandals. Shooting out the lights was one of their favorite sports. And spray painting the outside fence."

She turned to face him. "But always outside. Never inside. Why, suddenly, are they hitting from within? And how do they *get* in?"

He shook his head. "I don't know. Clyde and I searched

every way I ever could figure to get in. He patched them all. He checked again this morning, and they're still patched."

She crossed her arms and studied his expression, which was strained. "And so what do you make of it?"

He gave a harsh sigh. "That maybe that state trooper was right from the beginning. It must be an inside job."

"But this was a different security company. Somebody got to *both* of them?"

"That," he said. "Or it's somebody who works here. Who has access to the infield."

A shiver ran through her. "But that would mean it would have to be somebody like Morrie. Or Frederick, the head of the driving school. Or…"

She couldn't finish the sentence, so he did it for her. "Or Clyde."

"No!" she protested. "Never. Not him. Impossible. Don't say such a thing." But even the thought made tears sting her eyes and her chin quiver.

Kane was swiftly on his feet and close to her side. "I'm sorry," he said in a low voice, taking her in his arms. He held her close and put his mouth near her ear. "Don't cry. Forget I ever said it. Think of something else."

Her thoughts went tumbling out of control. His strength made her feel weak, filled with yearning to be held. All she could think was that she wanted, very much, for him to kiss her until she could think no more and escape completely into forbidden emotion.

CHAPTER ELEVEN

"LORI," he whispered, his breath a warm tickle in her ear.

Somehow she gathered her willpower and pushed herself away from him. "Don't," she said. "Please don't touch me like that. Don't hold me or hug me or kiss my forehead or—anything."

He let her go, but she saw the reluctance in his eyes. "Why? Scared of what might happen?"

"This summer's been emotionally battering," she said, and that, at least, was true. "I don't need any more complications in my life."

He took a step backward. "Me, either. Sorry. Old habits die hard."

Her feelings, tangled, were suddenly shot through with resentment. Is that how he saw her? *An old habit? A rut into which he could carelessly tumble, then right himself again?*

"Let's change the subject," she said, turning her back on him and mixing milk with the eggs. "Liz said an offer was made on the mills. The Hornings?"

"I can't confirm that."

"Do you deny it?"

"I neither confirm it nor deny it. I told you there are things I can't talk about."

"You don't want people to know there's going to be a real estate boom."

He shrugged. "We aren't at liberty to discuss that."

Lori wondered if *we* included Zoey Horning and working very, very closely with him.

"A discount mall," she said pensively. "And your talking to Charles Channing. I think I may know the common denominator of all this interest in investing."

"Yeah? And what is it?

"I couldn't sleep last night, so I got up and used Liz's secret weapon. The search engine. Channing's CapCity Credit Card is in the top five for being economical. And I bet he's going to make sure it becomes *numero uno*."

He touched his coffee mug to hers. "It's a nice theory. Go to the head of the class for imaginative theorizing."

"So Channing sponsors the track and spotlights the most economical credit card in the country," Lori said, nervous excitement rising in her chest. "The Hornings come in and put in a giant outlet mall. Maybe not even just an outlet mall. A value-oriented mall. Even lower prices than an outlet mall. Bigger bargains."

She took a deep breath. "Put in a theme park, a few music shows, offer discounts and coupons, and wham! You've got a low priced family destination for a weekend or a whole vacation."

He eyed her with a combination of admiration and amusement, but the mocking set of his mouth made her plunge on. "NASCAR projects a family-friendly image. Mall, theme park, shows could make this into a family-friendly destination that's superaffordable. You'd make Halesboro into a track in that same mold. Probably campgrounds and playgrounds, who knows what else? And it'd all be more economic on a CapCity Credit Card."

Lori's excitement wavered, turning into apprehension. She turned and started to scramble the eggs, trying to keep her hands steady. "But all that would cost a fortune."

"Just for the sake of argument, maybe the old saying's true," he countered. "You have to spend money to make money."

"You could also lose millions," she murmured.

"No guts, no glory," he said.

She winced. That had been her father's favorite saying. She took a deep breath and said, "Still, I can't get it out of my head. Forty percent of NASCAR fans are women. Suppose a couple with two kids comes to Halesboro, rents a tent at the campground, sees great racing, shops for great bargains, takes in a couple of shows and does the theme park. They could get more for their money here than almost any place in the Carolinas."

Her body tensed as she spoke, and she stirred the eggs vigorously. "But this can't spring from the ground overnight like a mushroom," she said. "It'd take time."

He shrugged noncommittally. "It depends on how well and how fast it's done, doesn't it?"

"I suppose. You said the mills are architecturally sound. They're still good-looking buildings. But they'll need to be gutted and cleaned up. They'll need new heating, plumbing, wiring and telecommunications systems. I read that it could be done in eight months. Another two and a half months to set up shop, maybe? The mall could be opened in early June."

He sat down, put his elbow on the table and rested his chin in his hand. "Your search engine must have nearly blown its gasket. What else did it tell you?"

Lori knew he was taunting her, but she didn't care. "I read about theme parks, too. If one was built on one of the old farm properties, it'd all have to be built from the ground up. But a core of old-time craftsmen and women could have shops and give demonstrations. A few simple rides, for starters, some shows throughout the day. It could be done. It'd be a start, the base for more to build on."

He gazed at her as if she were a naive and infinitely amusing child.

She didn't like it. "Stop looking at me like I'm an idiot."

"Maybe it's a diversionary tactic," he smirked. "To shake your confidence."

She pushed the bread down in the toaster and got out plates and silverware. "I'm sorry, but the whole project still reminds me of magical movie thinking—'If you build it, they will come.' What about glitches? They always happen. Think of the vandalism. Nobody'd counted on *that*."

His expression grew serious. "Plans have been discussed. They *might* fail. Partially or completely. That's the chance you take in business."

Tears welled again, and she fought them. If the plans failed, Halesboro would become little more than a ghost town. But if they worked, Halesboro would no longer be Halesboro. Her hometown would vanish, replaced by a big commercial machine with lots of commercial cogs and gears whirling and grinding.

She started to scrape the eggs onto the plates, but her hands trembled and she couldn't help it.

"Lori?" Kane said.

"What?" she asked, struggling to keep her voice steady.

"Don't cry on the eggs, babe. It'll make 'em too salty."

"Have you ever been smacked on the head with a skillet?" she asked in frustration.

"No. My mother used to threaten to, but I knew she couldn't. Booze screws up your aim considerably."

Oh, heaven, he'd had such an awful home life, she thought with a pang. Not a single advantage except his own brains and drive. But he'd overcome every obstacle. While she, who'd had every privilege, had amounted to so little.

The toast popped up, and she put the two pieces on his plate. "Since you cooked," he said, "I'll do the dishes. I'm a trained professional, remember? I'm good at it."

You were always good at everything, she thought. *That's why I fell in love with you.*

With all the force she could muster, she thrust that thought from her mind and made herself concentrate on business. "If you're up to all I think you're up to, it's ambitious. Very ambitious. Possibly too ambitious. You could fall on your face."

"It wouldn't be the first time," he returned, his expression suddenly serious. "But what if such a thing could work? And bring Halesboro back to life?"

Again she fought back tears. And she succeeded. "It

wouldn't be the way it was," she said quietly, forcing her voice to be steady. "That's all."

"Sit down and eat. I'll tell you something."

She sat, and stared at her eggs without appetite. "Okay," she said. "Tell me."

He put his hand near hers on the table top, but he didn't touch her. "A hometown is more than buildings or traditions. Above all, it's people. People need jobs. Do you know how many jobs could be created here? How much income for city improvements would flow in?"

He leaned forward earnestly. "Housing's affordable here, and the scenery—and the location—are great. Close to both Asheville and Charlotte. Business here would draw more business. Companies can headquarter here for less than in a larger city. A bigger population means more professionals. Doctors, nurses, dentists, technicians of all kinds. The hospital's inadequate here. But it would grow. And the schools.

"It's all going to be good for the *people,* Lori. Think of the people. And ask yourself this—What would your father want to happen? What would he want for the speedway's future? Would he want to see it thrumming with life again? See the whole town revitalized?"

She kept staring down at her plate. He was right, and she could think of no answer. At last she said, "Your plans are probably bigger than I imagine, aren't they?"

"You've done enough imagining for one day," he said, but his voice was kind. "Eat, doll. And then let's get back to the track. There's work to be done."

She raised her face and met his gaze. "Right."

"We've got another race to get ready for. And then head for the Poconos."

She nodded in resignation. She was seeing too much of him. Traveling together again would only make people speculate and gossip more. But she shouldn't care. There *was* work to be done, and she intended to do her part. For her father. For the speedway. And for the people of Halesboro.

Her nostalgia, her yearning for Halesboro to be exactly as it once was, this was selfish and childish of her. To her chagrin, she realized that she could still think and act like the town's pampered princess. The first time Kane had come into her life, he'd shaken it to its foundation. And he was doing it again.

BACK AT THE OFFICE, Lori began writing press releases for the speedway's next race. Her writing was choppy, her thoughts distracted. The Fulcrum team was practicing, and both Justin and Cork seemed to have calmed down.

But her mind was full of trolls and goblins. The trolls scuttled through her thoughts because of the new vandalism. She'd convinced herself that the damage to Kent Grosso's vehicles might have been a one-time fluke. But this second incident pointed at a campaign of malice and sabotage. Somebody wanted the speedway to fail—a faceless somebody whose motives she couldn't understand.

The goblins were smaller, capering and sniggering because of her feelings about Kane veered so wildly she did not know how he'd make her feel from one moment to the next.

"*Drat!*" she exclaimed, and deleted a sentence that made no sense. She took a deep breath and started over.

She'd left her door slightly open, and now someone rapped at it. It was Kane; she could sense his presence so clearly it was as if a live wire sent its charge through her body. "Come in," she said, her muscles tensing.

He entered, looking mysteriously calm. "Hi. I just talked to a technician from Vigil-Corps about the security system. This is a long track, it'll take a large upgrade. We're talking Matrix switchers, positioning systems, monitors, cameras, fiber optics and coaxial cable. This is the price range he thinks we'll be in."

He showed her a sheet of paper with a set of numbers that made her gasp. The lowest of them seemed astronomical. She looked up at him open-mouthed. "Wh-what will you do?"

He shrugged. "Get a few more estimates. But if it's going to be done, it should be done right, and these guys are good."

He folded the paper and slipped it into the back pocket of his jeans. "I don't want any more incidents like last night's."

She swallowed hard. "That's a lot of money. Are you sure…"

He leaned his shoulder against the door frame and crossed his arms. "That I can afford it? Can't afford not to do it. We want teams to test here. And then we want NASCAR to sanction at least one race here. We *have* to guarantee security."

"Still, you're investing a huge amount. How long will it take you to break even?"

"I don't know. We'll see."

"Kane, you're *serious* about this. You really do intend to put this place back on its feet."

He gave her a look of displeased surprise. "What did you think? That I bought it on a whim? Like I could return it within ninety days for a full refund? No. I came to play, and I play to win."

"I—I'm sorry," she stammered.

"Despite what you suspect," he said with a sarcastic quirk at the corner of his mouth, "I'm not Satan, come to buy the town's soul."

"I said I'm sorry." She could feel the goblins invading her mind again, gleeful at her see-sawing emotions.

"Okay," he said, raising an eyebrow in irony. "And I'm sorry about suspecting Clyde. He came to me and apologized for being 'muddle-headed' this morning. From midnight until four in the morning, he and his wife were at the hospital in Asheville. Their granddaughter had her baby a little early. The birth announcement's in the Asheville paper today."

"Their granddaughter? The one whose husband's in Afghanistan? Like A.J. was?"

"Like A.J. was. And she and the baby are fine. I'm sorry I had doubts about him, even for a second. But something like vandalism makes you suspect everyone."

"Me, too?" she challenged.

"No," he answered. "Not you. Unless you resent me even more than I think you do."

"Why should I resent you?" Of course, sometimes she did resent him deeply, but that wasn't the sort of feeling she could admit.

"Good question," he said, his sarcastic smile in place again. "Very good question. Maybe it's because I'm an agent of the force you like least in the world—change. I hope you get over it someday. If you don't, you're going to end up as a very unhappy woman. And I'd hate to see that, Lori. I really would."

He nodded in farewell and left, pulling the door nearly shut again.

She stared at the door, confounded. That he would even *think* of spending so much on a new security system amazed her. She'd kept doubting his commitment to the track was altogether genuine, but this proved it was. But why was he so determined? It couldn't be that he was saving something that she loved simply because she loved it.

Maybe it was to show her that although she'd failed, *he* could succeed. Everyone in Halesboro would be indebted to him, including her. He'd come back the conquering hero, and from the ashes of her defeat, he'd stoke a blaze of triumph that, in a very real way, made not only the speedway but the whole town *his*. He could feast on self-satisfaction. And the rest of the town could eat crow.

KANE DROVE HOME when testing was over. The vandalism infuriated him, but he was the sort whose fury was usually cold, not fiery. Mentally, he listed possible reasons for the damage to the NASCAR drivers' vehicles. Somebody wanted the track to fail. Why?

He could come up with a dozen scenarios. All were possible, but also seemed far-fetched or incomplete. And there was another complication, just as mysterious to him: Lori. When the Hornings got excited about the old mill buildings, they'd started talking of Halesboro's potential as a tourist destination.

The speedway was in bad shape, D. B. Horning said, but it could be restored by somebody who knew what he was doing. And Kane had thought, *I'm that guy.* He'd worked at Halesboro, he'd always followed racing, and he had clients who were first-class drivers. He knew racing from the inside out, and he knew an opportunity when he saw it.

What had put him off was that Lori's father had mismanaged the track, then died, and Lori had been forced to put it up for sale. For years his feelings toward her had been a two-edged sword. She was the first and only woman he'd ever loved. And she'd hurt him worse than any other human being ever had.

Part of him wanted to humble her, even punish her. Another wanted to come to her rescue like a knight on a white horse. And part of him hoped that as soon as he saw her, his obsession with her would die.

He'd been wrong. She still had her trim little figure and lovely face and red-gold hair. The only pathetic things about her were that she'd married that jerk Scott Garland, and that her father had set her an impossible task. But she was still sassy and vivacious; she thought fast and spoke her mind.

The old attraction still held him fast, and he hadn't expected it. He found himself toying with her, which made him feel like a lout. And, in turn, she seemed to fight her attraction to him, which made him feel vulnerable and uncertain. When he'd been poor and nobody, she'd taken his heart and stamped it flat. Was she proud enough to want to do the same thing now that he was wealthy? Or would she tolerate him now *because* of his wealth?

What he needed was a woman like Zoey, who had her own money, her own success, yet was surprisingly without complexity. He had enough complexity in his life. And always had.

LORI STAYED BUSY and wanted to stay busy to keep from brooding about Kane. But he was always hovering in her mind, like a handsome ghost who wouldn't be exorcised. So he was in her thoughts when she booked the pre-race entertainment, a motorcycle daredevil Kane had recommended, when she ordered the posters, when she checked on repairs to the infield.

In between, she had to plan for her trip with Kane to the NASCAR Sprint Cup Series race in the mountains of Pennsylvania. She wished she had something stylish to wear, but she wouldn't allow herself to spend the money. She'd pack her trusty crinkly sage-green slacks and the two matching blouses. She would not, she vowed, try to impress him. After all, he was seeing Zoey Horning, who was young, lovely and a millionairess. She probably had four thousand designer outfits. Lori had worn beautiful clothes once. What good did it do to dwell on it?

She had more important things to think of. The police had made zero progress on the recent vandalism. This was frustrating, as were the estimates coming in from other security companies. The lowest of them seemed outrageous. She worried about Kane losing a fortune and about the whole scheme of the mall, the theme park, all of it, failing miserably. And sometimes she worried almost as much that he'd succeed and view his success as a grim, ironic sort of revenge on the town.

She was nervous and on edge when she drove to the Charlotte airport to meet Kane early Saturday afternoon. He wore jeans and a cobalt blue polo shirt that set off his tan and showed his biceps. But even in jeans and a cotton shirt, he gave off an aura of elegance. People would think she was his frumpy country cousin. *So what?* she asked herself. She'd come to pride herself on living on a budget.

But traveling first-class still jolted her. And in Philadelphia, they checked into a hotel only a mile from the airport. It had a four-diamond rating, and her room seemed big enough for six people. Kane stayed on a different floor this time. Well, he was *acting* like a gentleman. But the room, too, overwhelmed her; it was so grand that she couldn't imagine what it cost.

Kane took her for supper in the hotel's beautiful restaurant, which had stained glass windows and a menu discreetly without prices. "I'll order for you," he suggested. "You'd order a slice of cheese on white bread if they served it."

"You…eh…live a bit high on the hog. I'm not used to it."

"You were used to it once. And it's no sin to enjoy life."

She shrugged helplessly and let him order her the filet mignon. Once she'd been used to such material luxuries. Now she felt her greatest luxury was being out of debt. It bestowed the kind of security and peace of mind she'd once taken for granted.

He'd ordered a bottle of red wine brought to the table. As the waiter left the table, Kane said, "I'd like to take you out to see Philadelphia. But we have to get up early tomorrow morning to beat the traffic. Then we fly out of here at 8 p.m. It's going to be a long day."

"I'm interested in this track," she said. "It's independently owned, like…yours." She's almost said *ours*. What a faux pas that would have been.

"Right," he said. "And it's got an interesting layout and an interesting history. I want to look closely at this one."

"This is the raceway they literally rebuilt," she replied. "Almost the way you want to eventually."

Kane said, "Not quite. The guy who started it realized it was built wrong. After a bunch of setbacks, he tore it down and began all over. Now it's a showplace and has two NASCAR races. I'd like even one race, but I don't want to tear down Halesboro. Just fix it up so it can be at its best."

The sommelier came, poured the wine for Kane to taste, then filled both glasses and silently slipped away. Kane touched his glass to Lori's. "To resurrection of the Pennsylvania track—and to one just as successful for Halesboro."

"I'll drink to that," she said, "but they poured a lot of money into the one here."

"Yep," Kane said without emotion. "The byword at the raceway here is PFC—pretty, friendly, clean. I want the same for Halesboro."

"It's a fine goal," she said. "If you've got the money to spare."

"Not to spare. To invest. And if I fail, I have job skills to fall back on. Waiting tables, sweeping floors, digging ditches. But my question is what do *you* do after you're finished helping me make the transition? Stay in good old Halesboro and go back to teaching?"

"I don't know," she said uneasily because she was reluctant to think of the future. "I suppose. It's home, after all."

"The only place you've ever lived," he said.

"Yes."

"But there's a big world outside it, Lori. Don't you want to see it?"

She smiled and said nothing. She was happy in Halesboro. Wasn't she?

THE ILLINOIS SPEEDWAY had risen up from the flatness of the cornfields, but Pocono was in the mountains, which seemed less alien to Lori. There was a lovely countryside and thick forests. The summer sky was blue and streaked with white clouds, and more than once she saw deer grazing beside the highway.

And the raceway *was* impressive. Lori loved the midway with its towering spruces, gazebos and picnic tables. The size of the track astonished her, although she'd known it was large.

The track's sharp turns and low banking dictated less speed than other tracks, but those who loved it said it was a driver's track, all the way.

Lori and Kane went to a sponsor's skybox above the main straight. More than forty people milled in the big room with its floor to ceiling glass overlooking the track. A caterer dispensed food and drinks, and there was tiered seating, as well as closed-circuit TV.

Kane was right. There was a large world outside of Halesboro, and, at last, she was seeing it, even starting to feel comfortable in it.

But then something unexpected happened. A beautiful girl came into the skybox with a tall man. She looked about, saw

Kane, smiled in delight, ran and threw her arms around his neck, hugging him and kissing him soundly on the cheek.

She had an astonishing figure, emphasized by her azure tank top and low-slung stretch jeans. She was someone completely different, with luxuriant blond hair and blue eyes. The blonde kissed Kane again. And she wasn't Zoey Horning.

CHAPTER TWELVE

KANE AWKWARDLY embraced the blonde, then disengaged himself.

Lori was almost certain that he blushed, ever so slightly. Kane blush? It seemed impossible. But he looked at Lori, nodded at the blonde, and said, "Er…do you remember my little sister Stacy?"

Lori, who'd been shocked at the blonde's forwardness, suddenly sped backward in time and remembered the pretty but skinny little girl who was Kane's half-sister. She had the same classic cheekbones as Kane, but otherwise didn't resemble him.

Stacy's blue eyes opened wider. "I remember you," she told Lori. "You taught at my high school. I was never in your class, but I knew who you were. It's great to see you again."

It was Lori's turn to blush. She'd been grateful Stacy had never been her student, and hadn't wanted to think about the girl. She'd brought back painful memories of Kane. Like him, she'd been poor, ill-dressed and an outsider. But now she seemed in full, healthy bloom.

"It's good to see you again," Lori said, and it wasn't exactly a lie, because at least this lovely girl wasn't one of Kane's paramours. "What are you doing these days?"

"I'm a fitness instructor," Stacy said. "I work for Cargill-Grosso."

"Cargill-Grosso?" Lori repeated, almost disbelieving. Why hadn't Kane told her?

Now, almost sheepishly, he said, "And now she and Nathan

Cargill are…seeing each other. That's Nathan over there, stealing all the cashews out of the mixed nut dish. Excuse me. I'm going to go make a citizen's arrest."

Stacy gave him an affectionate swat. "You're incorrigible. As usual." Kane headed toward Nathan, and Stacy turned her attention back to Lori. "Kane and I just sort of rediscovered each other," she said. "I'm really happy to have hooked up with him again. He's a super guy."

Lori blinked. Was there yet another facet of Kane she didn't know?

Stacy must have seen the puzzlement on her face. Lowering her voice confidentially, she said, "Our mother was a disaster. When he was home, he was my hero. I missed him something awful when he left. Sometimes I cried at night because he hadn't taken me with him. And finally, when I was fed up with Brenda's problems, I left. I wanted to find him."

"I can imagine," Lori said, feeling real sympathy for the young woman. "And you did find him. I'm glad."

Stacy gave a self-conscious shrug. "It took a long time to catch up with him. And at first Kane sort of kept his distance. I think he was afraid I'd turn out like Brenda. But he and I are cool now. We're family again. I've got my big brother again."

"That's good. Very good," Lori said.

"And it's good to see you with him," Stacy replied. "I know that he was crazy about you. Not that he ever told me. I found out from Brenda years later. Kane plays it close to the vest. He doesn't like to show his feelings."

Stacy's frankness was disarming. Lori said, "I…we're not exactly together. It's a business arrangement."

"Yeah." Stacy flashed a grin. "Sure. That's what *he* keeps saying."

Lori tried to change the subject. "Kane said no one has heard from your mother in a while. I'm very sorry. "

"Brenda wasn't stable," Stacy said, suddenly more solemn, "I know that she hit Kane up for money, but he stopped sending it when she just kept spending it on drinking. She did the same thing to me once I was older. I came to feel like Kane. I couldn't just keep enabling her, you know?"

Lori shook her head, feeling a tug of sympathy not only for Stacy but for Kane.

"I mean," said Stacy, "the money was one thing. But the emotional see-saw was worse."

No wonder Kane was so emotionally elusive, thought Lori. His mother had taught him to beware of caring. And Lori herself, in her youthful ignorance, had reinforced that painful lesson.

"I'm glad you and your brother reunited," she told Stacy. "Things must have been very hard on you both, growing up."

"He's strong," Stacy said. "He was always strong. Even though I was so young I saw that. It broke my heart when he left Halesboro, but it was the best thing he could do for himself."

She took Lori by the arm. "But I'm babbling. It's so strange to see a familiar face from Halesboro. Come meet Nathan. He used to come to Halesboro Speedway with his dad. Do you remember?"

"I do," Lori said with a smile. She kept the smile in place, but Stacy's words unsettled her. *He's strong. He was always strong.*

Was he strong enough to fight all the shadows gathering around them at Halesboro Speedway? And were either of them strong enough to face the complexities of their relationship?

ON THE PLANE back to Charlotte, Lori said, "I liked your sister. She told me how she missed you when you left. How glad she was to find you again."

"God love her," he said, but he didn't meet Lori's eyes. "I should have taken her with me or at least tried to provide for her better. I was wary about sending more money. I knew Brenda'd drink it all up, and that would only make things harder on Stacy."

"And you really don't wonder what's become of your mother?" Lori probed.

"I try not to think about her. I'll say one thing for Brenda. She made a person toughen up. If Stacy and I hadn't toughened up, we wouldn't have survived. But we did, and we're together again. Now let's change the subject. I talked to some NASCAR people."

Lori blinked in surprise. "Did they say anything about Halesboro?"

He turned and faced her. "We spoke in glittering generalities. Nothing concrete. They're smart about business, exceptionally smart. We have to prove that Halesboro would be good business for them."

"Did they say anything about the vandalism?"

"Just alluded to it. I said we're putting in a state-of-the-art security system. And they know that several teams are already testing there. In the meantime, our job is to ensure we get as many seats filled as possible. We need strong local and regional support to get us going and keep us going. And we'll get it—if I have to rent thirty elephants to stand on their heads in the infield."

"You're kidding, I hope."

"No, babe," he said, looking into her eyes. "I'm not kidding. I told you—I play to win."

She narrowed her eyes speculatively. "And what exactly, in the end, do you want to win?"

His gaze fell to her lips and lingered there. In a low voice, he said, "I'm still figuring that out." But he thought he knew now. Maybe he'd known from the day he'd picked up that old yearbook and bought it.

NO ELEPHANTS stood on their heads at the next Halesboro race. But the country-rock band was a huge hit, and so was the poster-signing session with Kent Grosso. The late-model race thrilled the crowd, and so did the twenty-five prizes of gas cards given throughout the night. Kane felt that the guests left happy and ready to return for more.

The security system people were still making estimates so

he'd hired a third company to provide a double complement of guards, as well as backup off-duty state troopers.

The only dark moment came when Lori's Mustang went cranky again. Kane said he thought it needed new spark plugs. She was exhausted, and he sensed that she was close to tears with fatigue from all her work on the race and her frustration at the car's continuing troubles. His heart contracted as he looked at her, realizing how strong she was in spite of her vulnerability.

"Come on," he said, as gently as he could. "I'll drive you home. I'll see that Clyde takes care of this tomorrow."

She seemed reluctant, but agreed.

He walked her to her door, and on impulse he said, "Could I come in for a while? There's something I want to talk to you about."

"Sure," she said, but uncertainty vibrated in her voice.

What am I doing? he asked himself. As soon as the door shut behind them, he knew he was getting into the very situation he'd sworn not to. But some inner force, too strong to resist, drove him.

She offered him a drink, and he accepted. She poured them each a glass of white wine, and they sat on the couch in her small living room.

"We made a lot of money tonight," he said, looking at her over the top of his glass. "Almost a third of what we spent."

Puzzlement crossed her face. "And that doesn't bother you?"

"You have to expect it at first," he said wryly. "If I'm still in the hole after ten years, I'll wonder if I made a really stupid mistake."

She cocked her head, the way she used to when they'd talk seriously. "I still don't understand. Why are you doing all this?"

He set his glass on the coffee table. He looked at her. He realized how tired he was of disguising how he felt, hiding it, especially from himself. The moment for truth had come. He took a deep but unsteady breath. "Why? For a lot of reasons. But the main reason? I guess it's you."

Her eyes widened, and her beautiful, so beautiful lips parted in surprise.

"I never got you out of my system," he confessed. "Ever." He felt as vulnerable as if he were standing naked on Main Street at high noon.

"But," she said, her voice quavering, "you and Zoey Horning…"

"I'm her friend. And a decoy. She's engaged to Rome McCandless. They want to stay out of the news. Rome's a famous guy, but he's also very private. That's why last winter I brought her and her father to Halesboro. She wanted to see where Rome grew up. He was at a game in Florida that day. I'm trusting you to keep this secret."

"Good grief," she said.

He put his hands on her upper arms, drawing her closer. "And I'm trusting you to understand this—when I left, I felt like you'd betrayed me. It poisoned me. I resented it for years. And I came here wanting to kick sand in the town's collective face. To do it with a vengeance. But vengeance doesn't feel so good. And you—"

He bent closer to her. "I wanted to show you what a mistake you'd made. I wanted to humble you, make you feel humiliated and ashamed. But I've come to realize what happened to us happened because we were too young to know better. As soon as I saw you, it all came back. The attraction. The affection. I guess I have to say it—the love."

He took her glass from her and set it aside. Then he pulled her tightly against him and kissed her until he got lost in it, just the way he used to. He was blind and deaf to everything else in the universe except her.

One tiny corner of sanity flickered in his mind, telling him this was dangerous. He was giving her the chance to hurt him again as badly as before, to reject him again.

But she didn't reject him. She wound her arms around his neck and kissed him back until they both were breathless, and once again he was hers. Completely.

HE MADE LOVE to her twice, and they dozed together, nestled like spoons, her back against his chest, his arm over her, guarding her, cherishing her nearness. She woke him in the early hours of the morning.

"You should go," she whispered, turning and touching his face.

"I don't want to." He kissed her, nuzzled her neck, her bare shoulder.

"You have to," she insisted, raising herself on her elbow. The room was shadowy, but he could make out her features by the light from the hall. "What will the neighbors think?" she asked.

He shook his head to clear it. "Aren't we old enough not to worry this time?"

"No," she said. "It's…it's different for a man. People will talk."

"They're already talking, if I know Halesboro. They'll imagine that we swing from chandeliers and—"

She put her fingertips over his mouth to hush him. "Please," she said. "I've always played by the rules. Except when it came to you. I don't want to seem brazen."

He laughed and tried to pull her nearer. "What you seem is *quaint,* love. I mean it's so old-fashioned it's cute, but—"

"Kane, I mean it. If I go back to teaching, I've got to watch my reputation. I've got civil duties, and—"

"All right, all right," he muttered. She drew away from him. She stood and quickly slipped into a robe—so modest.

She helped him gather his clothes. One of his socks had landed on the lamp shade. Then she and he spent so much time kissing goodbye that he wanted to take her back to bed, but she refused. "Please," she begged. "Let's be careful, that's all. I didn't expect for this to happen."

So he was soon alone in his car, thinking yes, her concern was practically Victorian and sort of charming, but it was also annoying as hell. Would she never outgrow this small town?

He slept uneasily in his motel bed, and when he awoke a few hours later, he phoned Clyde to tend to Lori's car, and then called her. He still had mixed feelings about her need for secrecy. He didn't ask her to breakfast; he *told* her they had a date. He didn't intend to take no for an answer.

He picked her up half an hour later, and when she came out of the house, his heart tightened with desire. She wore a dark green shorts outfit of some kind, and she always looked sensational in green. But she seemed self-conscious, almost shy.

He wanted to kiss her, right there on the front porch in the strong young daylight, in front of God and everybody. Then he'd like to pick her up and carry her back inside, straight to the bedroom. He wanted to make love to her until they were both sated and exhausted in each other's arms.

"Good morning," he said. "How does it feel to be a fallen woman?"

She managed a smile. "It feels surprisingly right. Somehow."

An unfamiliar knot formed in his throat, almost choking him up. "Yeah," he said gruffly. "It feels right. Are you my girl again?"

"If you're my guy." She gave him a bashful glance.

"I always have been," he said. He yearned to put his arm around her shoulders, but for the sake of what the town thought, he didn't.

IT WAS SUNDAY MORNING, and few people were yet in The Groove. Some would gather here after church for lunch or for coffee and pie. But for now Lori and Kane had it almost to themselves. Kane dropped coins in the jukebox and played "Got My Mind Set on You." The song had been a kind of anthem for him during the enchanted months of their romance.

He used to sing that in her ear, and he wondered if she remembered. She smiled at him, and he knew she did. He'd been wildly, crazily in love with her then, and he'd finally admitted that he loved her still. But not in the same heedless, reckless, hell-bent way. He needed to make that clear to her, and hoped she felt the same way that he did.

He leaned forward over his coffee mug and said, "I hate to use the term *you* hate, but after last night, things have *changed* between us."

She bit the inside of her lip, and then admitted, "I suppose they have."

"And they haven't changed. I love you."

She stared at him in panic. "Shhh!" She looked about to see if anyone had heard.

"I whispered that," he said in a low voice. "And there's music on. Nobody could hear."

"It's just…" her voice trailed off. She began again. "I…I feel the same about you."

"Can you say it?" he asked. "Can you say, 'I love you'?"

"Yes. But not here," she answered, clearly uncomfortable. "Not yet. I mean, we should be careful. We were so…so headlong before."

"I know that," he said as patiently as he could. "But I want to be with you again and again. The way we were last night."

She looked about nervously again. "I do, too, but…"

"But we should take it slowly," he supplied.

She gave a sigh of relief. "Yes. Exactly. Take our time."

He found this ironic since it had taken over twenty years for them to finally make love, but he understood what she meant. He could whisk her off to Las Vegas and marry her before the sun went down. But three months later, she might be back in Nevada getting an annulment. Because this could be a fluke, the way they felt now. It might not last.

"We need to be sensible," she answered softly.

"Right," he said, staring into his coffee. "Just see how it goes. I'm not asking you to make any commitment to me at this point."

"I understand." She looked solemn and lovely. "We need to find out if…uh…the relationship can work."

He hated words like *relationship,* but this was no time to quibble. "And I'm not making any commitment to you."

Suddenly, she looked hurt, and offended, as well. "I didn't ask you for any."

"I should have phrased that better," he said, thinking that he wasn't very good at this sort of conversation. "What I meant was—"

"I know what you meant." She sat up straighter, looked away from him.

He plunged on, praying not to bungle this. "But you want us to be discreet. So I have an idea."

"Yes?"

"What if I bought you a more private place here? Bigger. Nicer. Out in the country. Where nobody else is around to stick their noses in our business. And maybe sometimes you could come stay with me in Charlotte."

What he meant was that he wanted her mind, her heart, her soul—and her body, too. To know if they could make it as a couple in love, they had to be able to *act* like a couple in love. That, for him, included being intimate. It meant touching each other in ways they touched no one else.

But Lori turned and stared at him in disbelief. He realized he'd botched it, all right. Sparks flashed from her eyes, and she said, "That's a long way from being discreet. You buy me a *house?* In fifteen minutes everybody in the county would know."

"I mean I'd give you the money. It would seem like you're buying a place with your profits from selling the track. These things can be arranged."

She said, "I don't want a different house. I don't want to make sneaky 'arrangements.' I'd feel like a kept woman. And I don't want people thinking that I'm making up to you because of your money or that you're buying me—"

"Look, I suggested this out of respect for you. My attitude is different from yours. Just let people think what they want," he countered.

"Yes. It's *your* attitude. Not mine."

"The small-town mentality here," he said, "nearly smothered me when I was a kid. I don't want to be smothered again."

Lori gave a huff of frustration. The waitress set down a plate of eggs and bacon before her, but she didn't touch her fork. "This is already turning out wrong," she said.

"I'm sorry," he said. He put his hand close to hers, but didn't touch her. "Nothing I say comes out right. And I shouldn't have started this conversation in a public place. We should have gone for a drive in the country."

"You're right," she said.

"Let's do it tonight," he suggested.

"Yes," she said. "Let's. And now let's talk about something else."

"Fine," he said. "Kent's coming to test again. Next week. Dean will come, too. They're willing to do another signing. Some other drivers may join in. We'll arrange for some entertainment, a picnic."

She didn't look excited about that, either. He realized she was still worn out from making all the arrangements for the race last night. So he changed tactics. "But we'll worry about that later. First, I want you to eat, then get some rest. You've worked your heart out, Lori. You've gone above and beyond the call of duty. This afternoon, Clyde'll bring your car to you, and I'll drive him home."

He took a deep breath. "Then I'll come get you, and we'll take that drive. We've got a lot to work out. About you and me. And about the speedway. No matter what else happens, we have the speedway in common. You signed a contract that you'll cooperate with me for a year. A year's a long time. We can solve a lot of problems in a year."

Her eyes were full of wariness, and he knew what she was thinking. *We can find a lot of new problems in a year, too.*

And she was right.

He'd changed since he first fell in love with her, but he still belonged to her. And some things about her hadn't changed: she still belonged to Halesboro. She always had, and he feared she always would.

THEY DROVE DEEP into the woods that evening, and Kane brought a picnic of junk food and expensive champagne. The junk food from Halesboro's not-so-super supermarket consisted of chicken salad sandwiches from its small "deli," salt and vinegar potato chips and a plastic cup of coleslaw.

"Wow," he said, laying it out on the spare blanket he'd obviously taken from his hotel room. "Do I know how to show a girl a good time or what?"

They sat cross-legged on the blanket, across from each other, the food between them. He said, "What do you think? Is this too fancy?"

She gave him a mischievous grin. She felt far more comfortable now that they were alone. "I think you should have asked me to make something. You don't have to foot the bill all the time. What's that red glop?"

He stared at it with distaste. "It was two slices of cherry pie when I bought it. I think the crust disintegrated. The way it quivers, it may be trying to become a new life form. We can leave it for the raccoons—if it doesn't eat them first."

She laughed, feeling at home with him again. "Next time, I'll bring the food."

He cocked an eyebrow. "You mean you'd do this again?"

"Yes. I like it when we have privacy."

It was a peaceful evening, the breeze cool and piney, and cicadas singing in the trees. The sinking sun made the sky seem lavender and the clouds pink. She thought she heard one of their old friends, a tree frog. She saw Kane tilt his head and listen. He heard it, too.

"I had another idea," he told her. "First, I apologize for the bit about buying you a house. You're right. That *was* arrogant. But what if *I* bought a second home here? A place to stay instead of that motel room?"

"You mean like a cabin in the woods or on the lake?" she asked.

"I called Liz," he said, leaning back and half reclining while he nibbled a potato chip. "She said there're a couple of nice properties around. One sounds perfect. It used to belong to a federal magistrate from Pennsylvania. It was his retreat, but he decided to find something closer to home. It's about fifteen miles out of Halesboro on a private road, national forest on two sides."

"I remember," Lori said, brightening. "He had it built. Liz and I went to look at it. It's a charming little place, a white cottage in the middle of the woods, halfway up a mountain."

"Three bedrooms, two and a half baths," Kane said, reaching for another chip. "The furnishings stay. Ten acres with a creek and two waterfalls. Lots of azaleas planted around the house. What about it?"

He reached for the champagne bottle and refilled her glass. "If I bought it, would you come be with me there sometimes?"

She thought. "I'd try. If we could arrange it to be..."

"I know," he said, mock weariness in his voice. "To be discreet. Never fear. If I have to I'll personally dig an underground passage dug between your place and mine. Whoa, that'll be painful. The massages you'd have to give me. Oh—and there's a hot tub. You'd have to get in it with me and minister to my aching bod."

"It's a beautiful view," she said wistfully. "I remember."

"My bod?" he asked hopefully.

She swatted him. "The *property* has a beautiful view."

She tried to give him another swat, but he seized her wrist. "Oh, want to play rough, do you? All right. You've got it."

He easily wrestled her onto her back and pinned her wrists above her head. "I've captured you. And now I claim my prize."

He lowered his face to hers and kissed her, gently at first, but then with growing intensity. She liked it and kissed him back with the same fervor. "Let go of my hands," she finally managed to whisper.

"Why?" he teased and moved closer to kiss her again.

But she dodged him. "So I can unbutton your shirt," she said. "For starters."

It was the boldest, sexiest thing she'd ever said to a man,

but it felt natural and intimate, saying it. One thing led to another, and they made love once more.

Then she laid her head against his bare shoulder and they stared up through the trees at the darkening sky and the stars that seemed to wink down at them as if in approval.

I'm less inhibited, she thought with surprise. *A lot less inhibited.* It was because of Kane, she knew. All these years, her mind, heart, and body had craved him and him alone.

"You know," he said lazily. "If we practice enough, we could get really good at this."

She nestled against his chest, and he kissed her ear, her cheek, her throat. She put her hand on his shoulder and nuzzled the hollow of his neck. She thought, *I've never been happier. It doesn't matter if it lasts. I will remember this for the rest of my life.*

CHAPTER THIRTEEN

RELUCTANTLY, they left the mountainside, and Kane drove her home. He walked her to the front door. "I want to say something. If you're 'my girl' again, I don't want you being ashamed of me. It's too much like old times."

"I'm not ashamed of you," she said. "I'm ashamed of my own…cowardice. You were always a rebel. I was one for a few months, and scared and guilty most of the time. And…and I'm afraid of making a fool of myself over you."

"You think I might hurt you? I'd never want to do that. But I have the same problem. Love can be scary. Painful. Too painful. We both learned that the hard way."

"Yes," she said sadly. "We did. I don't want to learn it all over again."

"Me, either," he said. He kissed his index finger and placed it against her lips. "Will that scandalize the neighbors?" he asked.

"Probably," she said. "But I think maybe it's not so much we have an affair, but that we don't flaunt it. Don't fling it in everyone's face."

He wanted to touch her, draw her close again, she could tell. And she wished she could let him. But he shoved his thumbs into the back pocket of his jeans. "Just don't flaunt it?" he teased softly. "You've come a long way since this morning."

"I've *thought* a lot since this morning," she answered. "I don't know how this story ends. But even if it's a fleeting thing, it's something I want. I can't deny it."

"I want it, too," he said. "And it's killing me not to hold you. It's killing not to kiss you goodbye. I'd better start back for Charlotte because I feel my supply of willpower running down fast. But at least we could start going out together like a normal couple seeing each other. A…a courtship. I'll call you tomorrow. And see you on Tuesday at the testing."

She didn't want him to go. "I worry about those tests," she admitted. "You can't have the security system in place by then. You don't have all the final estimates yet."

"Not to worry," he said. "I'll have more guards still. And Kent and I came up with a plan."

"A plan? What?" She backed closer to her door, because the magnetic attraction of him was growing too strong.

"I'll tell you Tuesday," he said. "Look, I've got to get out of here. It's very hard for me, this 'being good' business. I'll see you soon and talk to you sooner."

Then he turned and loped down the stairs and back to his car. He waved at her casually, and she waved back, just as casually. Then she hurried into her house, not bothering to turn on the light. She drew back a curtain and watched him drive away. His absence already saddened her and left her feeling hollow and incomplete.

But then her phone rang, startling her. She switched on a table lamp and pulled out her cell phone. The caller ID told her it was Aunt Aileen.

"So you're home at last," Aileen said wryly. "I heard you went off with Kane. Your landlady was kind enough to call and tell me. She said he picked you up late this afternoon. And also that he came to your place last night. That he stayed a long time."

"Good grief," Lori muttered in disgust. It had started already. Mrs. McBeebee was like a one-woman broadcast system. "But why'd she call *you?*"

"She thought I should warn you. Said it was foolish for you to act so shamelessly, that everyone could see what was going on, and he just came back here to drag you down to his level, blah, blah, blah, and you should watch it if you ever wanted to teach here again, because you were setting a bad example for young girls, and that you need to come to your senses before you ruin your reputation completely. So I thanked her."

Lori's face grew hot with anger and embarrassment. Incredulous, she said, "You *thanked* her?"

"Indeed," said Aileen, "I said 'Thanks, but you really ought to mind your own business. It would be such a novel experience for you.' Still, Lori, I do have a warning for you."

Lori blinked hard in puzzlement. "Warning?"

"Advice. You and Kane cared deeply for each other when you were younger. Two decades have passed, but the spark is still there. You're single. He's single. But if you're having an affair, be circumspect."

Aileen paused. "I never told you this. After my divorce, I had an affair. It lasted seven years. A few people may have suspected. But nobody knew."

Lori was shocked. "An affair? For seven *years?* With whom?"

"Ben Sandoz. I met him on a theater tour to New York. He was a teacher, too. His wife had early onset Alzheimer's disease. She was in a nursing home. She no longer knew who he was. He was alone, and so was I. We kept it well-hidden. We saw each other only on school vacations, and never here or where he lived—a little town in Kansas as hidebound as Halesboro. It was emotionally very difficult for both of us. And then, suddenly, he died. Heart failure. I…I never got to say goodbye. But we'd stayed in love in spite of everything."

Lori couldn't believe her aunt's words. Aileen had hidden an affair for *seven years?* "When was this?" she asked.

"Twenty-five years ago. It was difficult," Aileen repeated, "we didn't want to be exposed to gossip and criticism. But you face more danger than I ever did. Kane's well-known. He moves among famous people. Your name could be linked to his not just in Halesboro, but spread all over the country. And you *don't* want that if you intend to keep living here."

Lori was struck speechless.

Aileen said, "And remember this. You may grow tired of him. Or him of you. Or you may both decide it wasn't meant to be. So for now, just don't be too reckless. Sometimes the hotter a romance burns, the faster it burns out. Don't let go of this chance to be with him. But, my dear, don't throw everything else away, either."

"I…I think I understand what you're saying," Lori replied.

"Maybe I should have kept my mouth shut. Not said anything to you."

"No," she answered. "You've always been honest with me. And I…I appreciate it, Aunt Aileen. I do."

"Anytime you want to talk, kid, just let me know. But beware—I've got a lot of opinions. One is that whatever you do, it's not as bad as what Mrs. McBeebee does. She loves nothing as much as spreading suspicion and ruining reputations. Don't let her sort hurt you. Take care. I love you."

"I love you back," Lori said, her throat tight. And when she hung up, she was more confused than before. What Aileen said made sense, yet it seemed contradictory. Be very, very cautious, but not *too* cautious. Love Kane, but not too openly—or too much.

Aileen's love affair came as a shock to her. How much secrecy and scheming had it taken to fool so many people for so long? And yet, how much comfort they must have brought to each other. But how much fear and bending of the truth, as well? How much duplicity? To keep from being criticized by people like Mrs. McBeebee.

A PICNIC, SO SOON after the barbecue, taxed Lori, but at least it was simpler. This time she chose another Asheville restaurant to cater, Carolina Style Cookin'. CSC specialized in chicken, ham, ribs and the most famous coleslaw and potato salad in the region.

She booked the High Lonesome Singers from Charlotte, and sent out announcements that not only the Grossos would be back, Roman McCandless would make a rare public appearance, and that he and the Grossos would be photographed with guests to raise money for the track's renovation.

Lori didn't like what her father had called "stunts," but she had to admit that Kane had a genius for promotion—genius and some very important and loyal friends. The tickets were selling out fast, and TV crews were coming from Charlotte, Raleigh and Winston-Salem.

Kane had promised an important announcement about the track, an announcement he was keeping even from Lori. She admired him and wanted, with all her heart, to trust him, but something in her held back, kept her wary. After all these years, their attraction had flared back into life, like a blaze that had died down to the embers only to spring into flames again. But would it quickly burn itself out again, as Aunt Aileen had warned?

If Kane wanted to prove he could have her again, he'd succeeded. Would he want to keep her?

She wasn't confident enough to believe that, and it was one reason she held back to keep their affair secret. She'd been humiliated by their first romance. She feared facing the same hurt and shame again. And in addition to losing Kane, she'd known the agony of being a betrayed wife, as well. But she did love Kane. For better or for worse.

She told him she loved him over the phone, and he said the same to her. But neither of them spoke any more of commitment—it was too soon, and everything seemed to be happening too fast.

Tuesday, he was back for testing with Kent Grosso, Roberto Castillo and team owner Dean Grosso. He asked her to meet him in his office, and they immediately kissed hello so passionately that Lori broke it off, fearful that their affection would go too far.

"My puritan," he said with both affection and regret.

"That was my grandfather's desk. It's giving off vibes of disapproval."

Kane kissed her on the tip of her nose. "Go to lunch with me? At The Groove, so I have to behave? I'll tell you about the security situation."

"Your and Kent's plan?" she asked, suddenly worried. She

knew that Kane could take care of himself, and so could Kent, but did they have any idea what—or who—they were up against?

"Can't you tell me now?" she asked. "I worry."

"I know," he said. "But I want time to explain everything. So you can *stop* worrying."

She nodded in reluctance. "At lunch, then. But, in truth, I'm surprised Kent agreed to this. He's putting himself at risk again. And he was really upset after the vandalism and I don't blame him."

"Kent's the type who'd rather get even than get mad," Kane told her. "He wants to get this guy and stop him for good. So do I."

He kissed her nose again. "And so do you, and you know it. If your dad was alive and well, he'd be going with us. You can't deny it."

My father would be proud of you, she thought.

ALTHOUGH TUESDAY WAS USUALLY a slow day in Halesboro, people were already coming to town for the speedway's picnic. The Groove was almost filled, but Kane and Lori found a booth in the back. Lunching business people eyed them with interest. So did the help.

Lori knew that she and Kane were now the town's hottest item of gossip, and the curiosity wouldn't go away. She felt intensely self-conscious, but Kane seemed unfazed.

They sat and gave their orders to the waitress. "All right," Lori said to Kane. She folded her hands tightly on the table top. "What do you plan to do tonight?"

"First," he said, "we think this has to be an inside job. A lot of people have been working around the speedway. One may have hidden when working hours were over—hidden anywhere, from a VIP suite to a janitor's closet. Our guess is the infield bathroom and shower building. The outside security doesn't see him simply because he's not outside. He spends the night there."

Lori frowned in puzzlement. "But what about the inside security?"

"He's already close to the vehicles. He strikes fast and hides again. The infield's a big area, and the lights keep being vandalized. The security guys don't stand like sentries; they're always on patrol. And even they can get bored, tired, steal a few winks. That's the only explanation."

"But how could he hide in the building? I'd think that's the first place guards would check."

"They'd look *around,* all right. But probably the last place they'd look is *up.* He could hide in the ceiling. I was going through your father's files. He had the bathroom remodeled in 1998—and put in a suspended ceiling. It has panels and runners. It hides pipes and wiring. An agile person could get in and stay concealed quite a while."

"You're sure of this?"

"Yes. It's been done in other places. Plenty of times."

"But how does he get in and out of the stadium?" she persisted. "It's locked when there's not a race or other event."

"Suppose he has a key?" asked Kane. "That somehow he got access to a set of keys, Clyde's or one of the maintenance men's? And had his own copies made."

It was possible, she thought. Several people had access to the keys. But it still made no sense to her. "Why," she asked, "is he striking out at the NASCAR teams?"

"Maybe he has a grudge of some kind. Against them or against this speedway. We'll find out when we catch him."

"And how do you plan to do that?" she asked, apprehensive.

"We're setting a trap. I'll say I'm going back to Charlotte, but I won't. I'll keep watch from one side, Dean and Kent from two other points."

Apprehension turned to alarm. "If you do that, I want to be there, too."

"No," he said firmly. "Because if somebody shows up, it might get rough."

"Yes," she said just as firmly. "I've got a stake in the speedway's future, too. Yours is financial. But mine's emotional, and my feelings are just as strong, probably much stronger than yours. I mean it, Kane. I have a *right* to be there. If you care for me, let me be there with you."

He looked conflicted, but he met her eyes. "*If* I care for you? I've cared most of my life."

"Then you'll let me be a part of it?"

"Yes," he said. "For a price."

"A price?" she asked.

"Someday bring yourself to show people that you care for *me*."

Startled, she set down her fork. "Yes? How?"

"Kiss me in public," he challenged. "Someday."

She thought of Aileen's cautionary advice. And she thought of her aunt's years of hiding and secrecy. She thought of being frightened by snoops and gossips like Mrs. McBeebee. And most of all, she remembered how fear and secrecy had helped tear her and Kane apart the first time. An urge to rebel went burning through her veins like liquid fire.

Aileen's affair had been decades ago. It had been in another century. The world had changed, hadn't it? Attitudes had changed. She looked at Kane and knew again that she loved him. Why should she be ashamed to show it? Didn't he deserve for her to show it?

"Kiss you in public?" she asked softly.

"Someday," he said. "Yeah."

"How about right now?" she asked.

His eyebrows rose in surprise. "What?"

"Right now," she said. "Right here. Stand up."

He stood, disbelief on his face, and slowly she, too, rose. She leaned toward him across the table, he leaned toward her. Her lips brushed his, then brushed them more slowly, and then she put her hands on his shoulders and really kissed him.

The café went completely silent except for the sound of the jukebox playing "Always On My Mind."

Now I've done it, she thought. *I've really done it.*

And she was glad. She felt strangely free, as if shackles

had fallen away from her. The town could disapprove all it wanted to. She was tired of fearing opinion. She was tired of hiding her feelings and hiding the truth. And she thought, in some strange way, Aileen might approve.

She drew back slightly. "So you'll let me go with you tonight?"

"You've got it," he said with a slightly crooked smile.

She liked that smile, she liked the pride and pleasure in his eyes. She leaned nearer and kissed him again.

THE PICNIC WAS both fun and festive. The infield was full of people, the serving tables were laden with food, and the High Lonesome Singers were in top form. Dean joked that he felt people weren't there to see Kent and him, that they were about to be upstaged when Rome McCandless appeared for a photo and autograph session.

Rome had always been shy, and Lori knew that he must respect Kane a great deal to make a public appearance like this. But nobody was going to ignore the Grossos, who were also Carolina heroes, a father and son who'd won back-to-back NASCAR Sprint Cup championships.

The Grossos, however, had other competition of their own sort. Special guests had been invited to be honored and hold autograph sessions of their own. Half a dozen old-timers who'd had legendary races at the speedway came to celebrate the rejuvenation of the track.

The flamboyant Flash Gorton was there, decked out in his famous purple and yellow uniform, so were Lightning Kinsky, Rolly Munson, the diminutive "Flea" Robbins, Bud Standing Bear and Gil Gilroy. They swapped stories of their favorite Halesboro races, shook hands, and grinned at all the fans who regaled them with memories of seeing them race.

"It's a lovefest," Lori whispered in Kane's ear.

"You're right," he said. "So can I put my arm around you?"

"Yes," she said with a smile, and when he did, it felt so right that she didn't care if people stared or what they thought.

She wasn't a frightened sixteen-year-old any longer. She was a woman who'd found the courage to follow her heart.

The drivers were introduced before the food was served, and all told funny or outrageous stories of their Halesboro days. Kent and Dean spoke last, saluting their comrades, and paying tribute to the track. Dean introduced Kane, who thanked everyone and announced that the next race would pay tribute to Andrew J. Simmons, who'd built the speedway and made it into a fabled track.

Then he introduced Rome McCandless. "Ladies and Gentlemen, let me introduce a true hometown hero, basketball great and winner of three most valuable player awards— Roman McCandless, the famous 'Roman Candle of the NBA.'"

Rome came out of Kent's motor home, where he'd been hiding. At six foot ten, with flaming red hair, people found it impossible not to stare at him, and his face had turned a darker shade of red than his hair.

He loped to Kane's side, took the mike and said, "I'm not much of a public speaker, but I came for this guy." He put his big hand on Kane's shoulder. "So later if any of you folks want a picture made with the Grossos and me, just step over to the photographer's van, and we'll be glad to oblige. Thanks for coming."

The crowd applauded, and he ducked his head to better hide his flaming face, and quickly made his way to the table where Lori sat with the Grossos. Kane remained standing. "At our next race, the Andrew J. Simmons 200, we're going to have a very special announcement that'll be very good not only for the track, but for the whole Halesboro region. So y'all come. And thanks for being here tonight. Enjoy yourselves."

He put down the mike and went back to his table and sat between Lori and Roman. "You did fine, Rome," he said, patting his friend's back.

"It's an honor for me to be here with these two guys," Rome said, almost bashfully, nodding at the Grossos. "And it's good of you to bring back this track. It was a big part of growing up here."

"His dad worked as part of a pit crew sometimes at the local races," Kane said to the Grossos. "Fine man."

Lori remembered that Rome's father worked full-time at the mills until they closed. With his fiancée's father buying the mill buildings and Rome helping focus attention on the track, he was helping preserve the two places where his father had labored. It was, she thought, a touching tribute.

At the end of the evening, the crowd oohed and aahed at another fireworks show, which ended, appropriately, with a volley of roman candles bursting and showering the night with every color of the rainbow.

And then it was time to close down the show. "I've got to start back to Charlotte," Kane announced. "Walk me to my car, babe?" He gave Lori an affectionate smile. She rose and went with him.

Roman came with them, clearly glad to be out of the public eye. Kane said, "I'll drive over and park by the stone bridge. Rome will drive me back and drop me off. I'll meet you in your office. See you soon."

He kissed her briefly, but with enough feeling to make her blood quicken. Then she stood and watched the two cars disappear into the darkness.

THE LAST OF THE GUESTS had left. Lori sat alone in her office, nervously wondering if the vandal would show up again tonight. Kane said things could get rough. She knew the vandal had a knife; the mutilated tires proved that. Could he have a gun, as well? She didn't like this plan, and she wished they'd left it to the professionals.

But then Kane rapped on her door and entered. He sat down in the chair next to her desk and took her hands in his. "I wish you'd stay in here," he said, staring into her eyes. "I'll let you know if anything happens. Go to the break room, lie down on the couch."

"No. I kept my part of the bargain today. You have to keep yours."

He smiled, remembering her kiss. "You *are* tough, aren't you?"

"You can't teach teenagers and be a sissy. Besides, I've got pepper spray. Suppose I have to come to your rescue?"

He sighed. "All right. Hold out your hand. I've got a present for you, Warrior Woman."

"What?" she asked, but put out her hand, palm up.

"Night-vision binoculars. Very compact, but powerful. Roman brought up four sets."

She examined them in amazement. They were light and sleek. "These really work?"

"Really. I promise you. It'll be like the night turns a luminous green. Hey," he said, "you changed clothes. You look like a ninja."

"So do you." She laughed. They'd both donned black slacks and long sleeve T-shirts.

"Here's the plan," he said. "You and I'll sit in the front row seats furthest west. Dean in front furthest east. Kent between us. We can see the whole field that way. Your job is to man the phone. If we jump into action, call the head of security right away.

"We've got six men walking the perimeter outside. Four more inside, but it's a big field to patrol, and they stop and make spot checks. But we can watch full time. Ready?"

Lori felt like a character in spy drama. She pulled on a black knit cap to hide her bright hair. Kane grinned at her. "I think you *like* this."

"I'm just trying to look the way they do in movies," she protested.

"Adorable is what you look. Let's go."

They exited the office, his hand on her waist to guide her. "Do you still believe somebody's hiding in the infield bathrooms?"

"I'm fairly sure. I kept watch on it during the fireworks. It was hard to keep count, but I think one man went in but didn't come out. And I know who."

"Who?" she demanded.

"I'm not going to say until we have him. I don't want to make any false accusations."

He shut off a light in a hallway, and they eased outside. It was a cloudy night, no light from moon or stars. He led her to the far west end of the stadium seating. Silently, he showed her how to adjust the binoculars to long or short range. She held them to her eyes and suppressed a gasp. The world had turned an eerie green, and she could see so clearly she was astounded.

The big stadium lights were off, only a few widely scattered security lights shone. Intermittently, Lori watched a security guard walk the edge of the track, but he would look up as often as he looked out, disappear into the pit area, reemerge and check the tunnel.

Kent's hauler and motor home, repainted and shiny, were parked near the bathroom by design, all the better to tempt the vandal.

"Kane," she said in her softest whisper. "What if he *is* armed? Have you thought about that?"

"Dean's got a gun. He's a hunter and a good shot. He'd shoot only to wound, not kill. Don't worry. And now we sit tight, keep our eyes on the field, and wait. It's going to be a long night."

He was right. At first the experience was so foreign, it was exciting, but excitement soon faded, and there was the long, quiet watching. Lori was amazed at how often the inside security guards were out of sight, but Kane said they had to check the stadium's interior from time to time.

The night grew cooler, almost chilly with the mountain breeze rising as midnight approached. Lori huddled close to Kane, and together they waited. And waited. And waited.

LORI GREW SLEEPY. Her watch told her it was 3:30 a.m., and her heavy eyelids told her it was long past bedtime. At last, Kane told her to stop watching a while and rest her head on his shoulder. She did so gratefully. She nodded off in an uneasy doze.

Then suddenly she felt his body tense and heard him whisper, "Bingo! He's there! Damn, he's been in that building the whole time."

Immediately awake, she jerked the binoculars into position and stared at the infield. Moving quickly from the shadow of the building, a slight figure, dressed in dark clothing, made its way toward Kent's motor home.

"Call security, babe," Kane said, and in a flash he was over the wall and running. The figure's back was to him.

Lori saw Kent vault onto the field, followed by Dean. She speed-dialed the head of security. "Somebody's on the field. Three of our men are closing in on him and need backup—immediately."

"You got it," said a gruff voice.

Lori looked through the binoculars again. Kent was fastest, and the dark figure stood a moment as if paralyzed. Then he began to run toward the grandstand. He had to get past Kane, but Kane tackled him and brought him down. Lori felt sick with helplessness as the two men scuffled in the grass.

The slighter figure managed to scramble to his feet and start running again, but Kent Grosso bore down on him. The fleeing man paused long enough to fling something away from him, but it was long enough for Kent to give a burst of speed, and bring the vandal down for the second time. Then Dean was over the interloper, his gun pointed at his chest. Security men were pouring onto the field, reaching for their revolvers.

Lori swept the binoculars back to Kane. He still lay on the ground, and though he struggled to rise, he didn't.

He's hurt! She panicked. She leaped from the seat, dropped the binoculars and rushed for the nearest entrance to the infield. She ran across the field so fast that twice she stumbled, and when she reached Kane, he was writhing on the ground, with Kent bent over him.

Kent raised his head and cried, "Somebody call 911. We need an ambulance! He's been stabbed!"

Lori fell to her knees beside Kane. Blood flowed from his

arm onto the grass, and a cut had slit open his shirt front, and when she felt it, it, too, was wet with blood.

"He needs a tourniquet on that arm!" Lori shouted, but Kent stared at her as if she made no sense. She ripped off her black T-shirt and started to tie it around his upper arm. "Help me tie it tight," she ordered Kent. "You're stronger than I am."

Kent snapped back to himself and began to knot the shirt around the wounded arm. Lori leaned over Kane. "Can you hear me? Help's on the way. Hang on, Kane. Please hang on."

He groaned, but his eyes fluttered open. She bent close to him, gripping his shoulders. "He cut your chest. How bad is it? Deep?"

"It's a scratch,' he said with false bravura. "Where's your shirt?"

She glanced down. Her top was covered only by a small, lacy black bra.

He stared groggily at her cleavage. "You've just shown me two wonderful reasons to get well," he said hoarsely. Then he passed out.

Sirens keened in the distance, growing closer.

Lori insisted on riding in the ambulance with him. One of the paramedics gave her a sheet to wrap around herself. "Will he be all right?" she kept asking.

"We'll see in the E.R.," said an ambulance attendant. "Calm down, calm down. The chest wound's superficial, but he lost a lot of blood fast. Must have cut an artery."

She sat by the gurney, holding Kane's good hand, feeling dazed and frightened. She hung on to him as tightly as she could.

She clutched the sheet more snugly around herself, stared down at his still face and realized, *I don't even know who did this to you. Or why.*

She bent down and kissed his forehead. His skin was damp with a fine sweat, and cool, too cool.

CHAPTER FOURTEEN

KANE SAT UP IN BED, looking pale, his upper right arm and chest bandaged. Lori and the chief of the Halesboro police stood by his bed, and Lori was there only because she flatly refused to take orders from the chief.

"All right," she said, holding Kane's hand and staring at Wally Taylor, a stocky man with his police shield shining on his broad chest. "Who did this? Is he charged?"

"He will be," Wally said. "As for who did it, I'm not at liberty to say—"

"I am," Kane asserted. "I saw him go into the building. And I saw him when we struggled. It's Jimmy Pilgram, isn't it?"

Lori's free hand flew to her mouth. "Jimmy? No! He's such a sweet kid. He works so hard."

Kane said, "My guess is that he found a way to make easier money, right?"

Wally Taylor sighed. "Now I'm not supposed to tell you anything yet."

"It's Jimmy," Kane persisted. "He's Morrie's assistant. Morrie has a full set of keys. Jimmy got them and copied them, right?"

Wally looked disgusted. "You're free to think whatever you want. Let's just say, yes, the perpetrator could get around pretty easy."

"He's a skinny, agile kid," Kane said. "Moves quickly."

"I liked him," Lori said, still stunned. "And so did Clyde and Morrie. Clyde even said that Jimmy reminded him of you when you were the same age."

"I'm flattered," Kane said sarcastically.

"Well," she said, embarrassed to have been so gullible, "he came from a broken home. And his mother's not well. But he worked his heart out. Clyde said he thought that Jimmy could go far, just like you. Maybe not as far, but at least make a success of his life."

"Look," Kane said to Wally Taylor, "now we all know it was Jimmy. And I reckon Kent told you about the theory of somebody hiding in the building, even about where we thought he was hiding. Skinny kid like him? He could get into the ceiling easy. What I want to know is why he did it? I've got a right to know. I own the place. Is he talking?"

Wally sighed harshly. "Yeah, he's talking. The public defender'll try to cut a plea bargain for him. The kid feels rotten. He's scared as hell. But they offered him more money than he'd ever dreamed of. And like Ms. Garland said, his mom's sick. She needs surgery."

"Who offered him money?" Kane asked, arching a brow dangerously.

"Hell, I can't say that, but who would you think put him up to it?"

"The Devlin Corporation," Kane said, all cool certainty.

"You got every right to believe whatever you want to believe," Wally repeated. "But it's not official yet, and you don't want to going around shooting your mouth off 'cause it will mess up the investigation, so I would greatly appreciate that you keep your piehole *shut*." He turned and pointed at Lori. "And you, too, Missy."

"My lips are sealed," she said.

"Mine, too," muttered Kane, "as with epoxy."

"But what happens to Jimmy?" Lori asked in concern. "He's just ruined his whole life."

"If he gets the plea bargain," Wally said, "that'll help him a lot. But then his big trouble is the stabbing and the vandalism."

Kane was silent a long minute. He looked deep in unhappy thought. "I'll have to think about this…"

Lori looked at him in a mixture of hope and disbelief. Would he refuse to press charges?

Did he remember all too well how desperate a poor, powerless boy like Jimmy could feel in Halesboro?

"It's a free country," said Wally. "Think what you want. Now there's some other people wanting to see you. Some of your high-speed friends. And remember, mum's the word about all this."

"We get it," Kane said with a resigned nod.

Wally shuffled out, and a nurse bustled in. "Mr. Ledger, you have visitors, but the doctor doesn't want them to stay for more than ten minutes. You need to rest. You'll have to leave, too, Ms. Garland."

Kane held Lori's hand more possessively. "Not her. She stays. And when do I get out of this place?"

"With luck, two or three days," said the nurse, her nose in the air. "And I'll send in the doctor to talk to you about Ms. Garland."

With a flourish of starchy scrubs, she left, and Dean and Kent ambled in, looking embarrassed. "You've got to work on your superhero act," said Kent. "Superheroes don't bleed. That's the first lesson, and you blew it."

"I'm too old to be running and aiming guns at people," Dean grumbled. He looked at his son and said, "*You* can be the superhero by your lonesome."

"This pretty lady going to come sit by your side every day you're here?" Kent asked Kane.

"I hope so."

Lori sighed. "I'll be here as long as you want me. But now we have even more bad publicity. How much will that hurt the speedway?"

"It won't hurt it at all, sweetheart. I told you, the first rule of publicity is that there's *no* bad publicity. The name Halesboro will be all over the papers, TV, the Internet—name it. This last was just another chapter in the Hellsboro legend."

Lori smiled weakly. Then she looked pensive again. "Jimmy Pilgram threw something last night. I saw him. Did they find it? Does anybody know what it was?"

Kent squared his shoulders. "I did. I saw the guard pick it up. A plastic jar. He sniffed and said it was full of drain cleaner. Jimmy probably was going to put it in one of the gas tanks."

Lori was horrified. "What would that do?"

"It supposedly causes an explosion. The cleaner eats through the plastic, mingles with the gas—and boom!"

"But that could cause enormous damage," Lori said, "even death."

"If it worked, sweetheart," Kane said. "But it's an urban legend. The kid was dumb enough to believe it."

At that point, the doctor walked into the room. "Have to ask everyone to leave. Want some tests done on this man. Come back during regular visiting hours."

"She stays," Kane said defiantly, holding Lori's hand more tightly.

"No, she doesn't," the doctor said, stone-faced. "You may own the speedway, but you don't own me. Sorry, everybody out."

Lori tried to give him a quick kiss that turned into a longer, more intense one. She was getting used to kissing him in front of people. And she liked it very much.

THREE DAYS LATER, Kane was out of the hospital and back in Charlotte. He and Lori talked daily on the phone, planning the August legends race in honor of Lori's father.

Finally the morning of the race arrived. Kane and Rome McCandless gave a press conference in Charlotte. Kane did most of the talking, and Rome, as usual, looked shy about being in the spotlight. Kane revealed that it was Roman who had bought McCorkle Castle.

He planned on turning over fifty of its four hundred acres to the Tomlinson Corporation to develop into a family theme park that would celebrate the heritage, traditions and crafts of western North Carolina. He would keep the upper floors of the castle as a family retreat, but most of the lower floor of the castle itself would be open for weekend tours.

"I want all of Carolina to enjoy the castle," Rome said at

the last, speaking without looking into the camera. "And I want to dedicate it to my folks, who told me with faith and hard work, I could grow up to be anything I wanted. And I'm going to build a chapel in their memory."

He paused and said, "And more business is coming to Halesboro. Horning Discount Malls is putting a super-value mall in the mill buildings where my daddy used to work. I think he'd be proud to see those buildings help Halesboro grow."

He was so guileless, so disarming, that Lori had to be happy for the changes he spoke of. They seemed to spring straight from Rome's gentle heart.

Rome cuffed Kane's hand. "You say the rest. You talk better."

Kane nodded. "Rome's a great benefactor to Halesboro. He's also donating a medical helicopter and copter pad that will serve the Halesboro hospital. He wants to give this gift in honor of A. J. Simmons, one of the first dreamers to invest in Halesboro."

Lori was so touched she cried all alone in front of her television set. Kane called her shortly after. "Now you can't dislike Roman trying to boost Halesboro," he said. "The guy's just so damn sincere."

"He is," she said, stifling a sniffle. "But how can he afford to *do* this?"

"He'll make twenty-two million bucks this season," Kane said wryly, "and that's before he endorses anything or makes any other deals. He's invested his money wisely over the years, and he'd rather spend it on his hometown than on yachts and diamonds or a private tropical island."

"So you and Rome and the Hornings have been in this together from the start," she said, feeling teary again.

"Yes, and I'll see you tonight. Rome won't come. He wants to stay home and watch mushy movies with Zoey."

"And you?" she asked.

"I want to give Halesboro a show it won't forget," he said. "Because the town's coming back. And so's the speedway."

BY THE TIME Kane arrived at the speedway, Lori was high-strung and shaken by waves of sentiment. She wanted everything to be perfect for this, her father's race.

And perfectly was the way it started out. There was a carnival atmosphere, the midway full of vendors, prizes to be given all through the evening, the specialty acts, a parachute flag jump, a famous singer come out of retirement to sing the national anthem—Kane had pulled out all the stops this time.

Everyone congratulated him on helping capture the vandal and for making Halesboro lively again.

In one of their few moments alone, Kane muttered in Lori's ear, "I think getting stabbed was the best PR move I ever made."

She grabbed his lapel in mock threat. "But don't *ever* do it again."

"I won't if I can help it," he said. "And I mean it. So here it is, Lori, the change *is* happening. Do you still regret it?"

"No," she said, but sadness tinged her voice. "What's past is past. The change is needed. And my father would *love* the excitement here tonight. And I'm glad things are moving on. I've learned my lesson." She glanced up at him, bemused. "And I guess I can thank you for that."

"Lori—" He seemed to want to say something, but he was interrupted by a reporter.

"We just got word that the Devlin Corporation's implicated in the vandalism that took place here. It's on the AP wire. Have you got a comment?"

"No," Kane said shortly. "I haven't been told any details. Until I have, I've nothing to say."

"What about the vandal, Jimmy Pilgram? Are you filing charges against him?"

"I'd rather not comment," Kane said. "Sorry. Have to go. Last-minute things to check. See you up in the suite, Lori." And he was gone, vanished into the crowd like a phantom.

Lori slipped away as rapidly as she could; she didn't want the reporter trying to corner *her*.

THE SPEEDWAY'S VIP SUITES couldn't match the luxury of any of the famous track suites she'd seen lately, but at least they were freshly painted, the chairs reupholstered, and she'd managed to have This Little Piggy cater snacks and appetizers for each suite in use and set up a modest table for drinks.

Dean and Patsy Grosso were there. Kent Grosso and his beautiful wife Tanya came, as well as a few of the old-timers—Flash Gorton, Rolly Munson, and "Flea" Robbins. "Damn," said Flea, looking out the big windows, "it's good to see this place full up again. Mighty good."

Lori was surprised and pleased to see the same NASCAR executive in the suite that she'd seen at the Illinois speedway, the man who took his tie off after the first lap, then his coat and let his fancy suspenders be seen. He'd been a pleasant man to talk to, so she went over and reintroduced herself, sure he didn't remember her.

But he did. Again he chatted easily with her, but he seemed tired tonight. He said he'd wanted to be here tonight but he was still jet-lagged from getting in from California early this morning. He made a statement that surprised and delighted her—but also turned the night into one of extreme imperfection.

"Yes," he murmured. "Excuse me, please, if I sit. I wanted to be here tonight because NASCAR's been interested in getting some regional series racing here. Been talking about it lately."

"A regional series here?" Lori echoed.

"Umm-hmm," he said wearily. "Mentioned it to Kane a while back. Last spring. Early April. He said there could be development up this way—and he was right. Bright man. Bright man."

Lori felt herself bristling. NASCAR had been considering sanctioning Halesboro all this time, and Kane had known it? He'd known before he'd made his offer, and never so much as *mentioned* it while she'd twisted in the wind?

The man might be fatigued, but he was observant. "You look

startled. Perhaps I mentioned this prematurely. Nothing settled yet, of course. Ignore me. My brain's still on west coast time."

"I know exactly how you feel," Lori said, improvising. "If I don't get my eight hours, I move around in a bit of a fog. Can I get you a cup of coffee?"

"I'd love one," he said. "You're a very gracious young lady. Black, please."

She went to the coffee urn, filled him a cup and looked about the suite for Kane. He wasn't there. Her temper rising, she stalked off to find him.

She felt angry and betrayed. Kane had *known* the track's fortunes would get better, he had known that NASCAR was interested and had hidden the fact. Acting on secret knowledge that could have helped her refinance, he instead used it for himself. Now her father's legacy belonged to *him*.

She was hurt not only by having lost the track, but by knowing that Kane deliberately held back the truth. He'd flimflammed her and charmed his way into her bed. She'd made a public display of her affection—and all the while he must have been laughing at her.

She found Kane in his office, talking spiritedly on the phone. "I know he should be punished, Justin," he said, "I'm not saying let him off free. But I don't want to ruin the kid's life, either."

He looked up, and Lori knew her expression was stormy. "We have to talk," she told him. "Right now."

"Justin, something's come up," he said. "We'll talk later." He gazed up at her, cocking an eyebrow. "You don't look happy, babe."

"I was up in the suite, and that NASCAR representative we met in Illinois was there," she said from between her teeth. "He was jet-lagged. He let slip that NASCAR's interested in scheduling some racing here. That they've been interested *for some time.*"

"They said they were interested, they didn't say it was going to happen," he said with a calm she found infuriating.

"You held out on me," she accused. "I might have gotten

help from the bank if I'd known NASCAR was interested. But no. You didn't tell me. Not even in June when you bought it. If I'd hung on just a little while longer—"

"You couldn't hang on any longer," he countered. "I repeat—how could I know a NASCAR offer would materialize? The track needed improvements—badly. I could have tried to find investors, but that's time-consuming. I decided to go it alone."

"You could have told me the truth," she accused.

"I didn't *know* for sure," he insisted. "I still don't know. And from the beginning I didn't know how you'd react to me. I didn't even know how *I'd* react to this whole deal. I'll tell you something, Lori. It wasn't easy coming back here. Never for a minute think it was easy."

"You wanted to get even with me. You admitted that. Well, I hope you're satisfied."

"Part of me did want to pay you back. But once I saw you, I had to forgive you. We were kids. *Kids.* Can't you forgive me for not telling you about an agreement with NASCAR that wasn't offered, might never be? What if I told you and it came to nothing? How much would *that* disappoint you? If it happened, I wanted it to be wonderful for you—and me. If it didn't, I didn't want you disillusioned."

"Oh," she said furiously, "you can talk so fast. You're such a wheeler-dealer. I wish I…I wish you'd never…I wish…" she burst into tears and covered her face with her hands.

"Lori," he said gently, "I've loved you since I was seventeen years old. Yes, I was arrogant when I came back. Yes, I sent contradictory signals. And no, I didn't understand my own motives."

He put his hands on her shoulders. She should have shaken off his touch, but she couldn't. Her emotions were a maelstrom, spinning wildly.

"But," he said, "I do love you. I'll stop trying to change you. I'll stop trying to test you. And I want to marry you. I said I didn't want commitments—yet I do. I realized that lying in the hospital, knowing if that knife had gone an inch deeper into my chest, I could have died. Life is short, too short…

"I can't stand to lose you again. Coming back like this was awkward. But I had to come back and see. And what I see is that it's time to get on with the future. We need to put the dark part of the past behind us. So say you'll marry me. It can be as long an engagement as you want. But I want us to be a couple. For the rest of our lives. And I'll say that to anybody in the world. You know, there's still even time for us to try for kids."

Children? She felt overwhelmed to the point of weakness. "I thought we were going to take this slowly."

"Twenty-one years is slow enough," he said. "If you don't want an engagement ring, I'll buy you an engaged-to-be-engaged ring."

"Maybe I should marry you," she retorted, giddy and trying not to cry, "just to get the speedway back in the family."

"If that's what it takes, I'll have a deed drawn up tomorrow giving you fifty-one percent interest. The controlling share."

He meant it. She could tell. "Then consider it a done deal," she said, a tremor in her voice. "But one more thing. Promise me you won't have the book thrown at Jimmy Pilgram. There *was* something in him that reminded me of you."

"Yeah," he said softly. "Me, too. Well, you saved me, Lori. And maybe we can help save him. Now come here."

She leaned against him, her arms around his waist. "I really was upset when I heard that up in the suite," she said.

"Be quiet, spitfire," he told her. "And kiss me. Kiss me till both our heads spin. Make this frog feel like a prince again. You did it once. You know you've got the power."

"You've always been my prince," she whispered. "From the moment we first touched."

She raised herself on tiptoe and kissed him. "Welcome home, your highness," she whispered against his lips. "Welcome, welcome home."

* * * * *

*For more thrill-a-minute romances
set against the exciting backdrop of
the NASCAR world, don't miss:
WITHIN STRIKING DISTANCE
by Ingrid Weaver
Available in August
For a sneak peek, just turn the page!*

"MR. MCMASTERS?"

At the woman's voice, Jake paused to look around. It was noon, and the first sunny day after two days of rain, so even a small park like this one was busy. Half the benches beneath the trees were already occupied by people eating their lunch. A pair of men in suits brushed past him, using the sidewalk to cut through to the next street. That's where Jake had been headed, with the intention of hitting the corner diner and adding a nice, greasy burger to the three cups of coffee that had been his breakfast. He shaded his eyes against the sun, trying to see who had called him.

It didn't take any special detective skills to spot her. With her wide-brimmed yellow straw hat, neon pink blouse and billowing, yellow and pink flower-splotched skirt, she would stand out in any crowd.

The fact that she waved at him helped, too.

Jake rested both hands on his cane and studied her as she approached. She moved with the grace of a dancer, her long limbs slender and in perfect proportion to her height. He estimated she was only a couple of inches short of six feet, another reason she stood out among the lunching locals. And the closer she got, the more striking she looked.

No, *striking* was an understatement. This woman was a knockout. Absolutely beautiful.

And she looked familiar.

That didn't make sense. He was certain he had never met her before. He would have remembered if he had—any man who possessed a pulse would remember meeting this woman—yet he felt an unmistakable tickle of recognition.

"Mr. McMasters?" she repeated, stopping in front of him. He nodded. "That's me."

"I apologize for chasing you down like this. I hadn't realized you closed your office for lunch. I meant to be there earlier but I was held up and by the time I got here it was already twelve and I must have just missed you. I was going back to my car when I guessed that must be you crossing the park and—" She stopped talking and pressed her palm flat against her midriff. She breathed deeply a few times before she extended her hand and smiled. "Sorry for rambling. Let me start over. I'm Becky Peters."

It didn't seem possible, but that smile made her look even more beautiful. It involved every part of her face, turning features that were already perfect into a harmony of…what? Honesty? Friendliness?

He was jumping to conclusions about her character. Aside from her outward appearance, he knew nothing about her. Realizing he was staring, he clasped the hand she offered.

And he was jarred by another round of recognition. Not from her name, but from her touch.

Her eyes were a warm, smokey blue. It was a memorable color, a shade that reminded him of a summer horizon at dusk. They widened slightly, as if she felt the same odd tickle from the contact of their palms that he did.

This was getting stranger by the minute. Jake leaned forward. "Miss Peters, have we met before?"

"No." The word came out rough. She cleared her throat. "No, we haven't met."

"Then how did you know who I was?"

"Mostly it was a lucky guess. I also asked my friend about you before I decided to come."

He returned his hand to his cane. Right. Sometimes he forgot about his most distinguishing characteristic. "I see. Is your friend a client of mine?"

"Not really." She looked past him. "You must have been on your way someplace. I hate to hold you up but I have to be at work later this afternoon, so would you mind if we talked now?"

His stomach did a little roll to remind him about the burger he'd promised it. He could ignore his hunger, but he couldn't afford to ignore potential business so he led the way to a vacant bench in the shade of a chestnut tree. He waited until the woman sat, then settled at an angle beside her, leaned his cane against the seat and stretched out his left leg. "It's lucky you caught up with me. Most days my work takes me out in the field. The only sure way to catch me in my office is to make an appointment."

"Of course. I should have guessed that a private investigator would be out, well, investigating."

"You must be anxious to employ my services."

"You have no idea." She took off her sunhat and laid it on her lap. "I've been waiting most of my life for this opportunity."

Jake allowed himself a few seconds to admire her hair. It was light brown, with streaks the color of honey. It flowed over her shoulders in lush waves, enough for a man to wrap around his fingers... He shifted on the bench to take his notebook from his pants pocket. "Which is?"

"Mr. McMasters, I heard you were looking into the Gina Grosso case and..." She took a deep breath. "I want to find out who I am."

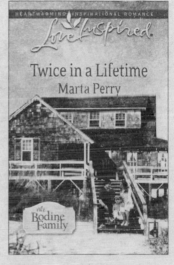

REQUEST YOUR FREE BOOKS!

2 FREE NOVELS
FROM THE ROMANCE/SUSPENSE
COLLECTION PLUS 2 FREE GIFTS!

YES! Please send me 2 FREE novels from the Romance/Suspense Collection and my 2 FREE gifts (gifts are worth about $10). After receiving them, if I don't wish to receive any more books, I can return the shipping statement marked "cancel." If I don't cancel, I will receive 4 brand-new novels every month and be billed just $5.74 per book in the U.S. or $6.24 per book in Canada. That's a savings of at least 28% off the cover price. It's quite a bargain! Shipping and handling is just 50¢ per book.* I understand that accepting the 2 free books and gifts places me under no obligation to buy anything. I can always return a shipment and cancel at any time. Even if I never buy another book from the Reader Service, the two free books and gifts are mine to keep forever.

185 MDN EYNQ   385 MDN EYN2

Name   (PLEASE PRINT)

Address   Apt. #

City   State/Prov.   Zip/Postal Code

Signature (if under 18, a parent or guardian must sign)

Mail to **The Reader Service:**
IN U.S.A.: P.O. Box 1867, Buffalo, NY 14240-1867
IN CANADA: P.O. Box 609, Fort Erie, Ontario L2A 5X3

Not valid to current subscribers of the Romance Collection,
the Suspense Collection or the Romance/Suspense Collection.

Want to try two free books from another line?
Call 1-800-873-8635 or visit www.morefreebooks.com.

* Terms and prices subject to change without notice. Prices do not include applicable taxes. Sales tax applicable in N.Y. Canadian residents will be charged applicable provincial taxes and GST. Offer not valid in Quebec. This offer is limited to one order per household. All orders subject to approval. Credit or debit balances in a customer's account(s) may be offset by any other outstanding balance owed by or to the customer. Please allow 4 to 6 weeks for delivery. Offer available while quantities last.

Your Privacy: Harlequin is committed to protecting your privacy. Our Privacy Policy is available online at www.eHarlequin.com or upon request from the Reader Service. From time to time we make our lists of customers available to reputable third parties who may have a product or service of interest to you. If you would prefer we not share your name and address, please check here. ☐

BOB09